SECONDHAND SPIRITS

Juliet Blackwell

AN OBSIDIAN MYSTERY

OBSIDIAN
Published by New American Library, a division of
Penguin Group (USA) Inc., 375 Hudson Street,
New York, New York 10014, USA
Penguin Group (Canada), 90 Eglinton Avenue East, Suite 700, Toronto,
Ontario M4P 2Y3, Canada (a division of Pearson Penguin Canada Inc.)
Penguin Books Ltd., 80 Strand, London WC2R 0RL, England
Penguin Ireland, 25 St. Stephen's Green, Dublin 2,
Ireland (a division of Penguin Books Ltd.)
Penguin Group (Australia), 250 Camberwell Road, Camberwell, Victoria 3124,
Australia (a division of Pearson Australia Group Pty. Ltd.)
Penguin Books India Pvt. Ltd., 11 Community Centre, Panchsheel Park,
New Delhi - 110 017, India
Penguin Group (NZ), 67 Apollo Drive, Rosedale, North Shore 0632,
New Zealand (a division of Pearson New Zealand Ltd.)
Penguin Books (South Africa) (Pty.) Ltd., 24 Sturdee Avenue,
Rosebank, Johannesburg 2196, South Africa

Penguin Books Ltd., Registered Offices:
80 Strand, London WC2R 0RL, England

First published by Obsidian, an imprint of New American Library,
a division of Penguin Group (USA) Inc.

First Printing, July 2009
10 9 8 7 6 5 4

Printed in the United States of America

Praise for the Art Lover's Mysteries
by Juliet Blackwell Writing as Hailey Lind

Brush with Death

"Lind deftly combines a smart and witty sleuth with entertaining characters who are all engaged in a fascinating new adventure. Sprinkled in are interesting snippets about works of art and the art world, both the beauty and its dirty underbelly." —*Romantic Times*

Shooting Gallery

"Lind's latest creatively combines mystery, humor, and interesting art tidbits. The unique characters—including aging art forgers, art thieves, and drug smugglers—add depth to this well-plotted cozy." —*Romantic Times*

"If you enjoy Janet Evanovich's Stephanie Plum books, Jonathan Gash's Lovejoy series, or Ian Pears's art history mysteries . . . then you will enjoy *Shooting Gallery*. . . . The book is a fun romp through San Francisco's art scene with some romance and a couple murders and car chases thrown in for good measure." —Gumshoe

"An artfully crafted new mystery series!"
—Tim Myers, Agatha Award–nominated author of *A Mold for Murder*

"The art world is murder in this witty and entertaining mystery!"
—Cleo Coyle, national bestselling author of *Espresso Shot*

Feint of Art

"Annie Kincaid is a wonderful cozy heroine. . . . It's a rollicking good read." —*Mystery News*

To Aunt Mem,
my first (and favorite) witchy woman

Acknowledgments

As always, special thanks are due to so many.

To my wonderful literary agent, Kristin Lindstrom, who has inordinate, obstinate faith in my writing; and Kerry Donovan, for her ongoing support and editing flair, and for encouraging me to explore my witchy ways.

To the supportive, boisterous NorCal Sisters in Crime (y'all know who you are). To Sophie Littlefield for always egging me on, and to Cornelia Read, James Calder, and Tim Maleeny for poker, dinner in bed, and long discussions of genre and mystery. I feel like I've been invited to sit at the cool kids' table.

To the warm and welcoming Come as You Are (CAYA) coven in Berkeley, California; the wonderful staff of the Sacred Well on Grand Avenue; and to all those witches, sensitives, and sorcerers who spoke to me and wish to remain anonymous. *Muchisimas gracias a todas las curanderas y brujas que me hablaron con confianza.*

To my mother's big, unabashedly Texan family for great expressions, bear hugs, and Southern food.

To my sister Carolyn—I missed you this go-round! Thanks for your unselfish help and laugh-out-loud suggestions. And to my sister, Susan, for her unflagging enthusiasm and novel suggestions.

Thanks to Jace, Shay, and Suzanne for their readthroughs and critiques. To Anna for *all* your help. And special appreciation to Bee, Pamela, Jan, Mary, Chris, Brian, the entire Mira Vista Social Club . . . and a thousand kisses to my guy Sergio.

And finally, a shout-out to Oscar, the suitably black cat, who insists that I *will* fall for his feline ways.

Tis the witching hour of night,
Or bed is the moon and bright,
And the stars they glisten, glisten,
Seeming with bright eyes to listen
For what listen they?

John Keats (1795–1821)

Chapter 1

Witches recognize their own.

So I could tell this customer was . . . *different* . . . the moment he walked into my store. Not to mention the bell on the door failed to chime.

He was gorgeous: golden hair glinting in the light of the amber sconces, eyes the blue of a perfect periwinkle, tanned skin with just a hint of whiskers inviting one's touch. Tall and graceful, he had the too-perfect, unreal beauty seldom seen outside a movie theater. And we were a long way from Tinseltown. This was San Francisco, where "silicon" referred to computer chips, not plastic surgery. Here, people were only too real in their endearing, genuine lumpiness.

But what really drew my eye was the energy he emitted; to a witch like me, he was as conspicuous as a roaring drunk at an AA meeting.

The stranger approached, the lightness of his step suggesting a talent for sneakiness. I waited behind the horseshoe-shaped display counter and fingered the protective medicine bundle that hung from a braided string around my waist.

"Lily Ivory?"

"That's me," I said with a nod.

He placed an engraved business card on the glass countertop and pushed it toward me with a graceful index finger.

Aidan Rhodes—Male Witch
Magickal Assistance
Spells Cast—Curses Broken—Love Potions
Satisfaction Guaranteed
145 Jefferson Street, San Francisco

"Male witch?" My eyes wandered up, down, and across his muscular frame. "Are you often mistaken for a female?"

This was San Francisco, after all.

"Rarely, now that you mention it." A glint of humor lit up those too-blue eyes. "But most people don't realize men can be witches."

"Sure they do. They just call them warlocks."

He winced. "Warlock" means "oath breaker" in Old English, and calls to mind the men who betrayed their covens in the bad old burn-the-witches-at-the-stake days. Some male practitioners called themselves "wizards" or "sorcerers," but most preferred "witch." It was a solidarity thing.

There are as many different types of witches—the good, the bad, the magnificently venal—as there are familiars. Still, the vast majority of us are female. I had an inkling of the power of a traditional women's coven, but in my experience male witches were wild cards with a tendency to stir up trouble.

Nothing about Aidan Rhodes suggested otherwise.

"Cute accent," he said. "You twang."

"It's not my fault. I grew up in Texas."

"I know. I knew your father."

"Really."

"We worked together."

"Is that right?" My tone was nonchalant, but my mind was racing. Aidan Rhodes was not overtly threatening, but if my father was involved, all bets were off.

I glanced over at my coworker, Bronwyn, who was across the room preparing a concoction for a middle-aged client with a nasty case of eczema and a nastier case of an unfaithful husband. The women's heads were bent low as Bronwyn ground up dried herbs with a wooden mortar and pestle. They appeared absorbed in the task. Too absorbed. Aidan Rhodes, male witch, must have cast a cocooning spell. If so, they wouldn't hear a single word we said; indeed, wouldn't be aware of his presence at all.

"It's not every day someone like you moves into the neighborhood, much less opens a shop." Aidan's long, elegant fingers caressed a pile of hand-tatted lace collars in the wicker basket on the counter. "A retail store, though—that surprises me. Unusual career path for one with your . . . talents."

"Is there a reason you're here?" I asked, upgrading the man from a curiosity to an annoyance. I wasn't usually so abrupt with potential customers, but it seemed unwise to use the shopkeeper's standard greeting—*May I help you?*—in case I inadvertently obligated myself to him. *There's many a slip twixt cauldron and lip*, my grandmother Graciela had drilled into me. Words mattered in the world of spell casting, and a slip of the tongue could have dire consequences.

"As a matter of fact, there is. I brought you a housewarming present."

"Thank you, but that's not necessary."

"I'm happy to do it."

"I'm afraid I can't accept."

"Oh, but I insist."

"I said *no*, thank you."

"You don't know what it is yet."

"That's not the—"

"Pleased ta meetcha."

I whirled around to find a misshapen creature perched, gargoylelike, atop an antique walnut jewelry display case. He was small and bent, with a muscular body and scaly skin, a large head, a snoutlike nose and mouth, and outsize ears like a bat's. His fingers were long and humanlike, surprisingly graceful, but his enormous feet had three toes and long talons. His voice was deep and gravelly.

"I'm your new familiar," it said.

"I'm afraid not; I'm a so—" I turned to give Aidan a piece of my mind, but he was gone, the door slowly swinging shut. The bell had once again failed to ring. I swore under my breath.

"A *so* what, mistress?"

"Excuse me?"

"Before you started swearing you said you were a *so*."

"I wasn't swearing."

"Were, too."

I blew out an exasperated breath. "I'm a solo act. I don't need a familiar."

"You're a witch, ain'tcha? Ya gotta have a familiar."

"Says who?"

"It's in the handbook."

"There *is* no handbook. Besides, I'm allergic to cats."

"I'm no cat."

"So I've noticed. But I'm probably allergic to . . . creatures such as yourself, too. Run along home to your master."

"Can't."

"Why not?"

"'Cause you're my master now, mistress." The creature attempted a smile, which took shape as a grimace.

"I'm serious. Now *scoot*."

The grimace fell from his gnarled greenish gray face. Had it been possible, he would have paled. "You don't want me?"

"It's nothing personal. I just don't need—"

"Don't send me away, mistress!" he begged, jumping down from the display case. Even at full height he didn't reach my belly button. He dropped to his knobby knees and clasped his hands, gazing up at me in supplication. "*Please* don't send me away. I'll be good, mistress, I swear."

"I can't have a goblin in the shop!"

"I'm not exactly a goblin."

"Gnome, then."

"Not really a gnome, either . . ."

"*Whatever* you are, you'll scare away customers."

"Howzabout a pig?"

"A pig?"

With a sudden twist of his scrawny shoulders, he transformed himself into a miniature Vietnamese pot-bellied pig. He grunted, wagged his curly tail, and darted around the counter.

"Hey! Get back here, you—"

"Bless the Goddess, isn't he *sweet*!" Bronwyn squealed, nearly knocking over a rack of 1950s-era chiffon prom dresses in her haste to cross the room. "Where'd he come from? I've always wanted one of those! George Clooney had one—did you know? They're *very* smart." Bronwyn scooped up the squealing swine and held him to her generous bosom, where, I couldn't help but notice, he stopped kicking and snuggled right in, his pale pink snout resting on her ample cleavage. "What's his name?"

I sighed. I had a million things to do today. Evicting a piggish gnome—or a gnomish pig—was not one of them.

"His name's . . . Oscar," I said off the top of my head, thinking of the *Sesame Street* character. The ugly little fellow seemed as if he would feel at home in a garbage can. "But he's not mine. He's a . . . loaner. He's just visiting."

Bronwyn and Oscar both ignored me.

"*Oscar*. Aren't you just a *darling*? Aren't you Bwonwyn's wuvey-dovey piggy-pig-pig?" She crooned to the creature in the high-pitched, goofy tone humans reserve for cherished pets and preverbal children.

Oscar snorted and rooted around in her cleavage. Bronwyn chuckled. I sighed.

A plump woman in her mid-fifties, Bronwyn had fuzzy brown hair and warm brown eyes. She favored great swaths of gauzy purple clothing, lots of Celtic jewelry, and heavy black eye makeup. The first time I saw her I couldn't decide whether she was a delightfully free spirit or just plain nuts. Shortly after I opened my vintage clothing store, Aunt Cora's Closet, she had approached me about renting a corner of the shop for her small herb business. I welcomed the company: Bronwyn was a so-so herbalist and an amateurish witch, but she had lived in the Haight-Ashbury neighborhood since its hippie heyday and knew *everyone*. She would be my entrée into a new and unfamiliar city.

Besides, Bronwyn had been one of the first people I met upon my arrival in San Francisco, and she had welcomed me with open arms. Literally. Bronwyn was a hugger of the bear variety.

Finding a safe place to call home wasn't an easy task for a natural witch from a small Texas town. For years I had traveled the globe, and finally came to the City by the Bay at the suggestion of a parrot named Barnabas, whom I'd met one memorable evening in a smoky bar in Hong Kong.

"The Barbary Coast," he'd said, gazing at me with one bright eye from his perch on the bar. "That's the place for you. But be careful!"

"Of what?" I'd asked.

"The fog," Barnabas had replied, holding a banana in one foot and peeling it with his beak. "Mark my words. Mark the fog."

"What about the fog?"

"Mark the fog! Mark the fog!" he'd screeched. "Hey! Son of a bitch bit me! Whiskey! Whiskey and rye till the day that I die! Set up another round! Who's buying?"

That was the problem with parrots, I had thought as Barnabas waddled off to harass the bartender. They're smart as heck and never forget a thing, but they do like their booze.

I can't normally understand animals when they speak, so I assumed he was either a shape-shifting elf—like the pig currently snuggling in Bronwyn's ample arms—or I had been drinking *way* too many mai tais. But either way, I took the incident as a sign. I packed my bags and headed to San Francisco, a city that is home to so many beloved lunatics and cherished iconoclasts that for the first time in my life nobody noticed me. Or so I hoped. The unsettling appearance of Aidan Rhodes the male witch and Oscar the familiar might make keeping a low profile a challenge.

I watched as Bronwyn embraced the wriggling pot-bellied pig with her typical unguarded, openhearted enthusiasm, wishing I could do the same. I didn't know quite what to make of my new housewarming gift. What might a male witch want from me? And why would he bring me a familiar, of all things?

The door opened again, its bell tinkling merrily as my inventory scout walked in.

"Maya!" gushed Bronwyn. "Come meet our sweet little Oscar."

"Jumpin' Jehoshaphat, what is *that*?" Maya recoiled. Twenty-three years old chronologically, but closer to forty on the cynicism scale, Maya had dark dreadlocks dyed bright blue at the ends, ears edged with silver rings and cuffs, and an aversion to makeup because, she'd explained earnestly, it was "too fake." Why the bright blue hair didn't strike her as equally artificial I wasn't sure.

Maya attended the San Francisco College of the Arts part-time, but her passion was visiting the elderly of her community and recording their stories for an oral history project.

I had met Maya a few weeks ago as she sat on a blanket on the sidewalk, halfheartedly peddling the 1940s-era beaded sweaters some elderly friends had given her in their attempt to "make a lady out of her." That quest was doomed to fail, but in the course of our conversation Maya and I discovered we had mutually beneficial business interests: Now she scoured her friends' closets and attics for inventory for my store, and I paid her a generous finder's fee.

"I believe it's called a Vietnamese potbellied pig," I said. "Apparently George Clooney has one."

"*Had* one," Bronwyn corrected me.

"Okay . . ." Maya said. "Why?"

"A friend couldn't keep it," I said. "It's only here temporarily. Sort of a foster situation."

"We *eat* things like that in my neighborhood," said Maya.

"Hush, child!" scolded Bronwyn, clapping her hands over the pig's ears and whispering, "He'll *hear* you."

"He's a pig, Bronwyn," Maya pointed out. "In case you didn't notice."

"He's not *deaf.* And he's a *special* pig. *I love* my little Oscarooneeroo."

"Hey, whatever floats your boat," Maya said with a shrug and an enigmatic smile.

Today Maya was taking me to meet a woman who had lived in the same home for more than fifty years and who, according to Maya, had never thrown away a single item of clothing. That description was music to my ears. Hunting down high-quality vintage clothing was a competitive sport in the Bay Area, and elderly pack rats were my bread and butter. Besides, I was on a mission lately: I needed to find the perfect wedding dress.

Not for myself, mind you. Me and romance . . . well, it's complicated, to say the least. But Aunt Cora's Closet was my first attempt at running a legitimate business, and I was so determined to do well that I wasn't above giving the Fates a nudge. On the last full moon I anointed a seven-day green candle with oil of bergamot, surrounded it with orange votives, placed malachite and bloodstone on either side, and, after scenting the air with vervain and incense of jasmine, I cast a powerful prosperity spell. Two days later the fashion editor at the *San Francisco Chronicle* called me with a *fabulous* plan: Her favorite niece was getting married, she wanted to outfit the entire wedding party in vintage dresses, and could I be a doll and help her out?

As my grandmother always said, *Be careful what you wish for.* After weeks spent haunting estate sales, thrift stores, and auctions, I had managed to rustle up several options for each of the eleven bridesmaids, as well as a half dozen gowns that could be altered to fit the bride. But, anticipating bridal jitters, I wanted to have plenty of options on hand. Maya's lead on two more gowns, if they were in good condition, would bring the selections up to eight. Surely one would catch the bride's fancy.

The bridal party was scheduled to arrive tomorrow at two o'clock for a mammoth try-on session, and Bronwyn suggested I make the afternoon an event by closing the store to passersby and serving mimosas, which sounded like a good idea. I hoped. I wasn't what you'd call an experienced hostess.

In fact, as we used to say back in Texas, I was as nervous as a long-tailed cat in a room full of rockers.

"Lily, you ready to go?" Maya asked.

"Sure am."

I grabbed my 1940s cocoa brown wool coat from the brass coat stand near the register and pulled it on, securing the carved bone button at my neck. It was only four in the afternoon, but a wall of fog was creeping in, dropping the temperature a good fifteen degrees in the past five minutes. Late-afternoon or early-evening fog is not unusual for San Francisco since it sits on a thumb of land between an ocean and a bay. Still, recalling Barnabas's warning—*Mark the fog*—I wondered if the weather had anything to do with Aidan Rhodes's visit. Spooks loved the fog.

The thought gave me pause. If Aidan's witchcraft was powerful enough to command the weather, I would have to be careful around him.

"Go ahead and close up if we're not back by seven," I said to Bronwyn, gently tugging on Oscar's ear. "And *you* behave yourself, young man, or I'll send you right back to where you came from."

"Don't you *listen* to her, Oscar Boscar Boo. Mama Bronwyn won't let mean old Aunt Lily send you *anywhere*," she crooned to my would-be familiar as Maya and I walked out into the cool March mist.

Shape-shifting creatures and meddlesome witches aside, the quest for really cool old clothes must go on.

Chapter 2

When we exited the store we decided to leave my vintage cherry red Mustang convertible sitting at the curb, instead choosing to take the more practical purple van in the driveway. The graphics on the side read:

AUNT CORA'S CLOSET
VINTAGE CLOTHING AND QUALITY ACCESSORIES
CORNER OF HAIGHT & ASHBURY
BUY—SELL—TRADE
IT'S NOT OLD; IT'S VINTAGE!

I steered while Maya guided me across town. Along the way, she gave me the scoop on what to expect.

"The source is Frances Potts. She's lived in her home near Hunters Point for fifty-two years, ever since she married Ronald. The Pottses lived together, one great big happy family, for years."

"Potts, Frances and Ronald," I repeated. "Got it."

"Frances and Ronald had two daughters. They lost one as a child—so sad; that just seems so wrong, doesn't it?—but the other married well and has a couple of kids of her own. Anyway, the in-laws died not long after the little girl, some thirtysomething years ago, leaving the house to Frances and Ronald. Ronald died not too long after that; don't know from what. Must've been pretty young, don't you think?"

"Seems like. So it's just Frances? She never remarried?"

"Nope. And she inherited everything from her in-laws, including from her mother-in-law's sister, Bessie. And like I told you, Frances has never thrown *anything* out."

My kind of woman.

"Where does she store everything?" Cloth could last for hundreds, even thousands of years if it was properly cared for. But as one soon came to discover in the vintage clothing business, that was a big "if."

"The basement."

My heart sank. Basements were rare in earthquake country—in a temblor the last place you want to be is belowground, where the trouble originates—and those that did exist were generally small and only partly finished, with the rest left in its natural state of dirt. Damp dirt.

"Don't worry—everything's hung up on racks; plus she's got a dehumidifier down there. She has a bunch of costume jewelry as well, mostly from the thirties. I think it belonged to her in-laws. Oh, and a swell collection of old Chock full o' Nuts coffee cans."

Maya and I shared a smile.

"One can never have enough of those," I remarked.

As we neared the Bayview–Hunters Point neighborhood the environs deteriorated, piles of trash increasing in inverse proportion to the condition of the cars lining the streets. Most of the storefronts were boarded up, and the only sign of commerce—other than the drug dealers lurking in the alleys—was a liquor store, its dirty neon sign flashing, —QU-R. Seagulls announced our proximity to the bay, but there were no expensive waterfront homes here. In its heyday, Hunters Point had been home to a working port and a naval station. It now qualified as a Superfund toxic cleanup site.

Most of the homes were two-story stucco duplexes with peeling paint and crooked shutters, interspersed with a smattering of 1970s bunker-style concrete apartment buildings. All in all, the ambience did not scream, "prosperous followers of high fashion," and I wondered what we would find at the Potts residence.

To my relief, Frances Potts lived in a once-grand Victorian that must have been built when the neighborhood's residents were middle-class. It sat high above the street on a huge corner lot, encircled by a four-foot-tall stone retaining wall topped with a crooked filigreed wrought-iron fence. The yard was dense and overgrown, but the varieties of rare plants suggested it had once had a Mediterranean theme. A widow's walk topped the main turret. Cheap metal grates covered the first-floor and basement windows, and a rain gutter had detached itself from the eaves and hung limply near the front stoop. Bright green moss obscured the elaborate design of the old roof shingles; it would be only a matter of time before they rotted away completely.

Throw in some cobwebs and a ticket booth, and the Potts home would be a dead ringer for a theme park's haunted house.

We reached the broad wooden porch and Maya rang the doorbell, which we could hear echoing inside the house. I looked out over the disheveled garden, trying to quell my nervousness. After a childhood of being shunned, I always felt butterflies in my stomach when waiting on someone's doorstep, hoping for admittance. It still seemed like a minor miracle when someone actually invited me into their home.

A child's high-pitched voice rang out on the other side of the door: "Who is it?"

"It's Maya. Is that you, Jessica?"

The door opened wide to reveal a little girl, maybe seven or eight, with long, glossy black hair and huge eyes to match. Her grin took up half her face.

"Hi, Maya! I was just helping Mrs. Potts peel potatoes and carrots for her dinner. She's having company."

"Yum," Maya said. "This is my friend Lily."

"Hi!" Jessica swung around and hopped away, holding her hands in front of her like paws. "Guess what I am!"

"A bunny rabbit?" I asked.

"A kangaroo!" She flashed a smile over her shoulder as she hopped down the shadowy hallway.

Maya and I stepped into the dim foyer and closed the door behind us.

"Jessica's a neighbor," Maya spoke in a low voice. "I get the sense that her mom has to work a lot; I met her last time I was here."

"Come in. Come in." A petite, white-haired woman

emerged through a doorway near the end of the hall and beckoned us into the kitchen.

The savory aroma of roasting meat greeted us in the bright kitchen, which featured high ceilings, large windows, and a worn terra-cotta tile floor. Old crockery, iron skillets, and copper pots adorned the shelves willy-nilly; huge mason jars full of flour, sugar, and pasta lined the green-tile counter. Stitched dolls sat high on a shelf along with several embroidered, heart-shaped pillows. A pan on the stove held raw peeled and quartered carrots, potatoes, and onions. A platter of sugar cookies sat under a glass dome.

"Mrs. Potts, this is Lily Ivory," Maya introduced us.

"So nice to meet you. Please, call me Frances," Mrs. Potts murmured in a soft Southern drawl. I felt an immediate kinship to her, though I couldn't put my finger on why. She wore a faded floral housedress, support hose, and fluffy pale pink slippers. By her slow, deliberate movements she appeared to be in her seventies. But there was a nervous vitality to her . . . a simmering energy just under the surface. Hard to say. I'm sensitive to auras and vibrations, but I'm no mind reader.

"You're here to look at the wedding dresses?" Mrs. Potts asked.

"And any other vintage clothing you might be willing to part with."

"*Vintage.*" She laughed and waved a hand. "They're just plain *old*. But they're yours if you'd like them. I don't quite know why I've squirreled them away all these years."

"For my sake, I'm glad you did," I said.

"Jessica, you'd best run on home, dear," Mrs. Potts

said to the girl, lifting the glass cover off the plate of cookies. "Your mother will wonder where you are. Take a cookie."

"M'kay. Bye, Mrs. Potts! Bye, Maya!" With a sugar cookie as big as a salad plate in one hand, the little girl hopped toward the back door, then stopped and looked back over her shoulder. Her big, near-black eyes landed on me, and she hesitated before adding, "Bye . . . lady!"

Frances led us down a short, high-ceilinged hallway to a door that opened onto the basement stairs. Her descent down the creaky wooden stairway was slow and arduous. Weak shafts of late-afternoon light filtered in through the high, grimy basement windows, but it was impossible to see anything clearly. Near the bottom of the stairs Frances stretched to her right, reaching out in the darkness to switch on the lights.

Women's clothes—mostly high-quality dresses and skirt suits—crowded a rack that ran the entire circumference of the concrete half basement. Dozens of hats, pocketbooks, gloves, and scarves wrapped in plastic rested on shelves above the rack. In the very center of the room sat a stack of cardboard boxes neatly labeled MOTHER POTTS and BESSIE POTTS.

I had met a lot of people who held on to a lot of things over the years, but this was truly impressive.

As I stepped off the stairs and into the confined space, I was hit by a wave of dizziness. The air reeked of mothballs and cedar, and like most homes that had embraced a number of souls over the years, the room swam with sensations, both good and bad. But there was something more—an undercurrent of bleak desperation. This went beyond the average vicissitudes of a typical human life.

I glanced over at the diminutive Mrs. Potts, wondering how her young daughter had died.

"There are the wedding gowns," said Mrs. Potts as she gestured toward two ivory dresses hanging on the end of one rod. "I had them dry-cleaned."

They were lovely, and in excellent condition. The older of the two was a 1920s flapper style made of Normandy lace, with a high neckline and long fitted sleeves. A sheer net-and-lace skirt fell from the drop waist, and featured at least seven inches of a floral embroidered area at the knee. The second underskirt then fell to a scalloped, embroidered hemline. Paired with it was an ecru net-and-lace veil with a flowered headpiece and an eight-foot-long lace-trimmed train.

The other gown was a tea-length early-1950s dress composed of two parts: a simple white satin sheath underneath, with a gauzy long-sleeved overdress that cinched at the waist before flaring out in a skirt made wide with crinoline.

Either dress might have to be lengthened with rows of lace or ruffles to accommodate my customer's measurements, but that was simple enough. I felt a small thrill of success . . . and relief. Seeing into the future wasn't one of my talents, but I had the definite sense that tomorrow's bridal fitting session would go well.

Frances took the simpler dress off the rack and held it up to her body with both hands, smoothing the fabric over the length of her torso and swaying slightly to make the skirt dance.

"Can you imagine? I once fit into this!"

"I have that very same reaction every summer when I put on my swimsuit for the first time," I said.

Frances and Maya both laughed and nodded, and I felt a wave of pleasant surprise. This was the kind of "girl talk" I had never been privy to, much less a part of.

"Where are you from, Lily?" Frances asked.

"West Texas. A small town not far from El Paso."

She nodded. "I'm from Louisiana originally, but I've lived here so long I've lost my accent."

I smiled. I always think I'm losing my accent, too, until I realize people keep asking me where I'm from.

Next we turned our attention to Mrs. Potts's impressive collection of everyday clothing. Maya went right to work opening boxes and pawing through "Aunt Bessie's" things, many of which had been carefully wrapped in dry-cleaning bags. Storing cloth in plastic wasn't the best plan, as it didn't allow garments to "breathe." Thus a lot of the fabric showed signs of rot and moth damage, but some of it could be salvaged. I had developed a careful multistep laundering process to gently bleach and clean even the most delicate silks and laces, and Maya's mother, Lucille, was an excellent seamstress who helped me with minor repairs. Customers who sought out rare vintage clothing usually took a mend or two in stride as the cost of wearing such beauty.

I started flipping through the hanging clothes, at the oldest end first, noting a number of designer names and labels from chic boutiques. Mrs. Potts must have been quite the clotheshorse in her day—this was high-quality stuff. The garments were primarily circa the 1950s and 1960s, with a few that harked back to the forties. These outfits would sell well; the clothes of the postwar decades were very hot right now. I held each one of the articles of clothing in my arms for a moment before setting them into one of the Hefty plastic bags we'd brought with us. As I cradled them, I felt for their vibrations, sensed their history.

I reached for a deep red shirtwaist from the mid-sixties. As I touched it, I felt a physical shock, as though I had been scalded. This was the garment responsible for those dreadful sensations I had felt at the bottom of the stairs. Letting go immediately, I dropped the dress in a scarlet heap on the ground.

Mrs. Potts looked up from the box of once-white gloves she had been matching and met my eyes.

"Perhaps we'd better leave that one," she said.

"Yes, perhaps," I murmured as I hung the dress back up.

In the vintage clothes business, there was a call for items that gave off less-than-positive vibrations. Some people are drawn to darkness, not in order to replicate it but because of a kind of deep understanding of, even kinship with, the shadow side that helps them resolve to set things right in this life. After all, without shadows, things lose their definition, their contours. A lot of perpetually sunny people don't understand that. On the other hand, a truly dark item in the wrong hands . . . That could be dangerous. As I knew only too well. As an impetuous young woman I had searched for the truth about my father, and when I found it, I barely survived. Even now the memory made me shiver.

Still, I would never sell such a garment to a customer. No one wearing that dress would be strong enough to overcome its tremors of grief.

With a sense of foreboding I looked up to see that there was no longer any daylight peeking in through the grimy panes of the high basement half windows. Glancing at my antique Tinker Bell wristwatch, I realized we had been down in the basement much longer than I thought. Evening was upon us.

A frisson of icy fear washed over me.

And then I heard it—a terrible wailing that turned my blood cold.

Chapter 3

Where are my children?

The keening cry sounded as though it were right on top of us. Everything else receded while I tried to fight off the terror and desolation of the wailing, clutching at my medicine bundle like a lifeline.

After a hideous moment, the crying subsided.

Maya was still rummaging through a box and humming an off-tune rendition of Bob Marley's "One Love," her butt sticking in the air. She hadn't heard a thing.

"What in all God's creation was *that*?" Frances asked, hand fluttering to her chest.

I looked at her for a long moment. Normal humans couldn't usually hear a demon's wail . . . unless they were marked for death.

"What was what?" I asked, not wanting to assume.

"You didn't hear that? I like to died just hearing such a sound."

"I didn't hear anything," Maya said, poking her head up from her task.

Frances gazed at me, sorrow and understanding in her eyes. "You heard it, though, didn't you, child?"

I finally realized whom Frances reminded me of: my grandmother Graciela. In that moment her tone of voice sounded so much like my *abuela* that I wanted to hug her.

"Must have been a cat," I said.

Frances just stared at me. She knew it was no cat.

Another scream erupted then, this one sounding young and all too human.

Jessica.

The little girl's smiling face came to my mind, unbidden.

"I heard *that*," Maya said as she ran up the basement stairs. I followed on her heels down the hallway, through the kitchen, and out the back door into the cool evening.

A small crowd had gathered about a block down the street in front of a run-down white stucco duplex, the front door wide-open. A distraught woman had collapsed on the concrete stoop. A young tattooed man held her and seemed to be speaking, but the woman was inconsolable. Several children of varying ages stood nearby, wide-eyed and silent, some softly crying.

"My baby!" the woman screamed. *"M'hija!"*

"What happened?" Maya asked as we approached the outer ring of the crowd.

A skinny young blonde with the pallid complexion and hollow eyes of a drug user gave us the once-over, apparently decided we weren't a threat, and answered. "Her daughter got snatched."

"Snatched? You mean kidnapped?" Maya demanded.

"Whatever."

"Did anyone see who did it?" I asked.

"Dunno. It was probably her dad or something." The young woman shrugged and turned away. An intricate tattoo of a snake ran up her bare arm, and as I studied it the reptile seemed to come alive, turning to me and staring in challenge, its forked tongue lapping in my direction.

There was evil in the air. I reached for my medicine bag and mumbled a quick incantation.

Much more grounded in the real world, Maya whipped out her cell phone and dialed 911.

The people around us murmured in a mixture of English and Spanish, rumors and speculation already beginning to ripple through the crowd. As I watched them, external sounds fell away until I was able to hear only two whispered words rising above the rest: "*La Llorona*."

My stomach fell. Those of us who grew up near the banks of the Rio Grande knew—and feared—*La Llorona.* According to legend "the weeping woman" was abandoned by the father of her children because she was of a lower social class, or because he fell in love with another woman—the details shifted depending on who was telling the story. This much was clear: The anguished mother took her children down to the river and drowned them, one by one, finally flinging herself in to join them in their watery grave. Now she haunts the banks of rivers and creeks, crying for her lost babies and abducting children who happen to be out at night, adding their souls to her brood.

La Llorona scared the *mierda* out of me.

"Maya, what in the world's going on, child?"

Maya and I looked up to see Mrs. Potts clomping toward us, using a walker to arduously make her way down the uneven sidewalk. The crowd parted, letting her through.

"We're not sure yet, but it looks as though a child was taken," Maya said.

Mrs. Potts gasped and held her hand to her mouth, then looked to the woman on the stoop.

"But that's Jessica's mother. . . . You . . . you're saying *Jessica* was taken?"

Maya and I exchanged looks.

"Maybe it's a misunderstanding," Maya said. "Sometimes kids hide, don't they? I'll go see if I can find out anything concrete."

Maya started moving through the crowd, talking to the bystanders. I stayed with Mrs. Potts, trying to lend moral support with my presence. Maya was right; there could be some sort of misunderstanding.

I would be more hopeful myself if only Frances and I hadn't heard *La Llorona*'s horrifying scream a few moments before in the basement.

As I watched the young tattooed man holding the sobbing mother on the stoop, his dark eyes focused on something across the street. Following his gaze, I noticed a small cluster of young men, all slouching in huge red oversize T-shirts and baggy jeans that sagged to their crotches. Strong, muscled arms crossed over their broad chests or stuck deep in pants pockets. Each one of them glowered at the young man on the stoop. When the wail of a police siren finally cut through the noise of the crowd, the men roused themselves and loped off down the street, unhurried.

Looking back toward the stoop, I watched the young Latino glare at the retreating men as though he were shooting daggers at their shoulder blades. Even from my position twenty feet away, I could feel his anger, almost smell its acrid scent.

A police cruiser pulled up, prompting the majority of the bystanders to disperse. A uniformed officer approached the mother, while another began working the crowd, taking statements. When he reached us I told him that Jessica had been at Frances's house earlier, and gave him my contact information. Frances did the same. Afterward, since we had nothing more helpful to add to the investigation, Maya and I walked Mrs. Potts back home and sat her down at the kitchen table. I filled the kettle for tea, but Maya unearthed a bottle of whiskey from a crowded sideboard and poured a shot into three small juice glasses, saying it was "for medicinal reasons."

Frances suddenly looked every one of her advanced years, and then some. She sat in a straight chair at the old pine table, clearly distraught but trying to fight tears. My heart went out to her as she smoothed her helmet of thick white hair and toyed with the buttons on her beige cardigan.

"Could I call someone for you?" Maya asked, placing her hand on Frances's stooped shoulder. "Your daughter, perhaps?"

Mrs. Potts looked up. "*No*. No, don't call her."

"But you shouldn't be alone—"

"Don't call Katherine." She grabbed Maya's hand. "Please, promise me."

"Of course. Whatever you like," Maya assured her, taken aback by her vehemence.

"I just . . . don't want to disturb her," Mrs. Potts said. "She's got her own family to worry about. There's no need for her to come sit with a silly old woman. I . . . I'm expecting my lawyer to come for dinner, anyway. She'll be here any minute."

"A lawyer who makes house calls?" Maya asked with a ghost of a smile.

Frances nodded, and returned a shaky smile. "I bribed her with a home-cooked meal. Herbed pot roast tonight. I have my own little kitchen garden, you know; never did know a frozen vegetable to come close to the taste of fresh."

"You remind me of my Grammy," said Maya. "I'll never forget her rhubarb pie, straight from the garden."

As I watched them both trying to rally their spirits, I had a profound realization: When I made the decision to settle down in San Francisco, I promised I would stop keeping myself at such a distance from people. Somehow I had failed to intuit that Jessica was in danger, but at least it was in my power to protect dear old Frances.

I asked to use the bathroom. Frances directed me to turn right down the hallway, then right again.

The corridor was so dark I had to feel my way to the doorway, my hand finally landing upon the light switch. The powder room retained none of the historic charm of the rest of the house; it had been remodeled some time ago—probably in the seventies—in ugly harvest gold linoleum tiles matched with avocado green fixtures.

I closed the door and started rifling through drawers. Collecting clothes wasn't Frances's only pack-rat tendency; I doubted she had cleaned out this vanity since the Nixon administration. In one drawer were boxes of generic tissues and Q-tips, in another an old tin coffee can full of spare buttons, air freshener, another heart-shaped sachet, and shoe polish. Pushing aside an ice-blue quilted satin glove box full of seriously old tubes of mascara and pale cakes of powder, I finally found something I could use: a hairbrush.

Carefully extracting several strands of white hair, I wrapped them in a tissue, and tucked the little package into the back pocket of my jeans.

I flushed the toilet to complete the ruse. When I opened the door to the hallway the light from the bathroom streamed out, illuminating a series of framed family pictures on the opposite wall. There was a photo of a much younger Frances, beaming beside a man with a crew cut and horn-rimmed glasses; a girl in cat's-eye glasses and bangs cut straight across her forehead; and a slightly younger girl in a matching dress. The sisters were towheads, with that pale, wispy hair unique to young children and forever mimicked by hairstylists. On either side of the family portrait were more pictures of the children. There was a series of school photos of the older girl as she grew, but only one more picture of the younger child, this time with her mother. They were seated on a bench near the water. Frances looked very stylish in a hat and gloves, and was wearing the deep red outfit that I had dropped in the basement. Beside her sat a cherubic-looking girl about Jessica's age.

I took the photograph from the wall and cradled it to my chest, concentrating. Pain coursed through me. This photo had been held often, kissed, and cried upon. This must be the daughter who had died.

I rehung the picture, feeling a new level of resolve.

Frances had suffered enough. I had no idea why she had heard *La Llorona*'s cry, but that demon would not nab two souls in one night. Not if I could help it.

I glanced down at my watch. I needed time to prepare a brew and cast my protection spell before the witching hour, when *La Llorona* would be strong enough to hunt down those she had already marked for death. Most folks think the witching hour is midnight, but in my experience it was three a.m.: the time between the night before and the morning to come, when humans were most vulnerable and the supernatural opportunities were ripest. The in-between time. When the spirit window opened widest between our worlds.

By the time I returned to the kitchen, Mrs. Potts's dinner guest had arrived.

"Lily, child, this is my lawyer, Delores Keener," Frances introduced us.

"Nice to meet you." She nodded with a warm smile. In her early forties, Keener was the type of woman often referred to as "handsome," the tall, solid kind who grew better-looking with age. She wore a beautifully tailored, immaculate cream-colored pantsuit and carried a maroon leather Coach briefcase overstuffed with papers. Her otherwise businesslike mien was belied only by her styled platinum blond hair, which lent her a rather incongruous, but not unattractive, bit of Marilyn Monroe glamour.

"Lily is here for all those old clothes in the basement. She seems to think someone might want them."

"Really? That's great," Delores said. "Frances here is like the Imelda Marcos of dresses."

"How you do go on," Frances scoffed, but smiled at the good-natured teasing.

"I was telling Frances how impressed I am with a lawyer who makes house calls," said Maya.

"Frances and my mother go way back. And I never could resist pot roast."

"It smells great," said Maya.

"Delores, I must tell you the most dreadful thing that just happened . . ." Frances began.

As Frances launched into the sad tale of the past hour, Maya and I excused ourselves and went back down to the basement.

"Angling for a dinner invitation?" I teased.

"I'm just worried about Frances, all alone in this huge house after . . . after what happened. But I suppose Delores will stay with her awhile."

"Besides, that pot roast smelled amazing. Must be the herbs."

Maya smiled. "Okay, I am getting hungry. I'll admit it."

"Let's take care of all this, and then we can stop for a bite on the way back." It was on the tip of my tongue to invite Maya home with me so I could cook for her, but then I remembered I had a spell to brew and a busy night of spell casting ahead of me. First things first.

We started hauling our seven Hefty bags of vintage clothing up the steep stairs of the basement, down the hall, and into the front foyer. The streetlamps shone through a stained-glass window near the parlor fireplace, casting jewel-toned light onto the worn Oriental rug. A sturdy oak grandfather clock ticked off the moments, the sound practically echoing through the empty rooms. Maya was right—how did Frances manage here all alone? This was a grand house meant to accommodate a big family, with children running about, parents busily taking care of business, and grandparents spinning tales of their youth. It was easy to imagine a day a few decades ago, when the home would have been filled with music and the voices of three generations. Then again, it was just as easy to envision the desperate, tragic day Frances's youngest daughter was lost forever.

Clothing is one of those things, like water, that you don't realize is heavy until you deal with it in bulk. Maya and I were panting by the time we lugged the last of our many bags out the front door, down the broad wooden stairs, along the cracked concrete steps to the sidewalk, and finally into the van. After our third trip I leaned back against the dusty vehicle, taking a breather.

I glanced down the street toward Jessica's house. There were now several police cars, both marked and unmarked, in front of the duplex, but the crowd had evaporated. I got the distinct impression that Bayview–Hunters Point was the sort of neighborhood where most residents did not knowingly put themselves in the path of authorities of any kind.

Maya and I returned to the kitchen to say good-bye and found Delores Keener comforting a weeping Frances.

Feeling awkward, I watched as Maya hugged the elderly woman, busying myself by writing Frances a generous check. I pay a lot more than the average secondhand shop, in part to get the best stuff, in part to help out needy seniors. Besides, the truth was that I ran Aunt Cora's Closet more for the sake of my own sanity than for the income. I had never been above using my special talents to develop a fat stock portfolio.

Maya and I climbed into the van and headed across

town. We were well out of the Hunters Point neighborhood before Maya broke the silence.

"What do you think happened with Jessica?"

"It could be anything," I said with a shrug. "Maybe it was her father, or some other relative. It usually is."

Her serious, dark eyes fixed on me. "Is that what you really think?"

I pulled up to a red light and hesitated. Maya hadn't heard *La Llorona*'s scream, thank goodness, and as far as I knew she had no idea I was a witch—had no knowledge of magic at all. So what was she asking, exactly?

"I don't know what to think, Maya," I said finally. "Let's just hope the police find something out, and soon."

Chapter 4

By the time we neared home, neither of us had an appetite, so we skipped dinner. I paid Maya her commission and dropped her at her apartment, just a few blocks off Haight Street. Bronwyn had long since closed up shop, and I was glad for the solitude. I brought Frances's wedding dresses with me to hang them up, but decided to leave the rest of the bags in the van until the morning, when I could sort through them with fresh eyes and decide which ones needed repair or embellishment, and which a simple cleaning.

As I let myself into the old two-story Victorian building that housed Aunt Cora's Closet I breathed deeply, sighing with contentment. The shop welcomed me with the scent of clean laundry, lavender, and sage. A bundle of rosemary tied with a black ribbon hung over the front door, inviting luck to enter, while charms in the form of dried flowers, wreaths, and herbal sachets hung over every doorway and mirror.

Several precious antique gowns too delicate to be out

on the sales floor adorned the walls like gossamer tapestries—their heirloom lace and exquisite hand-sewn ruffles were more suited to decoration than to twenty-first-century lives. The rest of the stock was hung on racks and divided by historic era: I carried clothing from the 1890s all the way up to the 1980s, from white cotton Victorian underthings to fringed leather vests. Though I preferred the older garments, there was a market among the youth for items just twenty or thirty years old, including the ugly polyester outfits I remembered from my adolescence. No matter, they all hummed with the energy and vitality of their former owners.

Aside from the overflowing racks of everyday skirts, dresses, and tops, I maintained an impressive selection of frothy lingerie, feather boas, hats, wigs, and even a few period stewardess, nurse, and cheerleader outfits. And though I carried only women's clothes, I liked to interpret that liberally: In the costume corner were several tuxedos and a number of Boy Scout uniforms, sailors' hats, and cowboy accoutrements. I couldn't wait for Halloween.

I love my shop and its contents. No matter how alienated I have felt my whole life, when I'm in the company of old things I sense the human connections through the ages. They have always helped ease the loneliness of my solitary existence.

A narrow staircase led off the rear storage room to a cozy one-bedroom apartment on the second floor. As in the store below, I had filled my personal space with much-loved used furniture, appliances, and artwork. The lace curtains in my bedroom window had been tatted by a British war bride who made her new home in the

Outer Sunset; the soft white sheets on my canopy bed were purchased at a Parisian flea market; even my stove was an old Wedgwood that had nourished three generations of a family in nearby Hayes Valley.

Unfortunately, like so much in the magical world, my sensitivity to vibrations was a two-way street. I hated the soulless feel of newly minted products that were factory-produced by poorly paid workers, and felt their despair every time I touched them. Even finding toothpaste whose vibrations didn't rattle my fillings could be a trial.

I crossed through the bedroom to the bath and took a quick cleansing shower with lemon verbena soap. Afterward, brushing my long chestnut brown hair twenty strokes, I was sure to capture any loose strands before tying it into a ponytail with a black ribbon. I then cleaned the brush carefully and brought the loose hair into the kitchen to burn.

My grandmother Graciela had hammered this habit into me: *Let not a single strand of your own hair fall into a brew,* m'hija, *for you will change the spell in ways you did not intend. Intention must always reign supreme while brewing. And never forget that hair and nails must always be burned lest they be captured for use in a spell against you.*

I often wondered how much of what I did was witchcraft, and how much superstition. To this day I couldn't shake the childish image of evildoers lurking behind every corner at hairdressers' and manicure salons, brooms in hand, just waiting to sweep up all that personal mojo lying around on the floor and manipulate it for their own evil ends. Last week my neighbor Sandra suggested we go for mani-pedis and I nearly hyperventilated.

No wonder I had a hard time making friends.

My favorite part of the apartment was its huge kitchen, which was at least as big as my small living room. The floor was tiled with 1950s-style black-and-white-checked linoleum, the cupboards were simple wood hutches painted a chalky blue-green, and unpainted wooden beams ran across the ceiling. From the beams dangled bunches of dried herbs, flowers, and braids of garlic; open shelves were crammed with jars filled with ingredients in a rainbow of colors; and a pot of fresh basil sat on the butcher-block counter to keep negative spirits at bay. The all-important lunar calendar hung by the sink.

Ready to begin spell casting, I filled my old cast-iron cauldron one-quarter full with fresh springwater and hoisted the heavy pot onto the gas stove to boil. A village "cunning woman" in the Scottish highlands told me that using an iron pot is an insult to the Fae, or the fairy folk, but I've never known any Fae well enough to ask.

"Whatcha doin'?"

I jumped and whirled around at the croaky voice of my wannabe familiar, perched on top of the refrigerator. My own personal outsize gargoyle.

"You makin' a spell?" he asked.

"You scared me . . ." I said, slapping my hand over my pounding heart. "What's your real name, anyway?"

"Oscar."

"No, it isn't. I just called you that on the spur of the moment."

"Then that's my name, mistress."

I realized I was arguing with a gargoyle, and tried to ignore him.

"I like it the way that lady says it. *Oscaroo*," he crooned.

"'Oscaroo' sounds like some strange Australian creature that evolution left behind."

He snickered. It was a disturbing sound.

I pulled a huge red leather-bound volume off a high shelf in the pantry. Every practicing witch has her own unique Book of Shadows, full of spells, recipes, and remembrances. Mine creaked when I opened it and smelled slightly of must, reminding me, not unpleasantly, of a used bookstore. Graciela had given me the book, already half-full of her own family recipes, when I was eight, and I had gone on to crowd it with notes and newspaper clippings for as long as I could remember. Besides spells, it contained mementos and quotations that I read to myself in moments of doubt and despair, as well as a few newspaper articles about events I would rather not remember, but that I must. The tome quite literally hummed with memories, knowledge, and awareness.

Though I knew almost all of my spells by heart, I always opened my Book of Shadows and double-checked before conjuring. It was part of my ritual.

Covering the counter with a clean white cloth, I started setting out the things I needed. Of primary importance was my *athame*, or spirit blade, which is a black-handled, supersharp, double-edged knife. Beside it I placed a length of blessed rope; a special kind of vinca known as Sorcerer's Violet; and dried stalks of Verbascum dipped in tallow.

"I like that lady that held me," Oscar said, a dreamy note in his voice.

"I'll just bet you do." I had never met a demon, male or female, who didn't possess a healthy libido. "Listen, I want to ask you about something. What do you know about *La Llorona*?"

He gave a little shudder. "She *scares* me. I hear she has empty sockets where there should be eyes, and her mouth is an open, voracious void, and—"

"*Enough*, thanks. I don't need a description."

"Then why did you ask?"

"I thought I heard her tonight. She's supposed to hang around riverbeds," I pointed out as I hung a basket on my arm and grabbed my white-handled *boline*, a special sickle-shaped knife used to cut magical herbs. "But there aren't any rivers in San Francisco, are there?"

"Nope." Oscar trailed me through a pair of French doors onto my terrace.

This was my essential rooftop herb garden: crowded with pots holding coriander, vervain, and even poisonous wolfsbane; and planters full of gingerroot, horehound, and damiana. Since it was only six weeks old my garden was still immature, but I had worked a fertility spell to speed the growing season up a little bit. I snipped off small sprigs of henbane and badger's foot and placed them in my basket.

"But water spirits are practical folk," Oscar continued. "They can't find a creek or a river, they use the bay, a backed-up storm drain, a swimming pool. Easy enough for drowning people, either way."

"Great. I finally find a place to settle down, and now *La Llorona*'s haunting the bay?"

He shrugged. "Everyone wants to live in the Bay Area. It's an active area, spirit-wise. New Orleans is getting crowded, and the climate's better here."

"Hey, what's the deal with your master, Aidan Rhodes? Does he want you to spy on me?"

"You're my master now, mistress," he repeated his earlier incantation.

"I don't need a familiar, Oscar. I'm not . . . not a normal witch."

"Well, you sure as heck aren't a normal human."

I glared at him.

"What'd I say?"

"Why don't you go be Bronwyn's familiar? She could use the help."

"Who's Bronwyn?"

"The woman you're so enamored with."

"Ooh, the *lady*," he repeated dreamily. Then he shrugged. "Can't. I'm yours. And she's not a witch like you. She one of those, whaddayacall? Wiccans."

"At least she belongs to a coven. I don't belong . . . anywhere."

In the old days—the burning times—there was a distinction made between sorcerers and witches. It was said that a sorcerer learned magic through training, while a witch was born with innate talents and connections to the spirit world. The latter was true in my case, to an extreme degree. I hadn't chosen this path; it had chosen me. One of the many curses my status bestowed was a near-perfect memory, and I could recall every alienating episode, every isolating incident, of my thirty-one years.

Oscar was following so closely on my heels that when I stopped to pick some cinquefoil grass he plowed right into the backs of my legs. He watched me for another minute while I gathered nine berries of deadly nightshade; then we both headed back into the kitchen where the cauldron was boiling.

"Whatcha cookin'?"

"A woman I met earlier may have heard *La Llorona*'s cry. I'm brewing a spell to protect her." I started crushing sempervivum leaves in the ancient stone mortar Graciela had given me when I left home.

"Ooh! How much is she paying you?" Oscar hopped around the kitchen in his excitement. "Firstborn? Life of duty? Web site?"

That last option threw me. "Web site?"

"Master Rhodes had a supplicant make him an interactive Web site. You should see it. It's awesome."

Times do change.

"She's not paying me anything," I answered as I dropped the black shiny berries, one by one, into the boiling cauldron. "She doesn't even know I'm doing it."

He narrowed his eyes, fixed me with an odd look. "Don't tell me you have a fetish for normal humans. They would have burned you not so long ago."

"Good thing we live in modern times, then, right?"

"I don't really like cowans," he mused, using the archaic derogatory word for a nonwitchy human. "They're fun to play with, but they're narrow-minded, quick to blame, can't see past their own—"

"Don't call them cowans. Besides, I'm just as human as the next person."

"Normal humans don't cast spells . . . at least, not well."

I threw my stone pestle down on the butcher block with a loud thud.

"For your information, familiars don't argue with their masters. And if you don't like humans, then you shouldn't hang around me. I *like* being around normal people. I'm a normal-people person. They just haven't especially liked me up till now. But all that's about to change."

"How will it change, mistress?"

"Because I'm not moving around anymore. I'm staying put, and I'm going to make friends, and sell great old clothes, and I'm going to use my powers to help people. But no one is ever going to know that I'm—"

"A superpowerful witch?"

"—a freak. I don't want to be seen as a scary freak anymore."

And with that I dropped a freeze-dried bat into the bubbling brew.

The matching of a witch with a familiar is supposed to be an intimate affair. A witch bonds to a special animal with which she feels an overwhelming sense of kinship and trust. Familiars are popular with witches because animals are often more in touch with the undercurrents of the spirit world than are humans, allowing them to be not only companions but magical intermediaries and helpers. But I had more than enough power all by myself, which was one reason I had never joined other witches in a coven. If I added my power to theirs, there was no telling what forces might be unleashed.

I glanced up at Oscar, who was back on top of the refrigerator, inspecting his scaly, clawlike toes. I couldn't say I felt much kinship. But as I brewed my concoction, I had to admit that I did sense a subtle shift in my power. It wasn't stronger, exactly, but it was smoother. Slippery, almost. As though finding the portals more easily.

I prepared the herbs carefully, mumbling incantations as I did so. I recited my spells precisely as I had learned them: in Spanglish, with a smattering of Latin and Nahuatl, Graciela's native language. After dropping in all the herbs, one by one, I brought out the tissue and added the strands of Frances's hair while intoning her name ten times.

My left eye started to itch, an omen that sorrow would soon find its way into my life. This wasn't unusual for me, and didn't necessarily have anything to do with the spell at hand. Still, I made doubly sure to do everything I could to repel negative influences. I stirred the brew only deosil, or in a clockwise direction. I cast the few leftover herbs into the fire under the pot. I chanted an extra ten minutes, just in case.

It took a full hour of boiling for the brew to come to readiness. I spent the wait time cleaning my implements carefully and thoroughly. Inspired, I used the rest of the time to straighten my sitting room. I was vacuuming the faded Turkish rug when a distinctive, rank smell began to permeate the air, signaling the brew's readiness for the next step: blood sacrifice.

I hated this part. Not because of the pain, but because it highlighted how different I was, even from other witches. The next step was beyond the abilities of any witch I'd ever known.

Gripping the black-handled knife in my right hand, I

cut a small X in the palm of my left. Holding the injured hand palm-down over the cauldron, I allowed four drops of my blood to drip into the brew, which was now swirling deosil on its own.

I braced myself. A great cloud of vapor burst from the vessel and streamed up to the ceiling, taking on the amorphous form of a face lingering above us, looking down. Graciela said one day I would learn who my helping spirit was, but I wasn't sure I even wanted to know. He or she . . . *it* . . . scared me, every time. Almost as fast as the face appeared, it melted back into the ether.

"*Wow!* Didja see that?" asked Oscar, who had fallen back onto his butt and was huddled against the cupboards in the far corner of the kitchen. I had that same reaction for the first year or so of learning how to brew. "Mistress is a truly great witch!"

I blew out a deep breath and wiped my sweaty brow.

Witchcraft isn't for the faint of heart.

I have a genuinely terrible singing voice, but I didn't let that stop me from crooning along to a Dido CD at the top of my lungs as I sped my cherry red convertible through San Francisco's quiet streets. Oscar had whined and pleaded and mewled until I caved in and let him come along. Now, ignoring my admonitions, he jumped back and forth over the seats like a talkative dog.

Sneezing be damned, a traditional black-cat familiar was sounding better all the time.

Bayview–Hunters Point, Maya had informed me, was one of the last affordable neighborhoods in San Francisco, in part because it was adjacent to 465 acres of prime waterfront property that had been declared a toxic waste zone after the military pulled out a few decades ago. While lots of San Francisco's lower-income and "marginal" folks—hourly workers, free spirits, and artists alike—had been driven by economic necessity across the water to the East Bay, many people in Hunters Point had stayed on, developing a strong, innovative neighborhood association and even establishing a flourishing artists' colony.

As I drove into Frances's neighborhood, I noticed small groups of young men lingering on corners and loitering in front of the liquor store, using the pay phone. Farther down the street, where Jessica lived, all seemed quiet.

I pulled up in front of the darkened Potts house a little before one in the morning. Taking a special charm from the glove box, I held it in my right hand, closed my eyes, and recited an incantation several times. A few minutes later a bleary, disoriented Frances opened the front door. I ordered Oscar to stay in the car, grabbed my big canvas carryall, jumped out of the car, hurried up the path, and took the stairs two at a time.

I shut the front door behind us. The house was dark, but my night vision is better than average, and diffuse light from the streetlamps outside sifted through the windowpanes, lighting our way. Frances moaned softly as I gently propelled her up the stairs and down the hallway. If she remembered any of this, she would think of it as a vague dream. She moaned again and I searched her lined face, hoping I hadn't given her a nightmare. People had unpredictable reactions to sleepwalking.

Strange . . . tonight the patterns of colored lights filtering through the stained-glass window seemed to have an ominous cast, and the ticking of the grandfather clock marked time too quickly, almost frenetically. The air held a stale mustiness that melded with the lingering aroma of pot roast and potatoes, the scent much stronger now than it had been earlier this afternoon. Ditto the general sensations of past souls, though this wasn't surprising. Old houses held all kinds of spirits. Like the vibrations I gleaned from clothing, these were primarily benevolent, but not entirely.

Still, all the sensations felt stronger. Had something shifted since this afternoon, or was it just the effects of being here, virtually alone, in the middle of the night?

Frances's bedroom was small and cozy. I imagined that she and Ronald never moved into the master bedroom after his parents died. The chamber was minimally furnished: a double bed with a simple maple headboard and matching side tables; a vanity covered in doilies, old perfume bottles, and a fine mist of baby powder; and a faded, rose-colored upholstered easy chair decorated with embroidered heart-shaped pillows like the ones I had seen in the kitchen. I noted with approval that both tall windows, looking toward the north side of the yard, were covered with heavy brocade curtains. That was good; it was best for me to be able to control the light.

I pulled the headboard out from the wall a few inches, then led Frances back to bed and tucked her under her worn sage green cotton duvet. She wrapped her arms around her middle and curled up on her side into a fetal position, let out another soft moan, and went back to sleep.

From my satchel I extracted a dozen hand-dipped white beeswax candles, candleholders, a widemouthed thermos, and my black-handled spirit knife. I lit a few candles for light and set them on the bedside table. Then I unscrewed the thermos and invoked the powers of the moon as I poured a thin stream of liquid in a magical circle around the bed. That done, I took my *athame* and used the sharp tip to trace a five-pointed star within the circle—a pentagram—in the air. With each point I acknowledged the five elements of life: Earth, Air, Fire, Water, and finally, Spirit.

I placed the ritual candles in sets of three on the watchtowers of the circle: north, south, east, and west. Finally, kneeling within the circle, I invoked my powers, focused my intentions, and began to cast my spell of protection against *La Llorona*, against evil demons of all sorts.

As soon as I began, I heard a scratching sound overhead, a rustling that indicated restless spirits. The bedside lamp flickered on, then back off.

"Evil be gone from my sight, gone from this place. I have wrought a circle of magical brew, a circle of light against the darkness."

The candles on the bedside table blew out. The flames on the circle wavered, but I commanded them to stay lit. Something was fighting the spell, aroused by it.

"There will be no trespass upon this soul, upon this essence. Evil be gone from here, for the good of all souls. This I compel you!"

I flinched as a heavy book flew toward my head, but it smacked into the invisible wall of the magic circle and fell to the floor. An insistent thumping began and grew louder until it sounded as though a small army were racing up a never-ending staircase, their footsteps echoing throughout the house. I closed my eyes and let myself relax into my power, confident in the strength of my focused intentions. The power coursed through me, using me as its vessel.

Suddenly the noise ceased. But then whispers began. A distinct but unintelligible voice murmured and chanted, invoking against me.

I opened my eyes.

Someone was there. Someone invisible.

Not a ghost. Ghosts didn't have this kind of power. This was an invisible someone.

And I was looking straight at it.

Using all my strength, I invoked the spirits of my ancestors, my helpmates, to maintain concentration on the spell. I chanted louder and tried to block out the insistent whispering, knowing the charmed bag on the braid at my waist, the power of the brew, and the magic circle would all work together to keep me safe.

I chanted, nonstop, until the house was hushed and my voice was hoarse. According to a quietly ticking clock on the bedside table nearly an hour had passed.

As I gathered my things, I reviewed the spell in my head. That invisible whispering presence had chilled me to the core. Had it really happened, or could it have been my imagination run amok? Though I was in touch with other spirit planes, I had an unfortunate tendency to freak myself out at the worst possible moments. Despite my years of study—or perhaps because of them—I knew only too well that much of the spiritual realm was still a mystery.

Physically and mentally drained, I left the Potts house shortly after two in the morning and drove to the edge of the San Francisco Bay, near the deserted India Basin Shoreline Park.

Time for a sit-down with a certain child-hungry demon.

Hunkering down on a muddy slope, I gazed out over the calm waters of the bay, feeling the effects of the "hangover" hum I always felt after working a spell, all my nerve endings alive, ultrasensitive, but weary. A blanket of fog hovered low over the water, but gleaming lights sparkled in the city of Oakland across the bay. The hills beyond were a sooty black against the deep purple of the night. Overhead, I noticed a red-tinged ring around the moon.

Blood on the moon. Another bad omen.

An hour passed. It didn't seem as though my quarry would be showing up anytime soon. Perhaps Jessica really had been a victim of an all-too-human form of evil—a drug deal gone sour, an estranged relative, a pedophile. Maybe it hadn't been *La Llorona*'s wail that Frances and I heard, after all, but just an everyday attic—or basement—ghost trapped in Frances's home. Clearly there was some kind of presence in that house, and I was the first to admit I wasn't great with standard ghosts. Though my energy stirred them up, I could never see them clearly or understand what they were saying. I could only feel their presence and note their effects.

Creatures like *La Llorona*, on the other hand, were much more malevolent—and straightforward—than your average ghost. I had no problem at all seeing and understanding her ilk.

A half hour later I decided to pack it in. I stood and

turned to brush some damp debris off the seat of my jeans.

A wave of icy dread washed over me. This chill had nothing to do with the fog.

Out of the corner of my eye, a flash of white. Someone—some*thing*—skittered by. I twisted around, but it was gone before I could focus. Again, on the other side, a cold breeze, as though a butterfly had rushed past. Or a demon.

I froze, caressed my medicine bundle, and recited a brief protective incantation.

"Did you see that?" I asked the darkness.

"What?" Oscar appeared at my side.

I immediately felt better. Maybe this whole familiar thing wasn't such a bad idea.

"I thought I saw . . ." I tried to shake off the willies. "Never mind. It was probably just my imagination."

Another skitter in my peripheral vision, this time on the other side.

"*La Llorona!*" Oscar cried in an urgent whisper. He jumped into my arms, wrapped his scaly limbs around my neck and waist, and trembled.

So much for comforting me with his presence.

Then the weeping began: the terrible keening of a mother so tormented and distraught that she would hold her own children, one after another, underwater while she watched the life drain out of them. The sobbing became a palpable energy enveloping us, swallowing us.

"*¿Has visto a mis hijos?*" the specter wailed. *Have you seen my children?*

The cry sounded far away, which meant that she was near. Demons were strange that way.

Now I could see her: a long-haired woman in a white gown, scuttling past.

Unpeeling Oscar from my body, I called out to *La Llorona*, then started chanting, trying to beckon her to return. It was no use. I was tired from working Frances's spell and didn't have the strength to compel her.

"What's happening?" Oscar whispered from behind a bush.

"She took off."

"Why? She was attracted to your energy."

"Hush, I'm going to try again."

I tried for another ten minutes before giving up, swearing under my breath. It had been a stupid move to try to summon the apparition while fatigued from the earlier spell. Caressing my medicine bundle, I took big gulps of the salty, chill bay air as I carried Oscar back to my car in the otherwise deserted parking lot.

What now? I wondered as I slipped behind the wheel. Go home and be glad that Frances was safe, try to forget little Jessica's smiling face . . . and try to convince people—children, especially—not to go near the water at night? All this without mentioning demons and ghostly phantoms? An impossible task in the City by the Bay.

Or should I go further and try to get Jessica back? Was it even possible? And could I then somehow banish *La Llorona*? Graciela used to tell me that I hadn't come anywhere near the limits of my abilities; she said I lacked the courage to explore my power. But I left home before finishing my formal training, and I feared unleashing powers I would not be able to control. Now that I was creating a home for myself, and even developing friendships, was I grounded enough to go further with my talents? Or would dueling with a child-stealing demon put everything I had been working for—my "normalness"—at risk?

Chapter 5

Back at my cozy apartment, Oscar ate a peanut butter sandwich and then curled up to sleep on top of the refrigerator. He was snoring within minutes. I wasn't so lucky; sleep proved elusive. I took a long shower, scrubbing myself with a natural loofah and olive oil soap, then tried to clarify my mind by burning a little frankincense and myrrh.

The incense made my apartment smell fantastic, but my thoughts were as jumbled as ever. Indicative of my desperation, I unearthed my heavy crystal ball from the old black steamer trunk at the foot of my bed. A gift from one of Graciela's wealthier magical friends, the crystal ball sat on a base of intricately worked gold inlaid with semiprecious stones. It was easily the most valuable item I owned.

I set it on the coffee table in the living room, sat cross-legged before it, breathed deeply to center myself, and gazed into the crystal ball.

Divination was not my strong suit. I often experienced a foreshadowing of things to come, as though my spirit guide were warning me, but that was about the extent of my fortune-telling talents. At times I suspected Graciela believed I was faking my lack of such an obvious skill, but it was no joke. My life would have been much simpler if only I had been able to foretell the future.

The art of seeing things in a reflective surface—a crystal ball, a mirror, or even the surface of the water—is called scrying. It's a classic tool for witches and seers, but I just plain wasn't any good at it. I concentrated on staying focused but open, willing my mind to concentrate while simultaneously allowing it to wander—no mean feat. This is the kind of skill that anyone can hone with enough training, but some practitioners are much more gifted than others from the git-go.

As was typical for me, I could see only fleeting shadows, silent and unfathomable, in my crystal ball. Plenty of portentous omens, but not a one gave me any clear sign as to what was going on in the present, much less the future. Nothing to shed light on Jessica's fate or to explain the presence of the dreaded *La Llorona* in San Francisco.

Not a single, cotton-pickin' thing. Frankly, if the spirits couldn't clarify things, I'd just as soon they kept their omens to themselves.

I stifled the decidedly unwitchlike impulse to throw my beautiful crystal ball through the window and watch it shatter on the street below.

I awoke to a gargoyle with questionable breath perched on my brass bedstead, staring at me upside down.

"Can I have the pizza?"

"What?" I croaked.

"Can I have the leftover pizza in the fridge?"

"It's *may* I have the pizza."

"*May* I?" He rolled his big green eyes.

"Surely. Help yourself."

He bounced onto the bed, then trampolined onto the floor.

"You really don't have to ask, Oscar; just make yourself at home."

The warmth of my cushy comforter beckoned me, tempting me to roll over and go back to sleep. But once I'm up, I'm up. Besides, bright sunshine streamed through my multipaned windows in San Francisco's version of a late winter's morning, and I felt my spirits lift. As my grandmother used to say, despite tragedy and grief, the sun will always rise.

The great thing about owning my store—and living above it—was that it was like having an enormous walk-in closet. My whole life I've been a blue-jeans-and-T-shirt kind of gal, but lately I'd developed an addiction to my own vintage clothes. I sneaked downstairs in the purple silk kimono I used as a robe and started poking around.

With bits of pizza crust and mushrooms decorating his snout, Oscar trotted along at my heels, in his piggy mode in case anyone was peeking in through the front plate-glass windows.

After some consideration I tried on a sleeveless late-1950s pink-orange-and-aqua floral dress with a scoop neck, wide skirt, and a narrow pink belt. It came from a garage sale in Marin, and its vibrations were comforting and mellow. I assessed my reflection in the full-length mirror. The outfit suited me. I'm of average height and weight, nothing special. Dark hair and eyes. I tan easily, but since I never take the time to sunbathe, I tend toward pale. Men don't drive into lampposts when I walk down the street, but I receive my share of appreciative glances and subtle once-overs.

I topped the dress with a soft turquoise cashmere cardigan, pulled my straight dark brown hair back in its customary ponytail, and tied it with a butter yellow silk scarf. Oversize pink, orange, and yellow Bakelite bangles finished off the outfit. A sweep of mascara and sheer pink lipstick completed my simple makeup regimen.

Compared to my earlier globe-trotting life, my current everyday schedule might seem a bit tedious to many. But after years of rootlessness, I reveled in my shopkeeping routine. I loaded an old Billie Holiday CD into the store stereo and sang along to *Lady Day*, imagining myself to be like any other merchant along Haight Street who started work early, straightened her inventory, washed her windows, and put the cash in the register.

Unlike most of my neighboring business owners, however, I always took time before opening to cleanse the shop of negative vibrations by sprinkling salt water counterclockwise around the periphery of the store, and then smudging deosil with a sage bundle. Afterward, I lit a beeswax candle, murmured a brief protective incantation at the front doorway, grabbed my usual marketing basket, flipped my hand-painted wooden sign to OPEN, and unlocked the front door to Aunt Cora's Closet at ten o'clock sharp.

On the curb directly in front of the store sat a tall, gaunt man-boy. Conrad was a neighborhood fixture who referred to himself in the third person as "the Con," though as far as I could tell he hadn't actually done any time in prison. Come to think of it, unlike most of the local youth, he had no visible tattoos at all, prison-inspired or otherwise.

He turned to greet me.

"Dude," which he pronounced, *dooooooooood.* "How you doin' this fine sunny day?"

"I'm well, Conrad. And how are you?"

"Fit as a fiddle and ready to roll. Want me to sweep your sidewalk?"

This was our unwritten rule: Conrad did an errand for me and kept an eye on the store while I went down the block to the café to buy him breakfast—usually bagels or a couple of cinnamon rolls—along with a drink called Flower Power, a trademarked mix of espresso, chai, and soy milk. I kept hoping the near-daily morning meal would put a little weight on his skeletal frame.

Since the 1960s the streets of "the Haight" have been a beacon to young men and women hoping to find—or lose—themselves among the open-minded citizens who people this town. They come from the mountains of Wisconsin and the streets of New York City and the suburbs of Kansas in search of a bohemian ideal of music, a non-materialistic life, and an ethos of tolerance. Unfortunately, a lot of them realize too late that high rents mean life on the streets, and many fall under the spell of easily available drugs. A lot of locals refer to them, as they do to themselves, as "gutter punks," but I hate the derisive tone of the phrase.

Conrad liked to say he was high on life, but his bloodshot, often unfocused eyes told a different story. I had offered many times to help him get off whatever he was on, but so far he had politely and consistently refused my assistance. I was tempted to hurry the process along by forcing him with magical intervention, but as with so much in life, "the Con" would have to be *ready* to change before he could succeed in any sort of lasting psychic transformation. The effects of enchantment are not all-powerful; rather, they are limited in the face of the dogged human pursuit of self-destruction. You have to believe, to *want*, in order to have a dream come about.

This is true even for us witches. Many's the time I've wished I could just wiggle my nose and make things happen like a certain television "witch" I grew up watching on after-school reruns. But real magic isn't that simple. A properly cast spell opens and broadens opportunities; it's then up to each individual to pursue them. Witch or no witch, there was no way around the fact that establishing a vintage clothing shop took a lot of long hours, hard work, and moving outside one's comfort zone. In some ways I wasn't so far removed from Conrad; I had to deal with my own daily fears and stubborn addictions.

Today I asked Conrad to unload the bags of Frances's clothes from the van rather than sweep the sidewalk. I led him over to the driveway I rented right around the corner from the shop, opened up the van's sliding side door, and then hurried down the street to the quirky, funky coffee shop called Coffee to the People.

As its name suggests, Coffee to the People is an unrepentant throwback to San Francisco's famed Summer of Love. Classic Bob Dylan or Grateful Dead tunes dominate the playlist on the overhead speakers. The walls are plastered with bumper stickers reading: DEMOCRACY IS A MUSCLE; USE IT OR LOSE IT!, HAS ANYONE SEEN MY CONSTITUTIONAL RIGHTS?, and YOUR SILENCE WILL NOT PROTECT YOU. Large posters feature Mandela, Gandhi, Einstein, and Harriet Tubman, and dated pins plastered to the tables read, STOP THE OCCUPATION OF EL SALVADOR, SUPPORT OUR BROTHERS IN VIETNAM, and FREE NICARAGUA.

Finally, the coffee drinks are made from fair-trade beans, and there are multiple vegan options for baked goods that succeed in making me feel guilty about being an omnivore. I'm always half expecting Angela Davis to pop out of the bathroom and deliver a lecture on issues of social justice.

Still, the times they are a-changing: The café now offers free Wi-Fi. As I swung open the dark wood–and-glass front door and walked in, few eyes looked up from the glowing screens of MacBook portable computers, and at least half the crowd wore earphones that attached them to electronic equipment while cutting them off from the people around them in a way I imagined must be anathema to 1960s ideals. This morning four bleary-looking students were already sprawled on the big, cushy couches near the back, while a group of young women sat at a large round table, chatting and knitting. All in all the café's a bit noisy, some of the people can be rather fragrant, and I wouldn't recommend leaving your laptop unattended for even a second. But it is just *so* San Francisco.

I took my place in line, knowing from experience that it would move slowly. The sometimes surly baristas existed in their own world, involving one another, the music, or their friends leaning on the counter telling loud stories over the noise of the steamer.

But I bided my time, enjoying the chance to people-watch. Bronwyn and I had started swapping our favorite "overheard" snatches of conversation from the coffee line. Today a tall, lithe wood sprite of a teenager turned to her slouching, purple-haired companion, put her hands on her hips, and declared: "He's just so *unabashed* when he talks about the theoretical aesthetics of commercial architecture. After all, it's just more . . . what's the word? I don't know, just I guess *essential* to live in a world of essence."

I tried to commit it to memory.

"What'll you have?" demanded the barista, Wendy, when it was my turn.

"Something chocolate," I said, hoping Wendy might jump in with a suggestion. Yesterday's events and three hours' sleep left me feeling like an emotional punching bag, and the only cure I knew for such a state was chocolate.

"I can't decide between a cayenne hot chocolate and the Chocolate to the People," I tried again when Wendy remained mute. "What do you suggest?"

Wendy tapped her black-painted, chipped fingernails on the counter, barely refraining from rolling her eyes. She didn't share much in common with her Peter Pan namesake. She was big and tall, her bangs cut straight across, the rest of her thick dark hair slightly curled under and cut to brush the top of her shoulders. A brave young woman who seemed quite at home in her own oversize-for-current-fashion body, she had a tendency to wear black satin bustiers and other lingerie items as everyday clothing.

"I'll just go with the Chocolate to the People, then," I said when it became clear Wendy wasn't going to be of any assistance. "And I'll take one Flower Power, two cinnamon rolls, and a bagel with cream cheese and avocado . . . and jalapenos."

My personal goal was to come here often enough so Wendy and the other regular barista, Xander, would recognize me, smile in welcome, and maybe even ask, "The usual?" as they did with their friends. Complicating this plan was that I never ordered the same thing twice. Still, a witch can dream.

Ten minutes later I emerged into the sunshine balancing my goodies in my handwoven Brazilian basket, and crossed the street.

"Lily!"

I looked around to see a neighboring merchant, Sandra, trotting out of her storefront and waving me down. A petite, pretty woman in her mid-thirties, she stopped when she reached me on the sidewalk. As usual, she stood just a little too close and stared just a little too intently.

"Good morning, Sandra. How are you?" I asked.

"I'm so glad I caught you outside your shop! I've been trying to get you over here for days! I believe you simply work too hard. Staffing the store every day plus buying and then preparing all the clothes—it's too much!"

"I'm sorry I can't really talk; I'm actually bringing this food back to Conrad—"

"He can just come right over and get it from you; you

buy it for him, after all. Conrad!" she yelled before I could stop her. For a small woman, Sandra had some impressive pipes. "Come on over and get your breakfast from Lily. We're going to visit for a few minutes!"

Unfolding his lanky frame, Conrad stood from his spot on the curb and trudged toward us with his hands stuck deep into the front pockets of his grimy jeans. I handed him his food and drink and he opened his mouth as if to speak, but Sandra beat him to it.

"What do you say?" she demanded, as though he were a child.

"Thank you ever so much, ma'am," he said in a truly terrible Texas accent, lifting an imaginary cowboy hat in my direction. I tried not to laugh.

Bowing to the inevitable, I asked Conrad to watch the door of Aunt Cora's Closet for a few more minutes and stepped into Sandra's shop, called Peaceful Things.

Like Coffee to the People, her store was exactly what tourists from around the world expected to find when they visited the Haight. Smelling strongly of patchouli, the inventory was a hodgepodge of tie-dyed classic rock 'n' roll T-shirts and paraphernalia, cheap but appealing Asian imports, brass hookahs, blown-glass ornaments, and inexpensive jewelry featuring peace signs and yin-yang symbols. She also carried what I secretly referred to as the lighter side of the supernatural—crystals, candles, pyramids, goddess figurines of all stripes, and a wide selection of New Age–inspired self-help books.

Peaceful Things, despite its name, made me uncomfortable. In the first place, I couldn't stifle the feeling that Sandra trivialized the mystical world, and second, I was afraid some of her customers might unwittingly invite unwelcome powers into their home. It was one thing to carry a protective quartz crystal around in your pocket, quite another to bring certain items—like the richly beaded and embroidered *pakets kongo* juju bag I held in my hand—into your home without understanding their nature and how to treat them with the respect they demand and deserve.

I put the bag back on its glass shelf and sipped my mocha while Sandra chattered on, nonstop, about the merchant association and how I really should get involved with the community and link together in an alliance, just as she had with her own residential neighborhood association. Of course, she had lived in her area forever and knew *anyone* who was *anyone*.

Sandra was the type of talker who rarely required a response. Still, just being in her presence tired me out. Since Sandra did not have her own energy centered, she tried to feed off others. Not intentionally draining, but with the same results.

"Just listen to me, rattling on and on. I brought you in here because I wanted to show you what I just bought off the Internet," Sandra exclaimed. She leaned down below her counter and brought out a large, flat cardboard box. Lifting it onto the glass surface, she opened the flaps and pushed back some rustling white tissue paper to disclose the contents: a large volume the size of a coffee table book.

I felt as though I had been doused in water: first hot, then cold. There was a bitter, burning smell.

The tome in front of her was the *Malleus Maleficarum* . . . the witch-hunters' bible.

I looked up at Sandra. Was that malice in her wide, searching, celadon eyes? Or merely excitement?

"Why do you have this?" I asked.

"You don't like it?"

"How could anyone like it? It's a vicious, misogynistic handbook for torture and murder."

"Lily, I'm so sorry! I didn't mean to offend you! Did I offend you? Is it because your friend Bronwyn is a witch? Or a Wiccan, as she calls herself?"

I swallowed hard and spoke in a measured tone. "I'm not offended, Sandra. I just think it's an evil book. I'm sure there are scholarly reasons to read it, just as there are for reading the Nazi propaganda that explained how to exterminate Jewish people. But I don't want to be the one to study it. Do you?"

"Well, I . . . I didn't realize. I mean, it's fascinating reading in a historical sense. It was published in 1487—"

"By the Dominican friars Heinrich Kramer and Jacob Sprenger, for the purpose of rooting out and destroying witches, as well as those who did *not* believe in them, through the use of standard 'tests' that were essentially torture. Yes, I know all about the book, Sandra."

"They say witches can't cry. And they can't drown."

"They also said witches stole men's penises."

She started flipping though the pages. "I didn't see *that* part. Penises?"

I slapped my hand down on the book, closing it. It hummed under my hand, and the burning smell once again assailed my nostrils.

"Why did you want to show me this, Sandra?"

"I just thought it was interesting."

I watched her closely, but for all her flightiness she was surprisingly difficult to read. Sandra was my neighbor on Haight Street, and I wanted to maintain a good relationship. But I had a hard time liking her.

"I have to get back to my store," I said.

"Could I come over with you and look through your new inventory?"

"You were just in yesterday morning. We don't have anything new up—"

"Maya mentioned you were getting some new clothes last night."

"We did just acquire a bunch of stuff, but we haven't prepped it yet. We still need to sort through it, wash everything, and make some repairs."

"I don't mind," she said, moving out from behind the counter to join me.

"Really, Sandra, it's not ready—"

"Don't be silly—I can wash clothes just as easily as you can. It's no problem."

"*No*, Sandra," I said as firmly as I could. "I have a process I like to follow."

Just then two college-age girls came into the store, wearing the uniform of the Haight Street youth: tie-dyed T-shirts over long skirts, faded zippered hoodies, their long hair tied in loose knots at the backs of their heads, worn backpacks slung over thin shoulders.

"Oh, okay," Sandra relented, peeved. "If it's like that."

"I'll let you know as soon as we put the new stuff out. I promise," I said as I slipped out of Peaceful Things, breathing a sigh of relief.

Making friends wasn't as easy as it looked.

* * *

I returned to find Aunt Cora's Closet blessedly free of customers. Weekday mornings are typically slow, which I enjoy. It gives me a chance to catch up on processing the clothes, and I had several Hefty bags full of new inventory awaiting my attention in the back room. I needed to sort through them carefully, making notes of the sewing repairs needed and setting them aside to send with Maya to her mother, Lucille, who did piecework for me at home. The rest I separated by laundering need: Some could be washed in the delicate cycle of my jumbo clothes washer in the back room; others needed to be sent out for "green" dry cleaning—our bill was terrible—and still others had to be washed by hand. Happily, I had a magical leg up when it came to stains: I could usually figure out what the offending article was, and therefore was better suited to deal with it.

But first things first. Determined to get to know my adopted city, I tried to make time to read the local paper every day. I grabbed the *San Francisco Chronicle* from the stoop, laid my bagel out on my horseshoe-shaped counter, and took a big bite. Staying up half the night casting spells and hunting demons gave a girl an appetite.

The bell on the front door rang, and for the second time in as many days I looked up to see a man stride through the front door of Aunt Cora's Closet. We get our share of transvestites wandering into the store—they love the old prom dresses—but since we carry only women's clothing, by and large ours is a female clientele. Men are noticed. Especially this one.

He was tall and broad shouldered, with shaggy dark hair, olive skin, and a five-o'clock shadow. He wasn't pretty like yesterday's male witch; quite the contrary. He reminded me of a painting I had once seen in the Louvre of a battle-weary medieval knight who had just removed his armor. I studied him as he stood inside the doorway and glanced around the shop, his piercing gaze taking in Bronwyn's herbal corner, the diaphanous lingerie on display along the back wall, and the hat stand full of feathers, bows, and net veils. He couldn't have been older than his late thirties, but his face displayed the lines and scars of an interesting life. His light gray eyes, startling in such a dark complexion, held a deep trace of sadness.

I tried to smile around the huge bite of bagel still in my mouth. My heart fluttered just a tad, and I was glad I had bypassed my comfy jeans this morning.

Finally able to swallow, I slid off my tall stool and stood.

"Good morning. May I help you?"

"I hope so." He took a notepad out of the back pocket of his faded jeans, leaned one elbow on the counter, and flipped it open. "I guess I need mugwort, something called Dead Men's Bells, and . . . what's that say? I can't read my own writing."

He held the dog-eared notebook out to me, showing a scratchy, intense script that tilted to the left.

"Elderberry shoots?" I ventured.

"Right. Elderberry shoots." He flipped the notebook closed and shoved it back in his pocket.

"I'm afraid Bronwyn's not in at the moment, but let's see what she's got on her shelves." I came out from behind the counter and headed toward Bronwyn's corner. I don't share my own potent herbal stash with anyone.

"Cute pig," the man commented as he trailed me across the store, squeezing his broad shoulders through racks of lacy negligees and poodle skirts. In his potbellied-pig guise, Oscar lay snoring on the purple silk pillow Bronwyn had given him for a bed. "You're not the resident witch, then?"

"*Me*, a witch?" I laughed, hoping my voice didn't ring false. "I repair and sell vintage clothing."

"Good. You're far too pretty to be a witch."

"Thank you, I guess." I slipped behind Bronwyn's counter and pulled a couple of neatly labeled mason jars down off a wooden shelf. A painted sign hung prominently on the wall with the amiable golden rule from the Wiccan Rede: AN IT HARM NONE, DO WHAT YE WILL.

"Real witches don't have green faces and warts, you know," I felt compelled to point out. "They're perfectly normal."

"Except for the fact that they think they're witches." He smiled and his face was transformed. The sadness was still there, but muted. His light eyes held mine, and for a moment I had a strong, inappropriate desire to try to control him. I forced myself to look away and started wrapping his purchases in a plain brown wrapper.

"You're looking for protection?" I asked.

"Excuse me?"

"Mugwort, Dead Men's Bells, and elderberry shoots. They're used in protective spells."

"I thought you specialized in clothing."

"I overhear things." I shrugged. "That'll be fourteen dollars and fifty-two cents."

He let out a little whistle. "They don't come cheap."

"These are very special herbs. You're not exactly making vinaigrette."

He chuckled. "If you want to know the truth, I'm going on a ghost hunt, and the ghost hunter, Gosnold, told me I needed this stuff. He told me I could get it here."

"Charles Gosnold?" I asked. I called him Charles the charlatan.

He nodded. "You know him?"

"A little. He's a friend of Bronwyn's."

"That would explain the recommendation. Anyway, that's what the magic herbs are for. Crazy, right?"

I returned the man's smile. Charles would no doubt take him to some rickety old building, figuring that age was the equivalent of ghostly goings-on. Ultimately they wouldn't see anything beyond figments of their own imaginations. What could it hurt?

"Where are you hunting these ghosts?" I asked.

"Out on the bay. Supposedly there's 'spectral activity' over the water lately."

Uh-oh.

"You shouldn't go out there with Gosnold."

"I've got to. I have a whole film crew lined up."

"I'm serious; it's not safe. Charles is all hat and no cattle."

"He's what?" the man asked with a quizzical half smile.

"He's a phony. He doesn't know what he's doing. You must have figured that out if you've spent more than five minutes with him."

He looked at me thoughtfully for a moment. "I'm Max, by the way. Max Carmichael. And you are . . . ?"

"Lily Ivory." I reached out a hand, and we shook. The

vibrations jumped between us, almost like a spark. His eyes flew up to mine and I snatched my hand back and smiled. After a moment he smiled back.

I couldn't help but notice that his spirit was completely on guard. Human, but tested. A lot of war veterans are like that—even normal humans can't experience repeated trauma without learning how to build a psychic shell to protect themselves.

"So, why are you going out with Charles, exactly?" I asked.

"I 'out' people like him."

"Like Charles Gosnold?"

"People who prey on other people's superstitions and fears."

"Ah. You're a . . . ?"

"Mythbuster, for lack of a better word."

"Is that like a professional skeptic?"

"Something like that."

"Someone pays you for that?"

"I even get benefits," he said with a crooked smile.

"But the bay . . ."

"What about it?"

Okay, Lily, get hold of yourself. It was true that I suspected something untoward was going on out near the bay, but *La Llorona* stole children, and this was a grown man. Still, the specter had been known to seduce handsome fellows, luring them to their doom when it struck her fancy. And, truth was, there was something out of the ordinary about this Max Carmichael, a distinct energy that was attracting me and might draw spirits. . . .

The bell tinkled as a tall, lithe brunette opened the door. Smartly dressed in a chic dove gray designer outfit that probably cost more than half my inventory combined, she hovered on the threshold as though afraid of catching something.

"Max? You about ready?"

"Be right there," he said over his shoulder. He looked back at me and winked. "We'll be careful."

Before he turned away to go I snapped the medicine bundle from around my waist and pressed it into his palm, cupping his hand with both of mine. I fixed him with my gaze. I felt his guard go up against me, but I was strong enough to make him listen, if not obey.

"Do me a favor and carry this with you? Just stick it in your pocket and forget it. Think of it as a lady's favor."

"*Max*," the woman in the doorway urged, annoyed.

Ignoring her, Max dropped his gaze to my hands holding his, then back to my eyes.

After a moment he blew out a breath and nodded.

"All right. But I want to talk to you about this."

"You know where to find me," I answered just as a premonition hit me. My eyes flew to the front door.

The bell tinkled as the woman left in a huff, and in her place entered two men, one of whom flipped the sign on the door to CLOSED.

Yikes.

Chapter 6

Out of habit I grabbed for my medicine bundle, only to remember that I had just given it away.

The two men hesitated in the foyer, just as the woman had. My daily protection spell gave a lot of people pause, especially if they weren't well-intentioned toward me or the store.

"Well, if it isn't Max Carmichael." The smaller man was the first to cross over to us, a shadow of a smile on his lips. Not much taller than my own five-foot-five, with a shaved head, trim mustache, and near-black eyes, he was attractive in a not-so-tall, dark, and handsome way. He wore black running shoes, khaki chinos, and a thigh-length black leather jacket. "I didn't know you were back in town."

"Carlos, good to see you," Max said with a nod but not much warmth. They shook hands.

Carlos turned to the man standing by his side. He was of medium height, husky, and so blond that his eyebrows disappeared against his pale skin.

"This is my partner, Neil Nordstrom. Neil, meet Max Carmichael. Max is a stringer for the *Chronicle*, among other things. Still on government contract?"

"From time to time," Max said as he shook Neil's meaty paw.

"What brings you here, Max?" Carlos asked. "Looking for a Mardi Gras costume?"

"Yep. I'm in desperate need of a ruffled Victorian petticoat."

Carlos grinned, teeth flashing very white. "That blue silk bustier would bring out the color in your eyes. Why don't you try it on, give us all a show?"

"Maybe later," Max said.

The smile dropped from Carlos's face as his dark eyes turned toward me.

"You Lily Ivory?"

I nodded.

"What's this about, Carlos?" Max interrupted.

"Actually we're conducting official business here, Max," Carlos said without taking his eyes off of me. "Mind waiting outside?"

Max's gaze shifted from Carlos to me, then back again. "What kind of business?"

"None of *your* goddamned business, Max, that's what kind. You two know each other?"

I shook my head. Max nodded.

A look of weary cynicism washed over Carlos's dramatic features.

"After I leave maybe you two can get together and get your stories straight." He flung an arm toward the door. "Out, Max. Now."

With one last curious look at me, Max strode out of the shop.

Carlos turned back to me, near-black eyes flat and unapproachable. *Cop eyes*, I thought to myself just as he reached into his jacket and pulled out a worn leather case, flipping it open to reveal a shiny SFPD badge.

"Are you and Carmichael involved in something together?" he asked.

"No, of course not. He just stopped by for some herbs."

"And yet you said you didn't know him."

"I meant in any significant sense."

The inspector blew out a long breath and looked over at his partner with eyebrows raised. The blond man shrugged.

"I'm Inspector Romero and this is Inspector Nordstrom. We need to ask you a few questions."

"Is this about Jessica?" I asked.

"Jessica?"

"The little girl who disappeared yesterday in Hunters Point?"

Carlos shrugged and shook his head. "Is that your old Mustang parked outside?"

"Do you need me to move it?" I offered, grasping at a final, slim straw of hope that these two might be plainclothes parking cops.

"Did you use the car last night?"

I nodded. "I . . . I visited a friend of mine who hasn't been feeling well."

"Who is this friend?"

"Frances Potts."

"How do you know Mrs. Potts?"

A terrible premonition washed over me. "Is something wrong? Is Frances all right?"

"Why don't you let me ask the questions, okay, Ms. Ivory? Now, how do you know Mrs. Potts?"

"I just met her yesterday through a mutual friend, Maya Jackson."

"Uh-huh. Any special reason this Maya introduced you two?"

"Frances has two generations' worth of old clothes stashed in her basement. I bought a bunch from her for the store."

"Was anyone else there at that time?"

"Little Jessica, though she left early. We told that to the police."

"You're saying something happened with a child and the police were brought in on it?"

I nodded and gave them a brief rundown of what had happened with Jessica's disappearance. Romero jotted down the particulars.

"Was anyone else at the Potts house?"

"Her lawyer, Delores . . . something . . . came later. She stayed for dinner."

"Delores something?"

"It'll come to me." This was the one area my memory failed. I was terrible with names.

"Frances Potts was found dead early this morning."

I looked from Romero to his partner.

"That's not possible," I croaked. "There must be some kind of mistake. . . ."

"Afraid not. Her daughter found her."

Guilt washed over me. On its heels came horror. How

had this happened? Why hadn't I stopped it? Why hadn't I sensed it?

"How . . . how was she killed?"

"Why would you assume she was killed? Perhaps she died in her sleep."

"Why else would you be here?"

He shrugged as though conceding me the point. "The city's trying a new pilot program in that area to combat drug trafficking. There's a street camera mounted on the telephone pole right outside the Pottses' home."

His eyes held mine for a long moment before he asked the obvious question.

"The tape shows someone pulling up in that Mustang and going into the house. You wanna tell me what you were you doing at Frances Potts's home at one in the morning?"

"I went by to check on her. She hadn't been feeling well."

"She called you?"

"No, I just thought I'd check on her."

"You don't think that's a little odd, to just drop by at one in the morning?"

"She told us she'd been having trouble sleeping."

He stared me down for another few seconds, not speaking. I could have sworn Inspector Romero was trying to read my aura, just as I was trying to read his. That surprised me. In my experience cops were by-the-book, logic-is-supreme sorts, with the possible exception of detectives, who relied a great deal on what they liked to call "hunches."

After a long moment his partner cleared his throat, breaking our connection, and handed me a piece of scratch paper with a five-pointed star inside of a circle, sketched in a dark pencil.

"You know what that is?" the blond inspector—Neil something—asked.

"A star?"

"Yeah, but it's a, whatchamacallit . . . It's used in satanic rituals, right?"

"Pentagrams aren't a sign of Satan; they're an ancient symbol of the human form." I hated how easily the craft was misinterpreted. I pointed down at the glass counter, to the display of several carved talismans and amulets. There were three in the shape of a pentagram. "You see? Head, arms, and legs. Pentagrams are used more for protection than for curses."

"Though they are used for curses sometimes, then, right?"

"Occasionally," I said.

"What are you, some kind of occultist?" interjected Carlos, frowning as he inspected the medallions in the display.

"No. I'm a shopkeeper specializing in vintage clothes."

"You seem to know a lot about the subject of pentagrams."

"I know something about the Mustang I drive, as well, but I'm no mechanic."

"So you're sayin' this star has nothing to do with devil worship?" asked the blond detective.

"It would depend upon who used it, and how. For instance, a lot of Wiccans use the pentagram in their rituals, but most don't believe in the concept of hell, much less the devil," I said. "Does this have to do with Frances Potts?"

The inspectors exchanged a glance. I had my answer.

"Were there any other signs of black magic or devil worship at the scene?" I asked.

"What kinds of signs?"

"The numbers six-six-six, animal sacrifice, maybe?"

"Those would be a sign of satanic ritual?"

"It's possible. Some people do associate the pentagram with the devil's work. If it's drawn upside down, with two points up rather than standing on two points like a person, it's thought by some to represent a goat with horns."

His eyebrows lifted in question.

"The goat can be a sign of the devil. It's called Baphomet."

"So this goat would mean there were satanists there?"

"It's really not that simple." I took a deep breath and tried to organize my thoughts in a way that would make sense to a cynical sensibility. "Most symbols and spells can be either positive or negative, depending on the intent of the person casting the spell. For instance, this candle"—I gestured toward the tall beeswax candle that I lit every morning with a brief spell of luck for the shop—"can be a simple source of light, or it can affect the course of someone's life, for good or ill, depending on the emphasis people give it."

Both men's eyebrows raised in a "hoo, boy" incredulous look. Blondie carefully folded the sketch and returned it to his breast pocket.

Inspector Romero resumed his questioning.

"How was Mrs. Potts when you last saw her?"

I swallowed hard again. How could my magic have failed?

"Ms. Ivory?" he urged.

"She seemed fine. She let me into the house, but went right back to bed."

"According to the security tape you were there for almost an hour."

"I was cleaning up a little."

"So that would explain any fingerprints we found at the scene?"

"If you found fingerprints, they aren't mine." I held my hands up palms out and splayed my fingers. "I was born without fingerprints."

"You were born that way?" asked Blondie.

"It's called dermatopathia pigmentosa reticularis. It's a genetic condition."

Romero held my hand, palm up, in his. He really was guarded; even when I concentrated fully I felt very little from him other than a pleasant, subtle throb. He scrutinized my finger pads, turning them slightly to the side to look at them in the strong light streaming in through the plate-glass windows.

"I'll be damned." He looked at his partner. "You heard of this?"

Blondie nodded. "They did a deal on it on the Discovery Channel. It's a pretty rare condition. I'm telling you, Carlos, you gotta watch more television."

"Spell it for me," he said to me, then made note of it. Romero's eyes remained on his notepad for several moments before flickering up to his partner. Finally, he continued. "I'll need your friend's information, the one who introduced you to Mrs. Potts yesterday. And the name of the lawyer you said was there. And we'll need to confiscate the clothing you took from the Potts home."

"The clothing?"

"It might be evidence."

"Of what?"

"Why don't you leave that up to me?"

With reluctance I led them to the back room, and then helped them to gather up the Hefty bags and cart them through the store and outside, to a battered silver Ford sedan double-parked in front of the store. As we walked by the dressing room alcove I realized that Frances Potts's two wedding dresses still hung on a separate rack. I warred with my conscience for a moment, then remained mute. The gowns wouldn't tell the police anything with regard to Frances's death, I felt sure. If they revealed anything to anyone, it would be to me.

"I guess that's it for now. If you remember anything else, call me." Reaching into the breast pocket of his black leather jacket, he pulled out a business card and handed it to me. *Inspector Carlos Manuel Romero, SFPD Homicide.*

"Oh, and Ms. Ivory?" he said over the roof of the car as he opened the driver's-side door. "Don't plan any trips in the near future. I imagine we'll need to contact you again."

He took the seat behind the wheel, slammed the door, and took off down Haight Street, turning toward Golden Gate Park.

I stood outside on the sidewalk for a long while after they left, gazing down at the inspector's card and concentrating on breathing. My hand again reached for my absent medicine bundle, which was no doubt already sitting, discarded, on the floor of Mythbuster Max's car.

Why had I given such a precious item to someone

who so clearly refused to believe? How could I have been so impulsive?

Was the lapse of judgment signaling some sort of shift in my powers . . . and could this have anything to do with my failure to protect Frances?

Frances's death was horrifying enough, but right on its tail came self-doubt. My magical talents had never before fallen short. On the contrary: Throughout my life my challenge had been to control my gifts, not to let them overwhelm me or those around me. Had I misjudged the situation with Frances? For that matter, why hadn't I sensed any foreshadowing of danger when I saw little Jessica yesterday? Could I be suffering under a black spell, conjured by someone more powerful than me? My mind cast back to the invisible force I felt and heard in Frances's house last night. What could it have been? Who—

Something rubbed at my ankles. I glanced down to see Oscar looking up at me with pink piggy eyes, the expression on his face eager and adorable. As reluctant as I was to admit it, it felt good to have someone—or some*thing*—on my side. I gestured to Oscar with my head and he obediently trotted back into the store. Locking the door behind us, I kept the Closed sign up in the window, then opened the glass case, where I had a number of consecrated protective talismans and amulets on display.

Every full moon, I fashioned the medallions from polished disks of wood in various sizes cut from the branch of a fruit tree, in this case apple. I carved ancient protective symbols upon them, hung them on leather straps, then charged and named each one in a symbol of rebirth by air and water, earth and fire. They hummed with protective energy. I grabbed one, hung it around my neck, and was about to close the case when, on second thought, I grabbed another.

Leading the way into the rear storage room, I sank into a vinyl chair at a jade green linoleum-and-chrome dinette set, circa 1962. I had grown up with a table just like this one in my mother's kitchen, but she never thought of it as cute or vintage. To her it was plain old ugly junk, a constant reminder that we couldn't afford better.

Which reminded me . . . I jotted down a note to myself on the back of an invoice book: *Send Mom money.*

Oscar shifted into his natural form and perched on the chair next to mine.

"This is for you," I said as I slipped the extra talisman over his head.

His eyes got huge as he looked down at the pendant hanging on his crusty chest. "For me?" he breathed.

"It's consecrated. It will help to keep you safe. I think you should wear it until I can figure out what's going on."

Tears welled up in his bottle green eyes. "Mistress is very, very good."

"You act as though no one's ever given you a present before."

He just shook his large head and repeated, "Mistress is very good."

I wondered about Oscar's background. I had known a few gnomes and goblins in my time, but I had never delved into their private lives. Where did he come from? Did he have a home? A mother? How did that work exactly? I should have some personal talks with the ugly little fellow. He was growing on me.

But for now, I had some vital issues to attend to.

"Something's going on, Oscar." I sighed and sat back in my chair. "Something not good. First a child goes missing, practically right in front of me, and then the spell I brewed—you saw me do it—fails. Frances . . . Mrs. Potts . . . she died anyway. How is that possible?"

"I'm supposed ta make things better, not worse." He shook his head. "Maybe it's my fault."

"It's not you. Do you think someone could be casting against me?"

"You know what you should do? Talk to Master Rhodes. He knows everything."

"Aidan the male witch? Are you saying he's involved in this somehow?"

"*No*, no. But he knows everything. He's in charge—" Oscar cut himself off and looked up at me guiltily.

"In charge?"

"He just knows everything."

I pondered that for a moment, then nodded.

"Good idea." I had hoped to stay clear of local witchy politics, but perhaps it wasn't possible. If there was another sorcerer casting against me, Aidan Rhodes might be the one to know about it.

I got up and retrieved Aidan's card from the top drawer of a cherry dresser that served as a catchall for my business papers. There was a Jefferson Street address embossed on the fine linen card, but no phone number.

"Do you know his number, by any chance?" I asked.

"He likes to talk face-to-face. Ooh, or you could check out his awesome new Web site!"

"In person is better, thanks." I had Internet access and a notebook computer, but cyberspace made me nervous. All those bits of code jumping around, unattended . . . In some ways I'm a pretty old-fashioned witch.

I considered calling Graciela for advice, but lost my nerve. I hadn't spoken to her, my mother, or anyone else from my hometown for several years. When it became clear I had to leave town before my training was finished, my grandmother sent me to study with a talented *curandera* friend of hers in Chiapas, but I went instead on an ill-fated quest to find my father . . . despite all her admonitions to the contrary. Not only was Graciela afraid of what I might encounter should I find my father, but she also knew that with a power like mine, not to be in complete control was dangerous. Of which I had plenty of proof. I rarely lost my temper, but I wasn't safe to be around when I did.

Over the years I had mailed Graciela presents and letters and money from various parts of the world, but she never responded. Now I was flat-out too chicken just to call her out of the blue.

"Yoo-hoo! Anybody home?" Bronwyn's voice rang out from the front door. "Lily? Is everything okay? Why are we closed?"

Smoothing my hair and taking a deep breath, I emerged from the back room. Little piggy Oscar trotted along at my heels as I hurried over to help Bronwyn with her many packages.

"Sorry about that," I said as I hoisted two "save a tree" cloth shopping bags onto the counter. "We had some unexpected visitors and I needed a moment to regroup."

Bronwyn put down her other bags and turned toward me.

"What's wrong?" she demanded.

"Nothing, really. I—"

"Don't tell me that. You look as though you've seen a ghost."

I laughed.

"It's not that. I—" I appalled myself by ending my protestation with a little hiccup.

Bronwyn turned and enveloped me in her plump arms. She was solid and good, full of warm vibrations and simple, straightforward compassion. I let myself sink into her tenderness for a moment.

"Lily, are you sure everything is okay?" she asked, stroking my hair. "Does this have to do with your being a witch?"

Chapter 7

I pulled away so quickly that I knocked over the hat stand.

"*Witch?*" I asked as we both crouched to gather up sundry caps and bonnets.

Bronwyn was aware that I had a working knowledge of herbs and the craft, but I had kept the truth from her, in part because I didn't want to be looked at as different, and in part because I was afraid she would be *too* welcoming.

Bronwyn belonged to an entirely unthreatening coven of women who practiced the genial religion of Wicca. In their version, at least, this essentially meant that they pledged to harm no one, to judge no one, and to learn about herbs and the ancient rituals surrounding the equinox and solstice. I let them have their meeting at the store during the last full moon, and from the little I witnessed from the back room, they burned a lot of candles and incense, cast a circle of women, chanted a few invocations, paid homage to the goddesses, and then visited over Bundt cake and herbal tea. Sort of like a Halloween-themed Tupperware party.

"You know I'm Wiccan, Lily. Why do you feel like you have to hide what you are?"

"I don't . . . I mean I—"

"I've seen you purifying widdershins every morning, then smudging deosil. That's Basic Site Cleansing 101. You think I didn't notice?"

I looked up into her soft brown eyes. From the moment of meeting Bronwyn I had been dismissive of her because of her lack of magical talent, but perhaps she represented something better, and even rarer: an endless supply of love and understanding. And I accused *non*witchy humans of being prejudiced.

"Thanks," I said with a loud sniff. "It's just that I've always felt—"

"Different? We all have."

But my version of *different*, I was sure, was slightly more dramatic than hers. For instance, she probably hadn't been run out of her hometown on a rail.

"Lily, sweetie, why don't you join our coven? We're open to all of goodwill."

However much power Bronwyn's coven might or might not have, I hesitated. I had no idea what my magic would be like added to that of thirteen or so believers, whether or not they had true supernatural abilities. The sad truth was that, as Graciela had warned me so long ago, I was not in complete control of my powers. The last thing I wanted to do was endanger a group of welcoming, well-meaning women.

"Thank you, Bronwyn. I'll think about it. But right now what I need is to get ready for the wedding party, which is supposed to be here in"—I checked my watch—"oh, jeez, less than twenty minutes."

"Relax, Lily. I brought plenty of champagne and fresh-squeezed orange juice. I guarantee you, get these girls downing mimosas in that communal dressing room, and all the little details will take care of themselves."

The bridal party arrived in two shiny black stretch limousines, which was enough to cause a minor outrage on relatively narrow Haight Street. A handful of street kids poked loud fun, a few homeless men approached to ask for spare change, and the trendy folk just wanted to see who the celebrities were. When they realized that there were no famous faces in the giggling assemblage, they walked on by with poorly concealed disdain.

Still, there was so much gawking and street clogging that Conrad felt duty-bound to step in and direct traffic. I gave him an old pair of orange mittens, and he carried out his duties with great flair. A couple of punk rockers stood behind and mimicked him, and a bearded, white-haired, self-anointed New Age priest blessed the limo and its inhabitants with the power of a pyramid made of Tinkertoys. All in all, the whole scene suited the carnivalesque quality of the Haight.

Twenty-three years old and only recently graduated from college, the bride, Natalie, bounced out of the limo looking more like a contender for the Oakland Raiders cheerleaders than a woman about to be married. Her sweatpants hung low on her narrow hips, giving us all peeks at her perfectly smooth, taut stomach. A cropped sweatshirt proclaimed her loyalty to her alma mater,

USC, and her shiny, well-brushed auburn hair fell long and loose about her shoulders.

Her friends dressed in kind. All wore sweatpants or gym shorts, and all gleamed with health, wealth, and leisure. Several were clearly also USC girls; one wore shorts emblazoned with the name UC Santa Barbara, while the others wore T-shirts that recalled spring breaks on sun-drenched Caribbean islands.

The twelve young women burst into the shop and started flipping through dresses and blouses with the high-spirited abandon of experienced shoppers. They squealed and cooed when they discovered Oscar, who led a couple of them on a merry chase through the racks of dresses and skirts until I caught his eye and gave him a Look, after which he stopped and allowed himself to be petted and adored.

Once their fascination for him waned, Oscar kept bumping around their ankles, trying his best to look adorable. I imagined he was hoping to be picked up, but since his pig form probably weighed nearly half what the gals did, his chances looked about as slim as their hips. Still, he enjoyed himself by sneaking under the dressing room curtain whenever I wasn't watching.

I took Bronwyn's advice and began pouring mimosas right away, handing each woman in the group a crystal champagne flute as they started to peruse the special rack of bridesmaids' dresses I had put out near the communal dressing room, which was essentially an alcove cut off from the rest of the store by heavy burgundy velvet drapes. Since I carry solely women's clothes, I have only two small private dressing nooks. Most people use the big communal space; even with strangers, once women get over their initial shyness, it becomes like a sorority party in there. Or so I imagined a sorority party to be.

This assembly didn't need much encouragement to make the try-on sessions a celebration. Bronwyn and I pushed the entire rack of gowns into the dressing room and they went to town, oohing and ahhing, laughing and giggling as they held dresses in front of themselves and their friends. The dresses ranged in age and style from the twenties to the sixties; I even had two gowns from the late 1800s, but these I kept on a special display behind the counter. The antique fabric was far too delicate to be tried on repeatedly.

While they enjoyed, I focused on the bride, Natalie. I shook her hand in welcome and concentrated on her vibrations, then led her to a gown I had won after a brutal bidding war at an estate auction in Palo Alto. In the end I had been forced to intervene with a little magic, as the sour-faced woman bidding against me was nearly as stubborn as I. But a determined witch is hard to beat. Afterward the woman wouldn't stop glaring at me, and called me a name that rhymes with "witch." Auctions, I had come to find out, were not for the easily intimidated.

As I looked at Natalie in the dress now, however, I knew it had been worth it.

It was a two-part ensemble from the turn of the last century. The ivory silk-and-satin bodice was lined with twelve real whalebones; the neckline was cut in a vee, decorated with ivory embroidery, and ruched; and it ended in a flattering point at the center front that dropped down over the narrow waist of the skirt. A large, lace-edged shawl-style collar wrapped around the neckline and attached with a satin bow at the side, and the full sleeves ended mid-forearm, while the inner sleeves extended to the wrist and matched the shawl collar. The voluminous skirt featured a full fourteen inches of narrow pleated ruffles at the bottom, along with two rows of ruched trim. To top it all off, a ruffled underslip attached to the skirt and ended with a velvet-and-lace hem protector.

The gown's vibrations were very subtle, and very calm. Putting it on took some effort—this was the sort of garment worn back when personal attendants were always at hand to help a wealthy woman to dress. But when Natalie assessed herself in the three-way mirror, she stood straighter, stopped giggling, and held herself with a kind of dignified maturity that made her seem, suddenly, ready to begin life with a husband and a new home.

She was immediately enthralled with her own image and refused to try anything else on. I was just as pleased. Not only was this the oldest and most expensive of the gowns, by far, but her decisiveness also meant I didn't have to bring out either of Frances Potts's two dresses as options. Now that Frances had somehow died despite my protection, I wanted a chance to study the gowns carefully. Perhaps they could tell me something. I hadn't felt anything troublesome when I held them in Frances's basement, but I no longer had confidence in yesterday's perfunctory appraisal.

Edith Piaf crooned on the stereo behind the register as I stuck a bunch of pins in my mouth and had the bride step up on a little raised platform covered with a silk rug. Maya's mother, Lucille, arrived and strapped on her wrist pincushion, and she and I conferred on the best approach to adapt the gown. Older garments were cut for much more petite dimensions than the average twenty-first-century woman possessed, so fittings could be a challenge. Occasionally seams could be let out, or carefully added panels sometimes did the trick.

Natalie was thin as a rail, but several inches taller than the original bride had been. Though the dress fit through the bodice—the most difficult part to modify— the skirt landed above her ankles rather than trailing slightly on the floor as it should. After some discussion we decided to add on another flounce at the bottom. I made a habit of salvaging antique material, lace, and ribbons from old dresses that were beyond repair; no doubt we had enough vintage ivory satin in the storage closet to finish the job. Happily, given the style of the dress, it would be easy enough to make such an addition appear part of the original design. With great care not to tear the delicate aged silk, Lucille and I pinned the dress where necessary and jotted down measurements for the alterations.

At long last we were finished, and Bronwyn and Lucille escorted Natalie back into the communal dressing room to help her remove the beautiful gown.

I downed a mimosa and set my energies to helping the bridesmaids decide on their own dresses. Since Natalie would be wearing such an antique gown, I assumed she would want the rest of her entourage to follow suit.

"Oh, nah," Natalie said as she stepped back into her sweatpants. "They can have any style they want. It'll be kinda like a vintage fashion show right there as we walk down the aisle."

"In that case, I totally want this one . . . I think," said a pretty redhead, the maid of honor, as she modeled an orange sherbet–colored gauzy confection circa 1955. It was sleeveless, with a Greek-goddess bodice, and fell just to her knees. Though the dress was lovely, I could tell it wasn't quite right for her.

"What do you think?" she asked.

Her friends weighed in loudly, and the consensus seemed to be that she needed to look around some more. One chose a lacy drop-waist flapper-style dress, while another was drawn to a slightly severe forties-style garment with a straight skirt and padded shoulders.

"Could you help me with this?" asked the redhead as she backed up to me in yet another chiffon, this one lemon yellow.

I zipped her up and smoothed the shoulders.

"I like those earrings," I said, gently cupping one in my fingers, using the excuse to feel for her energy. Despite her giggling air, I could tell she had been crying recently. "You might like these," I said, leading her to an inexpensive pair of beaded chandelier-style earrings in the glass case.

"Those are cute," she said. "But I don't really need any more jewelry. I've got hella earrings already."

"Oh, go on, Jasmine, try 'em on," Natalie urged. "It'll be like your bridesmaid gift. Everybody gets to choose stuff for their gifts—I just decided."

"The beads are tiger's eye. They're good luck," I added.

Tiger's eye helps people achieve clarity with desires,

and these particular earrings had a very definite, confident energy about them. The redheaded Jasmine needed to understand herself better before she'd ever find the right man. As soon as she tried them on I knew I had her. She felt better already. She wouldn't attribute it to magic, but to the little lift we feel when we know we're wearing something flattering. But no matter. They would help.

I then steered her to a sixties "London mod"–style dress that was better suited to her figure, and to her aura, before turning to the other bridesmaids.

"You have such a great eye," Bronwyn noted. "Before they even try something on you can tell who will look good in what."

"It's a knack. I've always had it. For instance, this deep purple would look great on you," I said as I held up a velvet tunic to her.

"You think so?"

"I know so. Take it."

Bronwyn came out of the dressing room a few minutes later, her cheeks rosy and her brown eyes shining softly. Her round face was radiant. She looked like a lovely, ample, sexy witch. Perfect.

"That looks great on you!" Lucille chimed in with a charming smile on her delicately featured face. Lucille looked exactly like an older version of her daughter Maya, save for the dreadlocks and ear cuffs. And like Maya, she had a deeply calm, comforting way about her that made me want to curl up next to her on the couch and watch old movies, with hot chocolate in one hand and a big bowl of popcorn in the other.

A loud knock shook the front door. I glanced over to see our neighbor Sandra trying to open the locked handle. Turning away, I cast an imploring look toward Bronwyn, who graciously went to the front door to explain why we weren't open at the moment. I couldn't hear everything she said, but it took some doing to get Sandra to leave.

"Isn't that Sandra Schmidt?" Lucille asked me.

"She owns the shop next door," I said.

"Oh, what a coincidence. She's head of our neighborhood association out near India Basin."

"India Basin? I was just over there. . . . That's near Hunters Point, right?"

"Oh, now that I think of it, Maya told me you were there yesterday when that poor little girl was snatched." She shook her graying head. "From right in front of her house. What a terrible thing. I swear, it's like that neighborhood is cursed."

"Did you know the woman we were visiting? Frances Potts?"

"Mrs. Potts? I guess everyone in the neighborhood knows of her, one way or another. The children are fascinated with her place—half of them thinking it's a haunted house, the other half running in and out of there, looking for cookies and company. It's always quite a scene on Halloween, I'll tell you that much."

It was on the tip of my tongue to tell her about Frances's death, but Natalie came to ask me about the selection of veils, cutting our discussion short, which was just as well. It felt unseemly to talk about a gruesome murder scene during a mimosa-fueled bridal-finery try-on party. Lucille helped me make note of the rest of the necessary alterations, pinning each ticket to its dress before leaving to shop for her niece's baby shower.

The bridesmaids' ultimate dress choices were as varied as the young women themselves, as were their selections of bridesmaid presents—they bought everything from antique jewelry to embroidered handkerchiefs to frilly garters. At the last minute the bride fell in love with a precious antique net-and-lace veil with a train that was fully ten feet long.

Natalie handed over a platinum credit card without once inquiring as to the price.

At four o'clock Natalie's aunt Susan, the fashion editor from the *San Francisco Chronicle*, showed up with a photographer. Susan's idea was to do a style piece on the store now, then cover the wedding that would take place three months from now, in June. The photo sessions began with each bridesmaid, and then the bride, showing off her new finds in the dressing room, in different sections of the store, and out front on the sidewalk.

Even Oscar made it into a few of the photos, which pleased him no end. As a demon he wouldn't be able to appear in photos, but as a pig he was front and center.

Susan gushed about my inventory and told me she simply *adored* the way I had set up the store. She asked a long series of questions for her article, promising she would be back when she had more time to look for her own dress, and that she would send the in-laws and various others from the party by to look for vintage treasures. With a weary but contented sigh, I saw her off, feeling sure Aunt Cora's Closet had made its reputation.

The bridesmaids took their time changing back into their street clothes, and hence back to their giggling, young ways. One reason I was so drawn to clothing was that, like cooking, it was a realm where non-witches experienced a little everyday magic. Put on a different outfit and your whole outlook on life could transform. There is a reason we refer to it as "changing": When you put on an outfit that is perfect for you, you change.

The entire process had taken much longer than I thought it would, as these things tend to do. As the women were dressing, a name popped into my mind, reminding me that I needed to talk privately with Bronwyn. I took her by the arm and led her away from the changing rooms, over near the counter.

"Did you know Charles Gosnold is leading a ghost hunt out on the bay?" I asked her in a low voice.

"Oh?" she asked, distracted as she picked up Oscar and gave him a kiss.

"He shouldn't be going out on the water. There's . . ."

She looked at me expectantly.

"A friend of mine told me that there's an angry spirit out there."

That got her attention.

"Really?"

"I don't think Charles is equipped for something like that. Do you?"

"I wouldn't be so sure. He was named 'Best Paranormal Sleuth' two years in a row in the *Bay Guardian* newspaper."

"Sleuthing isn't the same thing as dueling with an evil entity. This isn't some run-of-the-mill house ghost."

"He *did* ask me about some recipes for protection. . . ."

"Actually, he sent a man here for herbs while you were gone this morning. We got to talking, and it turns out he's a mythbuster. He's planning on 'outing' Charles."

"*No*," she breathed.

I nodded. *"Yes."*

Bronwyn frowned. "But there's nothing to 'out.' Charles is a real ghost hunter."

"*Ghost hunter?*" the redhead with the new earrings interrupted. "Serious?"

"Oh, yes," Bronwyn reiterated. "Best Paranormal Sleuth, two years in a row."

"That's awesome," said Natalie as she came over, walking while she brushed her long, gleaming hair and pulled it into a high ponytail. "I think I saw my Nana's ghost once, when I was at summer camp."

"Awesome," echoed Jasmine. Several other girls joined us and started talking at once, sharing anecdotes of supernatural encounters. Giggles all around.

"Still, you know how these nonbelievers are," I insisted to Bronwyn, lowering my voice. "Charles could arrange for a spirit to sit in the man's lap and he still wouldn't believe his own eyes."

"That's true. . . . Anyway, why don't you ask Charles about it yourself? He's supposed to stop by"—she consulted her watch—"any minute now. I thought the bridal extravaganza would be winding down by five."

Bronwyn and I got busy, carefully folding and wrapping the items the girls were taking with them, and hanging, bagging, and marking the dresses that needed to be altered and pressed before the wedding.

Fifteen minutes later the bell tinkled over the front door as Charles Gosnold walked in with a milk shake and an In-N-Out Burger bag that emitted the tantalizing aromas of French fries and hamburger.

"Good Goddess, Charles, must you insist on eating

that sort of thing?" Bronwyn exclaimed. "Surely you know it doesn't look right for your image."

"I was hungry."

"*Honestly*. Fast food." Bronwyn shook her fuzzy head.

"I like In-N-Out Burger," I said.

"Thanks, Lily," said Charles.

"Traitor," Bronwyn said to me with a slight smile before turning back to her friend Charles. "I gave you that information on the vegan lifestyle. It is physically as well as spiritually uplifting. Did you read it?"

"Veggies don't quite do it for a guy like me." Charles patted his generous stomach and shook his head. "Hey—what's with the limo? Is there a celebrity somewhere? I hear they like to shop in thrift stores these days." He winked, then looked around, I imagined hoping to spy some paparazzi. Charles enjoyed getting his face in the news.

"Sorry, it's just for little old us," said Natalie. The girls behind her giggled.

"Well, that's just grand," he said with a smile, giving them the once-over with a look that bordered on lascivious. "Grand indeed."

In his mid-thirties, pudgy with dark hair and a goatee, Charles had black eyebrows arched in a way that made him look eternally surprised—or as though he were spying something no one else could see, which I'm sure was the point. Originally from Arizona, he had hitchhiked to San Francisco at the age of seventeen and lived on the street for some time, scrounging for coins and food. One day he overheard someone asking which house Janice Joplin used to live in, and he started giving impromptu tours of the neighborhood to visitors, pretty much making up the stories as he went along. He soon realized that while rock-'n'-roll history had its followers, the more paranormal insinuations he made, the higher the tips. Thus his fascination with such things grew, and over the years he had transformed the pursuit of ghosts and ghost stories into a full-time gig.

Charles had an undeniable gift for storytelling, true, but so far as I could tell he didn't have the slightest sensitivity to spirits. Not so much as a haunted thimbleful.

"Charles," I said. "I met Max Carmichael today when he came in for some protective herbs."

"Oh, good, he came by."

"Yes. He said you sent him. But listen, he and I started talking, and he happened to mention that he's actually a mythbuster. Did he tell you that?"

"Mythbuster?" Charles echoed, a worried look on his face.

"He's fixin' to expose you as a fraud."

"You're kidding me." He paused for a moment before a calculating gleam came into his eye. "I must be doing pretty well if they're sending people to discredit me, don'tcha think?"

"What I think is that you should cancel your bay cruise."

"What am I supposed to do? He's prepaid. He's bringing a film crew."

"Just tell him something came up and you have to cancel, and give him his money back."

"Aw, I hate to do that. Professional reputation and all that."

"How about taking him to the Queen Anne Hotel instead?" I suggested. "That place has a great ghost." Several sets of eyes turned to gawk at me. "Or so I hear tell."

The Queen Anne Hotel, built in 1890, used to be Miss Mary Lake's School for Girls. According to legend the benevolent spirit of one of the dedicated teachers—perhaps Miss Mary Lake herself—never left the building; over the years guests reported awaking on chilly mornings to find that extra blankets had been mysteriously added to the bed sometime during the night. Nobody ever got killed or disappeared or possessed. That was my kind of ghost.

"*Really?*" asked Natalie, pretty hazel eyes shining with excitement. "I wanna see a ghost!"

"Maybe you should book a room at the hotel for your wedding night," suggested Bronwyn.

Charles was already fishing through his leather messenger's bag for a glossy ghost-hunting brochure. Handing it to the bride-to-be, he assured her of a "gen-u-ine" spirit sighting for a low, low price.

"After all," he reminded us all, lest we forget, "I was voted number-one paranormal sleuth in the entire Bay Area, two years in a row."

Chapter 8

After the bridal party took off in their shiny stretch limos, Bronwyn and I hung up dresses, put away hats and seamstress materials, and straightened up the store. I offered Charles the same amount Max was going to pay him, and in response much more to my financial bribe than to any professional consideration, Gosnold agreed to cancel their trip out on the bay.

The chaotic whirlwind of the dress fittings—and a couple of mimosas—had taken my mind off of Frances and Jessica, but once the crowd dispersed, their tragic fates hit me again with the force of an iron cauldron against my head. I couldn't keep from asking myself: What could have gone wrong with my spell of protection for Frances? Had I forgotten something? Was *La Llorona* much more formidable than I knew? Or was that invisible whisperer from the night before invoking against me with a magic stronger than mine? Frances had died in a pentagram, but not the one I had drawn—mine was invisible. Could it have been some sort of odd coincidence, a random break-in? As if there were a roving band of satanists just looking to break into houses and murder people.

According to Oscar, Aidan Rhodes knew everything. A nice trait in a man.

Bronwyn gave me directions to the address on Aidan's business card, mentioning that the office must be near Fisherman's Wharf. I set off in my Mustang, putting the top down to enjoy another sunny winter day. It was only as I neared my destination that I realized Rhodes's office was located smack-dab in the center of the bustling wharf area.

Aidan Rhodes must cater to the tourists, I thought to myself with some disdain.

A lot of witches use their powers to make a living, which is understandable, since so many of us are treated as lifelong freaks and outcasts, making things like college degrees and regular everyday employment difficult. In fact, some practitioners believe it wrong, across the board, to use one's powers for others without receiving any remuneration. Instead, they believe we should treat ourselves as professionals and our powers as a commodity in demand.

Still, the association of supernatural powers with circus sideshows and palm readers in carnival booths always made me feel as though these folks were selling out, cheapening things, like my neighbor Sandra with her trivialization of important vibrations.

The traffic on Jefferson Street inched along, slowed down by pedestrians and unfamiliar drivers, like me, seeking parking spaces and particular destinations.

As I pulled up to the address on the card, I realized

the situation was even worse than I feared: Rhodes's office address was the same as the Wax Museum. As Bronwyn would say, *Oh. My. Goddess.*

I used my glove-box charm and a brief incantation to run a hapless Hummer owner out of a good parking spot, then stood on the opposite curb for a moment looking up at the museum and double-checking the address on the card in my hand, hoping I had made some mistake.

These kinds of places made me nervous. Very nervous. Wax models of humans, often called poppets, are too easily transmorphed into other forms; they're used a lot in voodoo and other power systems that I don't fully understand. I don't really know a lot of witches, so I'm not sure whether it's normal to be so anxious around other supernatural systems. But they do put me on edge.

Graciela always used to tell me that true courage was found in fear. I hoped to blazes she was right, because I was finding a lot of things frightening lately.

Tourists thronged the sidewalk and spilled out into the street. There were families trying to corral laughing children, young couples in love with their arms wrapped around each other, older folks with bloated plastic shopping bags hanging from their arms and cameras at the ready. I know it's common for local residents to deride tourists, but I've always been partial to the vibrations of out-of-town visitors: By and large they are excited and happy, and uncommonly open to new and unfamiliar people and places.

Half a block up the street a man hunkered down in a leafy costume that made him look like a bush. When a hapless tourist would stride by, the bush-man would stand up, follow him for a bit, and kneel down again as soon as the victim turned around. Everyone was in on the joke but for the person the bush was following.

I stopped and watched for a moment, joining in the laughter of the crowd. I was always intrigued by the credulity of normal people. What would it be like to be that way? Not seeing beyond the obvious, not noticing the danger lurking behind every shadow . . . ? Nice, I would imagine.

Okay, Lily, time to face your fears. I squared my shoulders, took a deep breath, and crossed the street to the Wax Museum. Posters of the wax figures studded the walls, like old-fashioned movie stars. In fact, the whole front of the museum looked a bit like an abandoned movie theater, which only ratcheted up the eerie feel of the place.

At the front ticket window a bored-looking young woman with a nose piercing and kohl-lined eyes, very Queen of the Dead, put down her dog-eared paperback romance novel and picked up the phone when I asked for Aidan Rhodes. She had a brief conversation, looked me over a couple of times—not pleased with what she saw, I thought—and then waved me in.

"He's upstairs and to the left, right past the Chamber of Horrors."

Of course.

The modern glass-and-steel floating stairs were lined with exhibits and brief writeups of what the management referred to as the current wax "population." I passed by Elvis Presley, Abraham Lincoln, the Mona Lisa. It was interesting to note which historical or famous characters were deemed worthy of recognition: Austin Powers was prominent, for instance, but there was no Madame Curie. In fact, other than a handful of modern actresses, females were depicted primarily in the Vixens exhibit, which featured characters like Lucrezia Borgia, Jezebel, and Mata Hari. *Hmm.* I hoped Rhodes wasn't the one deciding on the "population," because someone had a rather twisted view of powerful women.

Two boys ran by me, excited to see a wax figure of local baseball legend Barry Bonds. Given the number of visitors milling about and enjoying themselves as they perused the exhibits, I guessed I was once again in the minority by finding the whole place much more sinister than entertaining.

When I reached the entrance to the Chamber of Horrors I peeked in. Just past faithful reproductions of an iron maiden and an electric chair, a wax figure of Dracula was looking up, blood dripping down his chin, his apparently willing victim swooning in his arms. I had to admit to a certain fascination with vampires. I always sort of wanted to dress as one for Halloween when I was a girl, but Graciela said it was inappropriate. Bronwyn told me Halloween was a huge adult holiday in San Francisco; maybe this year I would indulge myself and dress up as a vampire, like a normal person.

Lost in thought, I jumped when a pure white, long-haired cat ran toward me and rubbed up against my ankles. I'm allergic to cats, and therefore, since they're contrary creatures, they adore me.

I looked up to see Aidan leaning on the banister beside figures of Elvira and the Texas chain-saw killer.

"Lily!" he said with a charming grin on his face. "What a wonderful surprise. You look as pretty as a picture in that dress. Or is that politically incorrect?"

"You mean for me to wear the dress, or for you to notice it?"

I hadn't meant it as a joke, but he laughed.

It struck me, once again, how devastatingly handsome he was. It was more than mere surface beauty; in addition to being physically gorgeous, he had a surprisingly vulnerable, aw-shucks quality that made him much more intriguing than your average *GQ* cover model. Mere mortals didn't stand a chance. I didn't trust him—or that little-boy look in his bright blue eyes—as far as I could throw him.

The cat finally abandoned her efforts with me and ran to leap into Aidan's arms.

"What do you think of my place?" he asked as he stroked the beautiful feline.

"Isn't there an Edgar Allan Poe story about a wax museum?" I asked.

"Is there?"

"If there isn't, there should be."

"You don't like it?"

"It seems a little . . . I don't know . . . macabre? I thought modern-day witches were careful about being associated with such locales."

"My clients love it. Puts them in a receptive mood."

"You must have some interesting clients."

"You have no idea."

We walked down the hall to a thick mahogany door hidden behind an exhibit of European explorers. Aidan waved me into his office, closing the door behind us. Inside was a holdover from the Victorian days of the Barbary Coast: Fringed and tasseled green velvet curtains covered the windows, and a huge carved walnut desk, complete with claws for legs, dominated one end of the large room. Lots of dark wood, Oriental rugs, and upholstered club chairs. On the built-in bookshelves were tools of the trade, the stuff I usually kept out of plain sight: a crystal ball, pendulums, candles, feathers, and stones, along with a multitude of old, cracking leather-bound books on the history of witches, spells, and the craft.

"So tell me," Aidan said as he took a seat in the plush leather chair behind the desk, gesturing toward a high-backed brocade chair for me. "To what do I owe this lovely surprise?"

"A woman was killed last night."

He smiled and tilted his head. "By all means, get right to the point."

"Did you have anything to do with it?"

"Lily. I know you're wary of me, but you should know that I don't take souls."

The long-haired, pure white cat snuggled in his lap, and I watched as his long, graceful fingers caressed her. I couldn't keep from staring at him for a moment, even though I knew he was far too practiced to let me read his aura.

"What must you think of me?" A tiny frown of puzzlement developed on his otherwise perfect brow. "You're suspicious of me because I'm a man, am I right?"

"It has occurred to me."

"Come now, Lily. I would think you, of all people, would rise above simple prejudice."

"I have nothing against men being witches, per se."

Too nervous to sit, I stood and started inspecting the items on the shelves. I lifted something that looked like a monkey's paw, then caressed the crystal ball, all the while feeling for vibrations. They felt surprisingly warm and positive. On the other hand, a powerful witch can hide his surface vibrations easily enough with a sweetness charm. We, none of us, like to expose ourselves to strangers. Unsettled by the thought, I looked up to see Aidan's blue eyes, patient and searching, watching me.

It was clear to me that Aidan was no average witch; his power was palpable. And the fact that he discovered I was in town, and sought me out, made me think that he had an agenda.

"Am I right in presuming that you fancy yourself in charge of things around here?"

Aidan smiled and inclined his head just a tad.

"Don't you find it odd that with ninety-nine percent of witches being female, a man gets involved and appoints himself head of the whole shebang?" I asked.

"You know what they say: Nature abhors a vacuum."

"In my ideal things are a little less hierarchical."

"What about the pantheon of demons?"

"We're not talking demons, are we?" I put down the bejeweled pounded-copper chalice I was studying and returned to my seat. "I thought you were a witch. A *human* witch."

He grinned and nodded. "That's me. A mere mortal, just like you."

That wasn't very comforting.

"Have you ever heard of a woman named Frances Potts?"

"Doesn't ring a bell."

"Do you know any conjurers who might have intended her harm? She was killed last night in her house in Hunters Point. The police said something about finding a pentagram at the scene."

"Was the victim within the symbol at the time?"

"I assume so."

"What were the other signs? Herbs? Salts? Animal remains?"

"I don't actually know."

"I'm afraid I can't be much help without details."

I should have thought this through before coming. How could I get the information I needed without disclosing that I had cast a protective spell that did not succeed in saving poor Frances? If Aidan Rhodes, male witch, knew my magic had failed . . . Well, let's just say I shared one characteristic with the rest of the world: I was on my guard around witches.

Time to change the subject. "Speaking of demons, what do you know about *La Llorona* being nearby?"

His face shifted just the tiniest amount. I doubt most people would have noticed. His blue eyes widened a tad, the more innocent to appear.

"*La* who?"

"I thought you sort of ran things around here, or wish you did. You mean to tell me *La Llorona* is running around unsanctioned?"

"I don't know where you got the impression that I'm in charge of every two-bit demon in town." He allowed a tinge of annoyance into his voice. "How's Oscar working out for you?"

"He's fine. So you know nothing about *La Llorona*'s being in town?"

He gave a noncommittal shrug.

"She may be the one responsible for Frances's death."

"I doubt that."

"Why?"

"You said the victim was found within a pentagram? *La Llorona* wouldn't cross the circle, much less leave the victim there. Besides, she doesn't enter houses.... As far as I know, she *can't* enter buildings."

Well, duh. La Llorona left her adult victims on the shore of the water as warnings, and took the children down into the depths with her.

Aidan pulled a fat green gilt-edged book from a high shelf and placed in on the desk in front of me, tapping it.

"You need to bone up on your demonology."

"True," I said as I looked at the title: *Demons from A to Zed.* "Could I borrow this? I don't have much of a library, since I've been moving around so much."

"Be my guest."

"A child went missing right after Frances and I heard *La Llorona*'s cry. It seems a strange coincidence, Frances dying right on the heels of a child disappearing." I thought for a moment. "Presuming *La Llorona* grabbed the child, is there any way to get her back?"

He blew out a breath and shook his head. "That's a tough one. Even if you got her back she might be... different. Altered."

I nodded. "I was afraid of that. I guess time is of the essence."

"The only way I know of is to trade souls."

"Excuse me?"

"You heard me. A soul for a soul."

"That's the only way?"

"So far as I know. Would you like me to make some inquiries?"

"What will it cost me?"

"For you, not a penny."

"Uh-huh." I looked into the depths of his blue eyes. "I'd rather not be in your debt."

He smiled. It was a slow, sexy smile, making me tingle down somewhere deep. I knew the pull was probably due to his magic, that he looked at everyone—make that every *woman*—this way. But it reminded me, with sudden clarity, of how long it had been since I had had a man in my life. Unless you counted Oscar. Speaking of whom . . .

"How did you know I call him Oscar?"

"Mmm?" Aidan murmured as he stood and moved over to the sideboard, where he poured two glasses of wine. "*I* know what you could do for me. Are you familiar with the properties of mandrake?"

"Yes, I am. But to stay on subject for just a moment: I didn't tell you I named my new familiar Oscar," I said. "How did you know?"

"Witch's intuition."

"Is he reporting to you?"

"Don't be ridiculous." He handed me a glass of wine and hitched one hip on the desk, very close to where I was sitting. His energy was palpable as he looked down at me. "Is it true the mandrake root screams when you take it out of the ground?"

I nodded. "You have to approach it properly, obtain its permission. Then it's usually pretty docile."

"I have need of a mandragora. I don't suppose you could help me out?"

"A mandragora . . . as in a household imp?" A mandragora is a kind of familiar elf, made from the root of a mandrake plant. Though poisonous, the plant is associated with love, sex, and fertility. The mandragora is often kept in a closet or cupboard at home and helps in wish fulfillment and future-telling.

He nodded.

"Why would you need a mandragora?"

Aidan shrugged and smiled. "Just lonely, I guess."

"Can't you make your own?"

"I'm not particularly gifted with brews and herbs. My skills lie . . . elsewhere." He fixed me with a provocative gaze. "That's one reason I'm so sure our magical talents would cleave. We complement each other."

I had to smile. "Sounds like a pickup line at a coven meeting."

When he laughed he threw his head back slightly, and his blue eyes sparkled. "You're a powerful woman, Lily. We haven't had anyone of your abilities around here for years."

"What do you know of me and my abilities?"

"I told you, I knew your father. It's clear you take after his side of the family. You and I, we understand each other."

I took a sip of the wine—a full-bodied red, of course. Its robust flavors curled around my tongue, warming me from the inside. I could feel myself melting toward Aidan just a tad. There was something enticing about the idea of not having to hide my abilities, of being around someone who knew exactly who—and what—I was. Most of the men I've known in my life have been afraid of me. Most of the women, too, for that matter.

"Have dinner with me. We have a lot to talk about," he said, taking my hand in his. Sparks flew as we touched.

My eyes met his, and I could feel the seductive tug of his magic. I pulled away, managing to spill a little wine down the front of my dress. Aidan yanked out a monogrammed handkerchief and started to dab at the stain. My hormones shifted into overdrive.

"Thanks," I said, pushing the chair away and grabbing the hankie from his hand to dab at the wine myself. "But I'd really like to stay out of politics. I'm a solo act."

He watched me for a long moment, eyes assessing me, up and down, before nodding and inclining his head.

"I'll make some inquiries on your behalf. And please don't forget about my mandragora."

"Thank you," I said as I stood, wondering if I should shake his hand. The traitorous appendage tingled just thinking about it. Best to keep the physical contact to a minimum. I placed his stained hankie on the desk, turned toward the door, and let myself out.

Out in the corridor, I hurried by the figures of European explorers and passed the Chamber of Horrors, slowing my pace as I noticed a pair of tourists standing near the entrance to the exhibit. They were frozen in midstep, unmoving, just as still as the wax figures surrounding us.

A frisson ran up my back. Looking behind me, I thought it seemed like Elvira had moved toward me ever so slightly, lifting her slender arms. I took another step and looked back.... The arms were reaching out toward me....

My heart pounded. The power was tangible, running up and down my spine like an army of ants. I *hated* poppets. I looked back to see Aidan standing in his doorway, his bright blue eyes holding mine, a grin splitting his handsome face.

"Very funny," I said.

He laughed. "Come back anytime, Lily. For you, my door is always open."

Trade a soul. A soul for a soul.

Aidan's parting antics aside, I couldn't stop thinking about what he had told me about getting Jessica back from the demon.

The thought made me shiver. Even before he said it, I had known that would be the answer, could hear Graciela's voice in my head as clear as though she were sitting next to me in the passenger seat of my classic Mustang, big floral scarf covering the braided bun of her long gray hair and tied in a tight knot under her stubborn chin. *"Es la única manera, m'hija." The only way.*

But making that kind of decision—holding the balance of souls in one's hands—was beyond anything I could imagine.

As I stopped and started in the thick traffic that strangled the Fisherman's Wharf tourist area, I studied the people around me. Were any of them worthy of such a fate? I watched a drunken man staggering down the sidewalk with a huge tear in the seat of his pants; surely he was already mostly gone, his essence in the hands of oblivion. Or perhaps I could find an evil stock trader who was happy to drive elderly women into poverty for the sake of his own luxurious comfort. Or some despicable criminal—like the person responsible for killing Frances, for instance, or a child abuser—wouldn't that be justice? Could I rationalize forfeiting the soul of such a person to save that of a child?

No. Not even for the sake of a beautiful young girl with a huge, winning smile.

One of the fundamental principles my grandmother had hammered into me, from the very beginning, was to be wary of the "God syndrome." As the receptacle of truly astonishing abilities, a natural witch could start imagining herself to be in charge of things. But that path, sometimes called the left-hand or dark way, led to the corruption of one's powers and to evil deeds. Down that path lay spiritual and ethical ruin.

And on top of everything else, I wasn't even one hundred percent positive that *La Llorona* had snatched Jessica. There was still a possibility that it was mere coincidence. How could I find out? Would I hear back from Aidan? How would *he* find out? I really needed a sit-down with the old gal, but now that *La Llorona* knew I was here, she wouldn't come near me. It had been stupid to try to reach out to her when I was too psychically spent to hold her. A serious tactical error.

I had always been impulsive and overly confident in my own abilities, and now I feared Jessica was the one paying the price.

The fading evening light took on a pinky violet cast as I looked out beyond the Bay Bridge that led to Oakland and Berkeley. Rush-hour traffic was heavy as thousands of workers spilled out of San Francisco's financial district and flocked to their far-flung homes in places called Hercules, Pleasanton, and Livermore. I still didn't know the Bay Area well and looked forward to discovering the surrounding towns and wild spaces, especially the famed redwood groves and rugged northern California coast. I had hoped to make the Bay Area my home and stay here for years, not mere months, giving myself time to really settle in and explore.

But now I felt that familiar restlessness in the pit of my stomach, urging me to just cut and run. That was what I had always done before when things looked dangerous.

But if I ran away this time, would I ever stop?

You're staying, Lily; that's final, I told myself. San Francisco was my home now, and selling vintage clothes my calling. It might seem silly, but I felt as if I were making a contribution by working with my antique inventory, tending the store, adding to the crazy, one-of-a-kind Haight-Ashbury community. And I loved it. For the first time, I felt as if I were becoming accepted for who I was, rather than reviled for my special abilities.

So I was staying, come hell or high water. All I had to do now was figure out who had taken Jessica and get her back, then discover who killed Frances and help the police bring that person to justice. How hard could that be? I'm a witch, after all.

I pondered the events of the last twenty-four hours: Frances and I heard *La Llorona*'s wail while we stood in the basement. It was nothing new for me to hear a demon's cry, but it was a harbinger of death for Frances. Why had *La Llorona* singled her out? Then, moments later, Jessica disappeared. She could have been snatched by any number of people—I shouldn't rush to assume it was *La Llorona.* Then Frances had died despite my protective spell. Who could have killed her?

A human, no doubt. I had not protected her from humans, concentrating only on demons. Stupid. After all my experiences, how could I have underestimated the capacity for human evil?

And now the police suspected me.

That was the part that really spooked me. I remembered too well what had happened back in my hometown. And seeing the *Malleus Maleficarum* at Sandra's place made me feel as though I were being warned of a witch-hunt to come. Most people thought we witches were no longer in mortal danger, but I wasn't quite so sanguine. If I stuck around long enough, I feared I might find myself standing upon the modern version of the proverbial flaming pyre.

The pastel hue of the evening sky over the bay reminded me that Easter was just around the corner. I had a sudden, vivid memory of Jessica hopping down the shadowy hallway like a bunny—or no, make that a kangaroo. She wouldn't be going on any Easter egg hunts this year, or receiving any chocolate rabbits or candy eggs.

If I were going to go down in flames, at the very least I should save Jessica. It might be my final redeeming act.

Chapter 9

I wasn't sure I would remember exactly which of the nearly identical buildings was Jessica's home, but I needn't have worried.

Already a makeshift shrine had been set up on the sidewalk outside the duplex. Garish helium-filled balloons bobbed in the breeze off the bay, flames flickered on dozens of tall votive candles decorated with Catholic saints, and bright pink ribbons adorned fluffy teddy bears and stuffed animals. One sees these offerings by the road from time to time, memorials to lives lost in traffic accidents or by stray bullets in intense urban battle zones. Usually I was careful not to open myself up to their agonized sensations, but in this case I felt the sorrow resonate in me.

I mounted the stained concrete steps to the small stoop and rang the doorbell. A thin young man, probably a year or two shy of twenty, opened the door a crack. Dark eyes flickered over me with no change in expression.

"*¿Qué quieres?*" He asked what I wanted.

I hesitated, suddenly hyperaware of the wine stain on my inappropriate, brightly colored vintage dress. Through the opening of the door I could hear the sounds of a *telenovela* on the TV and smell the aroma of beans and *masa*, or corn flour. The scent made me think of Graciela on tamale-making day—she always wound up with a bit of corn flour on her nose. The memory gave me confidence.

"*Estoy aquí hablar de Jessica*," I said. "*No soy reportera.*"

My Spanish isn't great, but it was enough to get me in the door and to make it clear I wasn't a reporter. The young man stood back and let me in.

I paused for a moment in the doorway and took in the scene. The cramped living room of the apartment was lined with three twin beds that doubled as couches. A small linoleum kitchen table was surrounded by six vinyl chairs, and a single incandescent bulb in an overhead lamp provided the sole source of light. A television with rabbit-ear antennae was tuned in to a dramatic Spanish-language soap opera, its top adorned with items from a *botánica*, or herbal shop. There was a little Buddha in a Plexiglas pyramid, several pictures of the Virgin of Guadalupe, multicolored candles, and even a tall aerosol can of something that promised peace and harmony in the home. There were similar charms and icons scattered on every horizontal surface in the apartment, plus small sachet charms hung over every doorway.

Thumbtacked to the wall was a large colorful calendar from a local bakery featuring a handsome Aztec warrior holding a swooning woman in his arms, the glorious capital city of Tenochtitlán laid out behind them. We humans love to create mythical pasts. Interesting to think that this family could live in cramped, poverty-level conditions yet find solace in romanticizing the fierce, empire-building Aztecs as paragons of romance and justice.

"Please, have a seat," said a young woman with blond streaks in her otherwise loose, long black hair. She grabbed a chair from the small kitchen table and brought it into the living room for me.

Aside from the young man who answered the door, several people crowded the dim living room: An elderly man drank coffee at the kitchen table, five women of varying ages sat on the beds, and a half dozen children darted in and out of the adjoining bedroom. The adults had the red-ringed eyes and haggard expressions common to long, sleepless nights full of tears.

"Thank you for speaking with me," I addressed the group. What does one say, in any language, to people so recently touched by tragedy? Words were simply not enough. I concentrated on emanating empathy. "I know it's difficult, but I was hoping you could tell me what happened with Jessica last night. I think I may be able to help find her and bring her home."

"How?" asked the young man who had answered the door.

"I know some things," I said, keeping my words vague. "You can trust me."

"I'll go get my mother," said the streaky-haired woman before disappearing into the bedroom.

A young boy, a little older than Jessica, brought me a cup of instant coffee with sugar, and set it on the scuffed coffee table along with a jar of Coffee-mate and a spoon.

He crawled onto a plump, short-haired woman's lap. Then they all stared at me. The soap opera played softly in the background.

I sipped my coffee and allowed the silence to continue, letting everyone get used to my presence.

A few moments later Jessica's mother emerged from the bedroom and perched on the edge of one of the mattresses near me without meeting my eyes. The defeated slope of her shoulders and her blotchy skin told me all I needed to know. She couldn't have been more than fifty, given her young children, but she looked much older. Her black hair, drawn back in a disheveled ponytail, had only a few streaks of gray, but her face was etched with the trials of a hard life.

She told me her name was Felipa. Looking at her relatives rather than at me, she began to speak in broken English, talking as though she had recited the words before.

"First my son Juan, he died in an accident five years ago, right after he brought me up from Mexico. And now, *m'hija*, my daughter Jessica . . . Why has this happened? *How* has this happened to my baby?" She started to weep again and covered her face with a tissue, shaking her head. "You think you could find her?"

"My mother works for a housecleaning agency," interrupted the young man. "She always makes sure we learn English so we can do well here. And now . . ." He trailed off, shaking his head. "We thought we had left *La Llorona* behind—"

The young woman with the streaked hair made a sound between a hiss and a *tsk*, and glared at him.

"My brother don't mean nothing by it," she said with a shrug. "Superstitions."

"I understand," I said. "I know about *La Llorona.* I believe she may have been here."

Again they looked at me without speaking, their dark eyes assessing.

"Could you tell me what happened last night, when Jessica disappeared?" I urged.

"I just came home from work," Felipa said. "I brought groceries, mopped the kitchen before I made dinner. The front door was open, but I . . . I sent the children outside. I told them, 'Stay on the stoop.' They were supposed to stay on the stoop. . . ." She began to weep again.

"The other children began to scream, '*La Llorona*'; that's when we knew," the young man said.

I spoke directly to the little boy who had brought me the coffee.

"Did you see her?" I asked.

He nodded solemnly, huge eyes so reminiscent of Jessica's that I felt my stomach clench as I remembered what was at stake.

"Could you describe her to me?"

He craned his neck, looking to his mother for permission. She nodded.

I had to lean forward to hear him, for he spoke barely above a whisper. But he used his pudgy hands to clarify, holding them up to his scrunched-up face like claws. He described the ghostly spirit, her horrifying face, the gaping mouth, and the faraway-sounding cries for her children.

Presuming I could believe the child, I now knew for certain that *La Llorona* had absconded with Jessica.

Whether that meant more or less hope for the girl's salvation, I wasn't so sure.

Just then the door banged open and in walked a large young man in a bright white sleeveless undershirt and black pants slung low on narrow hips. Intricate tattoos ran up his forearms, biceps, and onto his neck. He was the one who was holding Felipa while she cried after Jessica's disappearance last night.

He walked in as if he owned the place. The tone in the room shifted.

"*¿Qué pasa?*" he demanded, lifting his chin in my direction. "What's going on? Who's she?"

Immediately Felipa and the man launched into a heated exchange. My Spanish was nowhere near strong enough to keep up with their intense discussion, but I understood the word *botánica*, and made out that the fellow was angry at Felipa for believing in "ridiculous magic" that wouldn't help. He scoffed at the mere mention of *La Llorona*. I also learned the man's name: Tomás.

Tomás was right that no amount of paraphernalia from a *botánica* would help bring Jessica back, but it could bring consolation to the family. In any event, it couldn't hurt.

I pulled a small black leather charm bag out of my backpack and gave it to Felipa, wrapping her hands around it, then my own around hers. I looked into her eyes and said a brief incantation of protection, comfort, and solace. Still weeping, Felipa thanked me repeatedly, and blessed me.

Tomás made a disgusted noise and stormed out of the apartment.

I thanked everyone for speaking to me, then hurried to follow Tomás into the night-shrouded street.

"Tomás, wait, please!" I yelled to his back as he strode down the cracked sidewalk. He didn't slow his pace. I jogged up behind him. "Tomás, is there something more you can tell me about Jessica's disappearance? Could it have something to do with the men who were here that day?"

He turned toward me as I caught up to him. "What men?"

"I saw you last night. Jessica had just disappeared; you were holding Felipa on the stoop. There was a group of scary-looking characters right over there, across the street, glaring at you."

He laughed. " 'Scary-looking characters'? Scary like me?"

"Scarier. You're not all that frightening." He was trying to be, but I sensed something else under the simmering anger: something almost noble.

"Who the hell are you, anyway?"

"I'm looking into Jessica's disappearance."

"Why? What do you care about my little cousin? You're no cop."

"No."

"Reporter?"

I shook my head.

"Then why? Someone hire you?"

"I was visiting Frances Potts when Jessica disappeared. Did you know Mrs. Potts?"

"Oh, yeah, I know her. That old lady's unnatural, is what she is." He turned and started walking away again.

Unnatural?

"That 'old lady,' as you call her, was killed last night," I said to his back.

He stopped, his shoulder blades contracting under his undershirt, revealing his tension. I couldn't help but wonder whether he was cold wearing so little out here near the bay. Why were young men always wearing either too much or too little? Down jackets in the summer, nothing but undershirts in the winter . . .

"I saw the police Do Not Cross tape. I'm not blind," said Tomás. "And I'm not surprised."

"Why not?"

"A lotta people wanted her dead."

"Dead? Why?"

"They wanted her land. And she was a snitch."

"A snitch?"

"Ratted out the homeboys. What the hell is she doing in this neighborhood, anyway?"

"She's lived here a long time. Why shouldn't she be in this neighborhood?"

"There's something wrong in that house." His hands low on his hips, he shook his head and met my eyes for the first time. "Last Halloween some kids broke in there. . . . You mark my words. She's like that . . . how do you call her? In the fairy tales? The evil witch that lures kids in and they're never seen again."

"We're talking about Mrs. *Potts* here? Frances Potts?"

Just then a beautifully detailed, candy-apple red Cadillac pulled up, bass pounding to the beat of a Latin rap song. Without another word, Tomás climbed in and was gone.

* * *

I jogged back to my car, got in, and reached for the ignition, but hesitated before turning the key. Frances's house was less than a block away, its silhouette a soft black against the evening sky. What had Tomás meant? Sweet little Frances, an evil witch? Impossible. Among other things, I was with Frances when Jessica was snatched; the old woman couldn't possibly have been involved.

Despite my fear of implicating myself further in the eyes of the police, I wanted—I *needed*—to take a good look around that house. The more I thought about it, the more it seemed to me that the vibrations were off on the night I was there. And then there was that invisible entity. . . .

I always carry several items in the trunk of my car for emergencies. Grabbing a dark blue cotton athletic bag from the trunk, I climbed into the backseat of my Mustang and transferred a flashlight, a few candles, a black silk bag, an extra couple of talismans, and a charm bag into my backpack. Finally, counting on the darkness to keep me from being obscene—luckily there wasn't a soul out on the street nearby—I pulled on a pair of old jeans under the skirt of my dress. Scooting down as far as I could into the footwell, I whipped the dress over my head and yanked on a worn UC Berkeley sweatshirt.

Feeling much more suited to the task at hand, I pulled an amulet over my head, tucked a charm bag in the front pocket of my jeans, and cast a quick protective spell over the vehicle. This didn't seem like the best neighborhood to park a vintage Mustang after dark, and I really love my car.

Then I jogged along the quiet street to the Potts

house, drawing the fresh salt air of the bay deep into my lungs.

I passed a couple small groups of young men gathered on stoops, but no one seemed to pay me much attention. One of the definite pluses of being "different" is not having to fear humans under normal circumstances, so I'm not frightened of wandering alone in the middle of the night, even in a not-so-great part of town. Don't get me wrong: As far as I know I'm as mortal as the next person, but I can hold my own against your average low-life/druggie/mugger, especially when prepared with a charm bag and a backpack full of consecrated amulets and talismans.

Conscious of the street camera Inspector Romero had told me about, I climbed over the low iron fence and slipped into the overgrown side garden of the Pottses' corner lot and lingered for a moment amidst broken beer bottles, crack vials, and cigarette butts. I didn't want to get caught on tape again—that would be tough to explain. I bided my time, assessing the structure from the safety of the brush. Just ahead, between where I was now and the back door, was Frances's small kitchen garden. In the light of the streetlamp I could make out what looked like neat rows of herbs, vegetables, and, as luck would have it, a mature mandrake plant.

That was a happy surprise. It must have been left over from the garden's old Mediterranean planting scheme, where plants such as mandrake and wolfsbane were common. Perfect for Aidan's mandragora. Mandrakes had to be approached carefully, however, and I didn't have the necessary supplies with me. I would have to come back for it later.

Hunkered down amidst the bushes, I waited, watching the structure for another ten minutes. Police tape crisscrossed the back door and cordoned off the gates in the iron fence, but no one was guarding the place. I imagined everything was locked up tight; I could probably unlock the doors magically, but I'd rather not take the time. Glancing up at the second story, I noticed a double-hung window was slightly ajar.

An old wooden trellis ran up the back of the building, supporting the fat, snaking branches of a vine long since dead. Leaving the protection of the bushes, I scooted to the back of the house and shook the trellis as hard as I could. It felt sturdy, the wood dry but sound. *What the heck* . . . If it was good enough for generations of actors in movies, it was good enough for me. I grabbed on, got a foothold, and hoisted myself up.

Hand over hand, step by step . . . the unfamiliar stretch and strain of climbing brought to mind a visceral memory I would just as soon forget: the moment I realized I wasn't just a simple misfit. The day I learned I was a witch.

I was in the third grade. We were on a school campout, the kind of event my mother eventually stopped forcing me to attend once she finally admitted her daughter was a freak. The morning had dawned cold and damp, and the camp leaders had made a great batch of oatmeal. My mother had raised me on oatmeal served with salt and pepper, the way her own Scottish mother had prepared it, but that morning I was handed a bowl that already had sugar and cinnamon on it. The idea of the sweet on what I knew as salty made me queasy, so I asked the girl next to me, Terry Buckmiller, to trade me for her still-plain bowl. She refused. Terry was a pampered violin virtuoso and had always been the smartest kid in class until I had displaced her. She had never liked me.

I concentrated, making her bowl so hot that it burned her fingers. When she dropped it I caught it, and I handed her my own in what seemed to me a fair exchange.

"You're a *witch* is what you are! A nasty old *witch*!" Terry pointed at me and shouted.

I was enraged. I had been raised with the same images as everyone else in our small Texas town: Witches were ugly hags in league with the devil. But her accusation struck a chord. Fear of the truth fed my fury.

A sudden gust of wind blew sparks and embers up from the fire, landing in Terry's lap and hair. As the grown-ups rushed to her aid, the other children moved in on me, accusing, shouting, pushing. Hating.

I backed away from them until I had nowhere else to go—our campsite was at the base of a sheer cliff. I turned toward the wall of stone as the children descended upon me, and I started to climb the steep, vine-strewn wall. The vines twined around my hands and wrists, helping me, pulling me up. When I made it to the top I looked down over the precipice, and with the perfect illogic of a young child cast a loud curse down upon the lot of them, even while denying I was a witch.

Every single child on that trip, except for me, came down with a virulent case of food poisoning. Officially the oatmeal was to blame, but soon afterward I was sent to live with Graciela on the outskirts of town. I spent the next several years learning to admit to myself that I was a witch, to control my temper, and to hide my talents from normal humans. I was still only partially successful at the latter two.

Which might explain why I was currently scaling the side of a house.

My mind came back to the task at hand. With much more effort than it had taken as a child—these vines were not helping me at all—I finally made it up to the second-story window. I hoisted it open and climbed inside the dark house, landing at the end of the second-story hallway.

Breathing hard, I stood for a moment and assessed the shadowed interior. There was a dank, closed-up smell, mixing with the still-lingering scent of pot roast. The last meal. And there was another odor, the sickeningly sweet aroma of death.

My skin tingled and again I felt the creepy sensation of ants running along my spine. The place was alive with spiritual energy.

I didn't bother with the flashlight, since there was plenty of dim illumination from the streetlamps outside, and my night vision is better than average. I started down the broad, high-ceilinged hallway toward Frances's bedroom, the next-to-last door on the left.

I had never before knowingly stepped into a recent crime scene. Perhaps they all felt this ominous. Maybe it was my imagination. If only I were a necromancer, I could call on Frances's spirit and ask her what happened. I felt sure that, since the death was so recent and had not been natural, her spirit would still be hanging around. But I have never been able to talk to the human dead. Sense them, yes, but not hold a conversation as though you were talking to your favorite auntie.

Since I was now sure Frances hadn't been killed by *La Llorona*, I wanted to know whether witchcraft had been involved, or whether it was just regular old homicide. I needed to see the murder scene.

A strong, stinging citrus scent assailed my nostrils. Something flickered in my peripheral vision. A sense of movement passing a doorway, preternaturally quickly. An entity flew over my head, taunting, making my hair stand up on end. There was a soft, barely audible *whoosh-whoosh-whoosh* sound, like a heartbeat on a fetal monitor.

A figure materialized in the doorway.

Chapter 10

Swallowing a scream, I held out my right hand and let fly a blast of energy.

In a scene worthy of an old Keystone Kops movie, Charles the charlatan crashed backward into Max the mythbuster and they both went down on their butts, landing sprawled on the threadbare bedroom carpet.

"What in the world are y'all *doing* here?" I asked in an urgent whisper, my heart pounding as I watched the two men climb to their feet.

It was rare for someone to be able to sneak up on me like that, but I had been so focused on the dead—and the undead—that I had once again forgotten to consider the living.

"I might ask you the very same thing," Charles responded, brushing off his pants. "I promised Mr. Carmichael here a haunted experience, and I'm a man of my word."

"Hi, Max."

"Lily." He nodded with a bemused smile. "What a surprise."

"Would you excuse us for just a moment, please? Charles and I have something private to discuss." I grabbed Charles by the arm and started pulling him out into the hall.

"What's your problem, Lily?" Charles demanded.

"*My* problem? You're trespassing for the sake of your ghost tours?"

"What's your excuse?"

"Someone was *killed* in this house, Charles," I whispered when we were several feet away from Max's curious ears.

"What?" Charles looked aghast.

"Just last night. So what—"

"But I had an arrangement with the owner of this house. She said I could lead tours as long as I made sure no one brought cameras."

"She did?"

"Yup. Your neighbor on Haight Street, Sandra, introduced us. It's my backup plan when other things fall through. Great old place."

"Let me get this straight: I paid you not to take Max out, and rather than give him his money back, you brought him here? You're a sleaze; you know that?"

"Lily, let's not be hasty. . . . The owner—"

"The owner was killed last night."

"You're saying *Frances* was killed*?"*

"Didn't you notice the fluorescent yellow police tape at the doors?"

He shrugged. "I thought it was part of the shtick. It lent an air of authenticity to the whole thing."

"Charles, this is a crime scene—"

"Someone was killed here?" interrupted Max, who had managed to sidle up to us without my noticing.

"Last night, a friend of mine—" I began.

A door slammed at the end of the hall.

Max crouched as though ready to fight, then reached into his waistband and pulled out a pistol.

"Put that thing away!" I said.

"Who else is here?" Max demanded, even while starting off in the direction of the noise. I grabbed his arm to stop him.

"You should both get out of here immediately," I said. "It's not safe."

Just then there was rustling overhead.

"Good idea," said Charles, his eyes fixed on the ceiling. He turned and headed for the stairs, speaking over his shoulder. "Max, I happen to know of a nice ghost over at the Queen Anne Hotel. You could even bring your film crew. You coming?"

"Either we all go," Max said, "or I'm staying with Lily."

The hallway light flickered on and off.

"Suit yourself," Charles said, scurrying down the broad stairway with impressive speed for a large man.

"Max, you really should go with him," I said. "I appreciate the whole gallantry thing, but I guarantee you I can take care of myself."

"What are you doing here?"

"I told you, a friend of mine—"

"A friend getting killed is reason to cry in your beer, not to trespass on the crime scene."

I heard a faint whispery sound, and saw a subtle flash of light in my peripheral vision. We weren't alone.

"Are you in some kind of trouble?" Max asked me.

"Max, do you still have the medicine bundle I gave you? Is it in your pocket?"

"As a matter of fact it is." He patted his breast pocket.

"Keep it. And here." I rooted around in my backpack until I felt a smooth circle of wood. I slipped the medallion over his head.

"What is all this?"

We both froze when we heard scratching and rustling overhead.

"*Bad spirits*," I whispered.

"Or rats in the attic," Max, the cynic, replied. He strode down to the end of the hall, where an attic access door was apparent in the ceiling, a string dangling down from it. Before I could stop him he yanked down the retractable stairs and climbed halfway up, his head and shoulders disappearing into the hole. He shone a large, powerful flashlight around the periphery.

"Nothing," he declared.

"How much nothing?"

"Some old picture frames, chairs, kid stuff."

The black rectangle of the opening swallowed him whole as he climbed the rest of the way up.

After a moment of hesitation—this was where the scratching sound had come from, after all—I followed.

Aside from stacked cardboard boxes and miscellaneous furniture shoved under the eaves, the area was set up as a child's playroom. A rocking horse, a small easel with a chalkboard, a stack of board games. What surprised me was the number of dolls and toy cars strewn about the floor as though abandoned where they lay, not stored away in boxes. But everything was covered in dust and cobwebs. No one had been up here for a very long time. Using the beam of my flashlight I studied an intricate Victorian dollhouse, a detailed replica of the house we were in. It held a family of dolls: a man and woman and two girls. A chill ran up my spine.

The man was hanging from a beam, a black string around his neck.

A child's gruesome imagination or something more sinister?

I reached out and picked up a discarded, wild-haired Barbie. I concentrated. The sensations from the doll were strong, but almost unrecognizable. What *was* it? Unsettling to be sure, but they reminded me of the danged shadows in my crystal ball, like a dream you're trying to remember the next morning . . . tantalizingly close yet still out of reach. One thing was sure: It had been a long while since this doll was last held.

"Lily? Are you all right?"

I dropped the wretched doll, wiping my hand on the thigh of my jeans. It itched. "Yeah, sure, I'm fine. See anything?"

"Nothing."

I swung my flashlight beam around the stuffy attic room. In the opposite corner was another trapdoor in the floor. I walked over to it, hoisted it open, and focused my flashlight beam down the hatch. It looked as though the steps led to a closet.

"Let me go first," said Max.

I was already starting down. "Why?"

"It could be dangerous."

I smiled and continued down the steep ladder. "Somehow I think I'm more prepared than you are for what we might find."

Max followed immediately behind me.

We landed in a cramped closet that smelled of mothballs and cedar. Obviously Frances hadn't packed up all the old clothes she had access to. The door was ajar and led into another bedroom. This one was much larger than Frances's chamber, and appeared to be the old master. The busy printed wallpaper and duvet cover were in old-fashioned tones of pinky beige, brown, creamy yellow. Cobwebs adorned the corners, and a layer of thick dust lay undisturbed on the furniture, as though the room had been closed off for some time. But dark powder also marred a few of the surfaces: the residue of fingerprint dust.

And on the broad-planked wood floor: a chalk outline of a body, spread-eagled within a pentagram.

Talk about your haunted houses.

Max pulled out a small digital camera and began taking pictures.

I knelt. The pentagram had been drawn in salt and what looked like blood. It had been kicked and smeared, no doubt by the feet of countless police officers and coroners. My hand shook as I reached out to the remnants of the circle. I could feel nothing more specific than anger, and pain, and diffused magic.

A hand touched my back, making me jump. I turned to see Max right above me, a finger to his lips, motioning toward the closet. I followed his eyes to see that he had pulled the clothes on the rod to the side, revealing a small door at the rear of the wardrobe.

A dim light shone under the door.

Max and I looked at each other for a long moment. He held his hand out to me and helped me up, and we both moved as quietly as possible to the closet. Max brought his gun back out and held it at the ready. Standing on either side of the door, we waited for a moment, listening. Nothing.

I reached out carefully; then as quickly as I could I twisted the knob and pushed the door in, then leaped back. Nothing happened. After a moment in which we could hear only our own ragged breathing, Max held his gun with both hands in front of him, police officer–style, and jumped in the doorway.

It was a shallow subcloset cut out under the eaves, with a sloping ceiling that descended quickly.

Empty.

Except for an elaborate altar.

The surface had been covered in a fringed black cloth, with dozens of candles, all lit. There had been an animal sacrifice—a chicken, by the looks of it. Feathers and blood adorned the altar and had dribbled onto the floor. By the stench, it appeared to be at least a day or two old. A stitched doll sat at the back. There were a few blackened bones, cut-up fruit, carved gourds, candy, seashells, plastic beads, and an open bottle of expensive Puerto Rican rum. Sparkly foil paper, a fan, symbols on paper, herbs, and powders were scattered about. Amongst other notes, there were a few downloaded prints of articles about me in Texas—the accusations, the lack of a trial.

One large lit candle was cradled in something claw-like. The tallow yellow wax had dripped so much that it was hard to tell, but it took the form of a human hand.

Max came over, frowning down at the altar, gun at his side.

"Put that gun away, Max. The only thing you're going to hit is one of us."

"I'd feel a lot better about this whole thing if—"

Suddenly the door behind us slammed shut, blowing out the candles. Both our flashlights flickered out at the same time, plunging us into inky darkness.

Max threw himself against the door, twisting the knob . . . to no avail.

"God *damn* it!" Max yelled, banging on the solid door in frustration.

We were locked in the pitch-black room. I heard Max clicking his flashlight, and I did the same. Neither functioned.

Holding my right hand out in front of me, I envisioned power flowing through me, from the top of my head to the tips of my toes, and out of my right hand.

"What is dark be filled with light; remove these spirits from my sight."

Even amongst witches, I'm a freak. Most sorcerers' hands create a blue-white light, but mine is orangey red. I let the light from my hand fill the room and instantly, like a darkroom during photo development, everything was bathed in a soft red light.

I looked back down to study the altar. This was no witchcraft as I knew it. My guess was voodoo. Like witchcraft, there was the good and the bad, the evil and the benevolent in the practice of magic connected to the voodoo religion. But unlike with witchcraft, I wasn't sure I could tell the difference.

"Could I borrow your camera?" I whispered, my gaze

still fixed on the scene before me. When Max didn't respond, I looked back at him.

He stood frowning, staring at my hand. I guess he wasn't used to seeing light emanating without benefit of exterior power sources.

"*Max*. The camera."

Still frowning, he handed it to me. Keeping my right hand up for light, I used my left to snap pictures of the altar and its contents. The flash created a strange strobe-light effect in the confined space.

While my attention was diverted, several of the altar candles flickered back to life, and things started to jump upon the altar. Then papers began to fly around the room.

Intent on what I was doing, I ignored them. Bad mistake.

"Lily!" Max yelled as a ritual knife flew through the air toward me.

Max jumped in front of it.

It turned its blade at the last moment and plunged into his side.

"Max!"

The candles flickered out again, and the light from my hand stopped as I crouched to help him. I reached up to the altar and grabbed the hand-shaped candleholder. Suddenly all the candles lit up again and the locked closet door swung open.

Max lay sprawled on the floor, barely conscious. Blowing out the flame, I shoved the candleholder into my backpack, grabbed Max under his arms, and pulled him as hard as I could. I grunted and slid but at long last managed to drag him through the closet and into the main bedroom.

I looked at the gash in his side. It shouldn't have knocked him out, but all bets are off when injuries are sustained due to magic. I had a silk sack in my backpack, which I folded up and set beside him. Taking a deep breath, I yanked the knife out of his side, stanching the flow of blood with the folded sack as a compress on his wound, securing it with his belt. Thank goodness Max still had my medicine bundle in his jacket pocket—the knife had sliced through his shirt, but the blade had glanced off the magical bundle. A small slit in the bag showed that it had caught the full brunt of the attack.

"*Max!* Max, look at me." His gray eyes finally opened and met mine, dull and unfocused. I took him by his shoulders and stared at him, unblinking.

"Listen to me, Max. You need to get up and walk. Ignore the pain in your side. I need you to be a real macho man right now. Use all your energy to stay upright and walk. Let me lead you, Max. You can trust me. Do you believe me? *You can trust me.*"

I pulled him up by the arm, and he struggled into an upright position, hunching over slightly to hold his side. I pulled his arm around my neck and helped him to stand up. Finally I led him as quickly as I could down the main staircase, across the front room, down the hall to the kitchen, and out the back door. He stumbled occasionally, and I could feel his head loll from one side to the other. He was in bad shape.

We staggered down the back steps and through the dark garden. My heart pounded, my breathing was ragged, and I was sweating up a storm. Just as we reached the sidewalk he stumbled and fell to the ground. My heart sank. Could I get him to his feet again?

Black-clad legs suddenly appeared in front of me.

I looked up. Tomás.

"What the hell . . . ?" he said.

"Thank goodness!" I gasped. "I need your help. Will you run and get my car—it's the red Mustang outside your house—and bring it back here?"

"What's going on?"

"I have to get him home. But Tomás, watch out for the surveillance camera across the street."

He smiled. "Bunch of kids took that thing out of commission yesterday."

"Oh, good," I said, cringing at the breathless tone of my voice. "Hurry with the car?" I held out my car keys.

With a quick nod he grabbed the keys and ran.

I heard a hoarse laugh and looked down to see Max struggling to get his elbow underneath him to sit up.

"He's gonna take off with that antique car of yours."

"No, he won't. Relax. He'll be here in a jiffy."

"I tell you what, Lily. You have far too much faith in your fellow man."

Just then, the Mustang screeched around the corner.

"A lot you know, Mr. Cynical."

Tomás helped me finagle Max into the passenger seat.

"What happened to him?" Tomás asked.

"It's . . . a little hard to explain."

"I told you that place is no good."

I thanked him for his help, then sped through the streets of San Francisco like a NASCAR driver to my shop, where I repeated my earlier performance and convinced Max to half walk up to my apartment. He was really flagging by the time we hit the stairs, and I wasn't faring much better. I'm strong, but Max had a good fifty pounds and six inches on me. I called for Oscar, who got behind him, put one outsize gnome hand on each cheek, and pushed until our motley trio finally careened through the door at the top of the stairs.

"Fill the cauldron about halfway with springwater and put it on to boil."

"I'm not meant to actually *assist* in spells, just—"

"Move!"

"Yes, mistress."

Grumbling about my mixing him up with Igor the lab assistant, Oscar did as I asked as I laid Max down on the living room rug. I knelt over him.

"Max, pay attention." I held his face between my hands. He looked so vulnerable. I felt a surge of helplessness that I hadn't experienced since Graciela was accidentally laid low by one of my spells gone wrong, when I was just sixteen. "Listen to me, Max. You'll go to sleep now. You can trust me. Go to sleep, and do not awaken until you are told to. Do you understand me?"

His eyes seemed to come into sudden focus. He lifted one hand and touched my cheek. He mumbled something, but I had to lean closer to hear.

"What?"

"You're . . . okay? Not hurt?"

"I'm fine. Hush now, and go to sleep."

He closed his eyes. I brushed the hair from his forehead under the guise of checking for fever, studying his features for a moment: five-o'clock shadow, the hard planes of his face, long black lashes, kissable mouth . . .

Then I sprang into action. His wound was serious—not only physically, but there was no telling what kinds of supernatural power might be attached. I would need a three-pronged approach: a brew, a poultice, and a circle with incantations.

I rushed outside to gather herbs, chanting the whole time. The water was boiling by the time I was finished, so I added herbs, essential oils, and goat's milk. Finally I snipped a lock of Max's hair and clipped his nails, then added these to the concoction. I chanted over it, stirring it until it stirred itself. Then I left it to boil.

I mixed a poultice of herbs, mustard, and essential oils.

I stitched Max up with black silk thread boiled in the brew.

I cleaned his wound with witch hazel and applied the poultice. By then the brew was ready. I forced him to drink a cupful.

Then I began to cast a circle, drawing down the moon and calling on my helpmates.

I knelt within the circle, rocking and chanting. By the time I finished, my little Bavarian cuckoo clock was chiming two in the morning. Oscar had long since curled up in his bed atop the refrigerator. Max was sleeping peacefully; his pulse was strong and steady.

As we said back in Texas, I felt like I'd been rode hard and put up wet. I could barely keep my eyes open. With a sigh of relief, I curled up next to Max, and slept within the safety of the circle.

I awoke with the sensation that I was being watched. This time it wasn't by a hungry goblin, but a shirtless man with one strong arm wrapped around me.

"What the hell happened?" Max frowned down at me.

"I told you not to wake until I told you to."

"What?"

"Never mind. How do you feel?"

"In dire need of coffee."

"I mean your . . . your side. Let me look at it."

Pushing on his chest until he lay back on the floor, I lifted the bandage from his wound. I noted with relief that it had already started healing.

He looked at me as though struggling to remember something. Then he started looking around. "Where the hell am I? What happened last night?"

"What do you remember?"

"Rats in the attic, that altar in the closet, then . . . nothing."

Good. "You were injured."

"Obviously." He was leaning over and trying to inspect the wound, but it was at an odd angle for him.

"I brought you to my place to fix you up."

"So, you're a doctor now?"

"Not exactly. Let me get you some coffee."

Oscar snorted and trotted off to look for food. I followed him into the kitchen, fed him a leftover half sandwich, and put the kettle on. Filling my single-cup cone filter with ground beans, I brewed two strong, fragrant cups of French roast.

After sitting up for a few minutes, Max got to his feet and started swaying. He seemed confused and a bit vacant, a common reaction to his wound and my spell.

"Be careful," I said as he collapsed back onto the couch.

I brought him his coffee and set my own on the side table.

“I need to change your bandage.” Bringing my basket of gauze and tiny jar of poultice over to the coffee table, I knelt in front of Max and found myself face-to-face with his bare chest. I could feel him looking down at the top of my head.

If the wound had been over to the left just slightly, it might have been critical, beyond my abilities. I felt waves of guilt and self-doubt. I should have *made* him leave the house with Charles, but the truth was, I had wanted him to stay with me. He made me feel safe. And then my magic hadn’t been strong enough to protect us.

“I’m so sorry,” I whispered.

“Are you the one who used me for target practice?”

I shook my head.

“Then why are you apologizing?”

“I got you into the situation.” I looked up at him. “If it wasn’t for me—”

“If I recall, I followed you into that closet. I’m a big boy, Lily. I take my own chances.”

“Yes, but—”

“Shh.” He put his index finger on my lips to stop my protests. Rather than taking it away immediately, he let his finger remain a moment, then rubbed slowly, gently across my lower lip.

Our eyes met, our breath coming harder.

“You’re so . . .” he said as his gaze fell to my mouth.

The phone rang.

It was Aidan. It was important. It was just as well.

I stood. “I’ll be right back.”

I picked up the phone extension in my bedroom, sinking down into the bed.

“Hi, Aidan.”

"You knew it was me?"

"I'm like a walking caller ID."

"Ah, that makes sense. Hope I'm not waking you."

"Not at all."

"I've made some inquiries. Frances's death seems to have been human, not demonic."

"Yeah, thanks. I'm getting that, too."

"But there were no local witches involved, at least none under my auspices. So you could be dealing with out-of-towners, or, more likely, with someone trying to make it look like a magical or ritual death."

"Why would they do that?"

"To cast suspicion elsewhere? Who knows? Anyway, I want to dissuade you from going after *La Llorona.* There have been some recent developments."

"What kind of developments?"

"I'm not sure yet. Suffice it to say, you'll be in over your head. Unless you take me with you, of course."

"Would you work with me on this?"

"Only if we could reach some kind of agreement. This would be asking a lot. And in any case, I need a few more days to assess the situation."

"All right. Thank you, Aidan. I do appreciate it."

I hung up the phone, feeling as though Aidan was something of a witchy Godfather, making me an offer I couldn't refuse. I sighed, then brushed my teeth and hair, and took a moment to change into a fresh sweater and straight skirt—circa 1960—before returning to the living room.

When I saw Max, I stopped short.

Chapter 11

Max held my Book of Shadows in one large hand, steadying himself with the other. Since I never bring anyone to my apartment, I'm not in the habit of hiding things. Stupid of me. I had left my Book of Shadows out last night, wide-open on the counter.

"What's this?" he asked.

"A, um, recipe book."

"Uh-huh. Here's a recipe that includes gecko skin."

"A lot of people eat reptiles. Bugs, even. I used to travel a lot, and I wrote things down."

"And eye of newt?"

"That's actually an herb. Sounds creepy, though, huh?"

Max fixed me with a long, searching look. Then his light gray eyes scanned the room, noting the charms over the doors and mirror, the gazing ball, and the cauldron washed out and left to dry near the sink.

He snapped the book closed, tossed it onto the counter, crossed his arms over his chest, and blew out a breath.

"Why does every interesting woman in this town have to be into witchcraft?"

"How do you mean?"

"For chrissakes, Lily. This is what I do. I may have been blinded to it for longer than usual because I . . ." He shrugged. "I was distracted. But I've done my homework. I recognize the signs."

"Then I reckon you know that historically, 'witch' was a derogatory term for a woman healer."

"And I take it you fancy yourself a healer?"

"Good thing for you, or you'd be at San Francisco General with a cotton-pickin' tube down your throat and a catheter up your—"

Max let out a loud bark of laughter. I couldn't help but notice the sparks in his light eyes.

"I think I forgot to thank you," he said, holding his side.

"You're welcome. Come sit down, let me fix you some breakfast, and I'll tell you what you want to know."

Max brought a chair into the kitchen and watched me as I prepared a quick omelet with fresh vegetables from the farmers' market, artisan Gruyère cheese, and thin-sliced imported olives. I boiled a batch of grits and whipped up some scrambled eggs for Oscar. I put thick slabs of my homemade whole-wheat bread to toast and squeezed oranges for juice. Finally, I poured us each second cups of coffee.

Any witch worth her salt, in my estimation, is a good cook. In fact, people who possess no magic at all can instill their home-cooked meals with love and security and health, transforming ingredients and bringing disparate people together as family and friends. There's a reason that when opening one's home to guests, the first thing you do is offer food and drink. Cooking is a kind of everyday magic.

As I brought the coffee to the table, I saw Max sneaking Oscar a bite of omelet and patting him on the back.

"He's already eaten twice this morning," I said. "He's going to get fat."

"He's a pig. He's supposed to be fat. He's a cute little fellow—reminds me of a dog."

At which Oscar reared back and glared at Max.

"Do you have a pet?" I asked.

"I used to. And it looks like I'm on the verge of inheriting my father's old mutt. She rides around with me a lot. Loves the truck."

I smiled and picked at my own food while I watched Max dig in, eating heartily. I told myself I was interested because an appetite was a good sign after such an injury. But the truth was, it fascinated me to watch big men eat with abandon. This one, in particular. Finally, Max sighed, leaned back, and wiped his mouth with his napkin.

"You're quite a cook."

"Thank you."

"All right, I'll repeat my question: Why do all the interesting women have to be witches?"

"I might as well ask why all the interesting men are married or gay."

"Not *all* the interesting men."

He smiled and held my eyes.

"So assuming you're not gay," I played along, "it begs the question: Why aren't you married?"

A shadow crossed over his face. He stirred a lump of

raw sugar into his coffee, licked the spoon, and leaned back in his chair.

"My wife died four years ago, August eighteenth."

I reached out and placed my hand over his, casting a comforting spell without even thinking about it.

Max looked up at me, startled. We both seemed at a loss for words.

He took his hand away, leaned back, and I felt his guard slip up.

"Tell me what happened last night."

"You remember the altar?"

He frowned. "Just barely."

"We were attacked."

"By whom?"

"Not whom, exactly. More like what. You don't remember?"

"Nothing after the door slamming and locking us in."

I avoided his eyes, taking our dishes into the kitchen. He stood up to help but I waved him back down. He might not be feeling the effects of his wound, but it was more serious than he thought. My magic was making it numb.

"You should lie down."

"Just tell me, Lily."

I stood at the counter, my hands flat on the cold tile.

"Forces attacked us. Spirits, demons, maybe. I'm not sure. I'm not that familiar with the voodoo pantheon."

He fixed me with a look. Several seconds ticked by.

"What happened is that somebody jumped us," Max asserted. "What are you trying to cover up? Was it Gosnold?"

"Of course not. Listen, it's not that simple, Max—"

He snorted.

"I know it's hard to understand. I—"

"Lily, please." He pushed the chair out with a screech and stood up. "It's one thing to play around with gecko skin and charms, quite another to pretend that something clearly human is on a different dimension altogether."

"I really think you need to keep an open mind in this case, Max. There is evil in the world, and—"

"I couldn't agree more. Look at what's happening in Darfur. Hell, you don't have to go that far. Look around any city: drug addiction, mothers neglecting babies, fathers molesting their kids, people shooting each other—that's true evil." He leaned in toward me and spoke very softly. "But it's plain old human evil. Nothing magic about it."

I was at a loss for words in the face of such disbelief. I wasn't accustomed to trying to convince people of the supernatural world; usually it was the other way around. But after what we'd survived together in Frances's house, it seemed ludicrous to deny it.

"Tell me what happened, Lily."

"I don't know. But whatever it was wasn't human."

"You're saying we were attacked by ghosts?"

"Not ghosts, but spiritual forces of some sort."

Max let out a loud breath and drew his hands through his hair.

"I can't deal with this," he grumbled, stalking to the door.

Oscar shifted to his gnome form and stood beside me. Together we watched as Max strode out without a backward glance, slamming the door behind him.

"Sheesh. You were up all night tending to him, and that's all the thanks you get?" Oscar growled. "Cowan ingrate."

I couldn't have said it better myself.

"*Dude.* The walk of shame."

"The what?" I had trailed Max down the stairs of my apartment, through the store, and out into the cold morning sunshine. By the time I got outside he was already halfway down the block, striding along as though he hadn't been seriously injured a very few hours ago.

Sitting with his back up against the wall of Aunt Cora's Closet, Conrad elucidated. "Duuuude. When they leave early in the morning wearin' last night's clothes, it's called the walk of shame. Least, that's what we used to call it back at school."

I had to smile. "It's not like that."

"No? Too bad. He's cute."

"You think he's cute?"

"Oh, yeah. Tall, dark, and handsome—standard hottie. Watch out, though. He must have a jealous wife or something. Those dudes across the street were taking his picture when he left. Prob'ly private eyes."

I followed Conrad's gaze to the beat-up silver sedan parked outside the shoeshine store across the street. Inspectors Romero and Nordstrom were eating bagels and drinking coffee, making no effort at subterfuge. In fact, Romero gave me a little wave. Clearly they had been watching as Max left the store.

That was just great. I had no idea what dealings Max had with Carlos Romero, but I had the sense it didn't help my case to be considered too friendly with Max the mythbuster.

"You want me to sweep?" Conrad offered.

"That would be great, thanks. Would you like something other than a bagel this morning? I could make you an omelet."

"Nah, thanks. A bagel would just hit the spot."

On my way to the café I stopped by the silver sedan. Just because they were investigating me didn't seem like a reason not to be neighborly. I tapped on the driver's-side window. Inspector Romero rolled it down.

"Hi," I said.

"Hey," said Romero with an amused half smile.

The blond practically choked on his old-fashioned glazed.

"Can I get you boys anything? I was just on my way to the café."

"You want anything, Neil?" Romero asked his partner.

Still clearing his throat, Neil shook his head.

"I guess we're good. Thanks for asking."

"Anytime. Don't work too hard, now," I said as I turned to walk away.

"Ms. Ivory," I heard Romero call out, and the sound of his car door opening.

I stopped and he walked toward me.

He looked at me for a long time, dark eyes assessing, then glanced around as though to see if anyone would overhear us. When he spoke, he kept his voice low.

"Let me ask you something straight out: Are you some kind of witch?"

"Witch?" I hesitated. Despite my recent coming-out to Bronwyn, and even Max for that matter, this wasn't the sort of thing I bandied about. "What does that have to do with anything?"

"I called up the sheriff in a little town called Jarod, in west Texas. Isn't that where you're from?"

I looked away. Even the name of that town hurt my heart.

"People there sure as hell think you're a witch, or some other freak of nature."

"Gee, thanks so much, Inspector."

"And there was an incident. . . ."

"Those charges were dismissed and found to be baseless."

"They were dismissed, but whether or not they were baseless is a matter of opinion. A lot of people seem to think you cast some sort of spell to change the mind of the county prosecutor."

"I never understood how people claim not to believe in witchcraft, and then accuse witches of casting spells. How does that work, exactly?"

He shrugged. His intelligent eyes seemed to be mulling something over.

"So are you going to charge me with a decade-old crime, Inspector, or arrest me for practicing witchcraft without a license?"

"I just want to know what the hell's going on."

"That makes two of us."

"Ms. Ivory—"

"Please call me Lily."

"Ms. Ivory, as far as I know it's not against the law to practice witchcraft. Just tell me: Do you consider yourself a witch?"

"A lot of people call me that. I don't know what I am,

exactly." I blew out a breath and came to a decision. "I know I have certain abilities that set me apart. I've had them since I was a child."

"Abilities?"

"I imagine you've seen a lot of unexplainable events in your line of work, Inspector. Is it so hard to imagine there might be something more out there?"

He pinched the bridge of his nose and leaned back against the brick wall of the building next to us, looking very tired. Suddenly I realized: He believed me. Who knew a homicide detective could believe in witches?

"Prior to the other night, did you have any relationship at all with Frances Potts?"

"No. I just met her."

He nodded. "So what motivation could you have to kill her?"

"Is that why you're stalking me? Because you think I'm a witch, or you think I killed Frances, or both?"

He shrugged, looking like Mr. Innocent. "Just needed a place to sit and eat breakfast," he said with a smile as he moved back toward the car. "No reason at all."

Overnight I had become a minor celebrity at Coffee to the People. As a measure of my new status, a few students even looked up from their laptop computer screens when I walked in.

"Hey, Lily, did you see the paper yet?" asked the barista Xander. He was tall and thin and dressed in a sort of Bavarian punk style, favoring black leather, silver spikes, and so many facial piercings that I cringed when I looked at him. Still, he had sweet eyes and an appealing though frenetic energy. He reminded me of a lanky, self-mutilated puppy.

Wendy waved her copy of today's *Chronicle*.

So much had happened in the past twenty-four hours that I had forgotten all about the article in the paper. Aunt Cora's Closet was right there on the front page of the Style section, with a huge color photo of Oscar ringed by lovely young women in their vintage attire. There was even a photo of yours truly helping to fit one of the bridesmaids—I'm not very photogenic, but I was happy to see that this picture wasn't bad.

I was just starting to read the article when Sandra rushed into the café, waving the newspaper section in one hand, an empty coffee mug emblazoned with, *My other car's a broom*, in the other.

"Lily! You must be just *swooning* over this," Sandra said eagerly, wide eyes fixed on mine.

"Yeah, it's pretty amazing."

If only I could work up the appropriate enthusiasm. I hadn't slept much for the past few nights, but truth to tell, that didn't usually affect me very much. My funk, I felt sure, had more to do with the fact that I was either losing my powers, or up against something much stronger than I was. Never before had I so regretted not finishing my training at the feet of a master. There was a tiny part of me that wondered . . . would Aidan help to train me? Could I trust him enough to learn from him?

"Where was *I* when all this was happening? You should have called me over; I could have helped," continued Sandra, bouncing up on her toes. Her restless energy wrapped around me. "I would love to show her—what's her name? Susan Rogers?—I wanted to show her my store. Do you think you could mention it to her?"

"I'm sure I could—"

"I just think this sort of attention should be for everyone, don't you?" Sandra interrupted.

"Leave it alone, for God's sake, Sandra," said Wendy, rolling her eyes and snorting. Wendy had wandered into Aunt Cora's Closet once or twice and always stopped to chat with Bronwyn, but hadn't shown much warmth toward me. I had the sense she was wary about new businesses in the neighborhood. Like many in the Haight, she was protective of the rare sense of camaraderie here.

"Maybe we could get the paper to do a story on the whole Haight," I said. "All of the merchants' association members."

"What a fabulous idea! Let's do it. Will you call her?" said Sandra.

"I'll try to mention it next time I talk to her," I said, then ordered bagels for Conrad, and drinks for both of us. Xander asked me about Oscar, and I invited him to come over anytime to say hi. Wendy tossed a vegan cookie, on the house, into the bag before handing it to me with a smile and the directive to "have an awesome day."

I felt a little thrill. Was I finally "in" with the Coffee to the People crowd?

"Thanks for the bagels, Wendy. Bye, Xander. Bye, Sandra."

"I'll walk you back," said Sandra as she shadowed me out the café door and across the street. "Could I take a look at those clothes yet?"

"Clothes?"

"You got a bunch of new stuff in, remember?"

"Oh, right." I hesitated, not wanting to tell her the police had confiscated the whole lot. I had the sense that anything Sandra discovered, the whole world would soon know, and just as I was starting to fit in, the last thing I wanted was for the merchants' association to find out I was under suspicion of murder. "Things have been really busy lately, so I still haven't done much."

"What is there to do? Run them through the wash? I'd be glad to give you a hand."

I tried to swallow my annoyance. Sandra wasn't a bad person. She was just needy. And pushy. And what with a demon snatching children and people dying under my protection and Max being skewered with a ritual knife and cops breakfasting outside my store, I wasn't in the greatest mood.

"Thanks, Sandra, but as I told you before, I'll let you know when they're ready. I have my own process, and I'd like to keep it that way. I have to go now and get ready to open for business. Nice to see you; good-bye."

I traded the little paper sack of bagels along with the Flower Power drink to Conrad in exchange for the broom, then hurried back into my store, hoping Sandra would take the hint and go away. I headed into the back room to put the broom away, but on second thought I tucked the old-fashioned straw-bristled sweeper against the wall right behind the door, then crossed over to Bronwyn's counter for a small pinch of salt. Placing the salt on the broom, I concentrated on Sandra. The next time she came into the store, the broom should keep her focused more on her own shop than on mine, and help motivate her to leave promptly. I might need to do a stronger spell to keep her at bay, but I decided to wait for a few days to see what happened. I didn't yet trust my assessments of interpersonal relationships.

Next I performed my cleansing ritual, flipped the painted wooden sign, and officially opened my door to customers. I spread the *San Francisco Chronicle* out on the counter to read the article about Aunt Cora's Closet thoroughly.

It was a glowing assessment, not only of my store and the fashion possibilities of my inventory, but of all the "green" reasons to shop vintage—who knew that textiles are the number-one filler of landfills? Simply by shopping and wearing vintage, you could show off your environmentalist stripes. I liked that.

I carefully clipped out the article and pinned it up, along with the photo, on the bulletin board behind the counter, right next to my business license. Stepping back, I assessed it with a certain thrill of pride. This was my first attempt at making a living in a legitimate business, and I had pulled it off with only a teensy bit of magic. I was feeling more normal all the time.

As I flipped through the rest of the paper, I noticed an article about Delores Keener, Frances's lawyer, announcing her candidacy for San Francisco district attorney. Funny how you could meet a person in someone's kitchen one evening, and before you know it you're friends with the district attorney. I guessed this was how a person became connected to one's community. And such an association could come in handy in the case of, say, being charged with murder, right?

Don't think that way, Lily, I admonished myself. *You'll attract the negative.*

I was almost ready to close the paper when I came across an article about the disappearance of Jessica Rodriguez. The article wasn't simply reporting the known facts; the reporter, Nigel Thorne, linked Jessica's disappearance to others that occurred in the same area over a period of years. It even mentioned Elisabeth Potts, Frances's daughter. My stomach clenched. I rubbed my temples and sighed in frustration. Despite my powers, I couldn't even keep Frances safe—or Max, for that matter—much less rescue the girl. What good was it being a witch these days?

I pulled myself together as the door opened to admit the first of the day's customers. By twenty after the hour, a steady stream of visitors began dropping by. First it was mostly Haight Street neighbors, many of whom had never taken the time to stop in or hadn't yet realized we were open. Some came simply to introduce themselves and to congratulate me on the article. A few shop owners made a point of stopping by as well to discuss the merchants' association.

And many came to visit with Oscar, who had become something of a celebrity—and knew it. He was in piggy heaven, preening before his fans like a porcine Brad Pitt.

I watched him, amused, as he strutted in front of a small crowd of shoppers.

"I hear you're the vintage fashion maven," said a vaguely familiar woman with curly reddish blond hair and freckles. She wore a long-sleeved T-shirt under faded denim overalls. Cute, but she did look a bit like a refugee from a 4-H meeting.

"If it says so in the papers, it must be true," I answered with a smile as I straightened a display of sequined clutches. "May I help you with anything?"

"I hope so. I work at home, perfectly happy in my solitude, telecommuting into work. But now I have to show up in a command performance at a big company party, and I can't bear to set foot in the mall. I need to look decent, but I can go a little artistic, if you know what I mean."

I felt a little thrill. I adored this kind of challenge.

As we moved through the dress racks, the woman told me her name was Daphne, that she had moved to San Francisco from a small community in California's Central Valley, and that she loved the Haight—she was a Coffee to the People regular, which explained why she seemed so familiar—and didn't mind her computer job with a big investment firm, except that she hated showing up there in person.

"I work in my pajamas most of the time," she said as we flipped through some early 1960s swing dresses. "No matter what you're wearing, you can sound businesslike on the phone. But socializing with colleagues is a different matter altogether. . . . I don't own a single little black dress."

As the words came from her mouth, my gaze alighted on the perfect Little Black Dress. It was a crepe rayon forties cocktail dress with beaded details at the shoulders, ruched at either side of the flattering squared neckline. Daphne, much more drawn to the bright patterns of the later-era dresses, was unsure, but I insisted she try it on.

When she emerged, she was transformed from a country mouse to a 1940s movie star. She had tucked her reddish curls behind her ears, thrust her chest out a bit, and looked sexy and artsy and strong, all at the same time.

Standing in front of the full-length mirrors, she laughed.

"Wow. Is that me?"

"It sure is." I met her eyes in the mirror. "That dress is *you*."

I dug up a pair of chunky-heeled 1940s shoes to complement the dress, and even found a small alligator-skin clutch to complete the outfit. By the time I was ringing up her purchases, Daphne was flushed with pleasure and confidence, and I felt a sense of deep satisfaction.

Demons be damned. At least I loved my job.

The rest of the day stayed busy, not only because so many people had seen the article, but because Mardi Gras was just around the corner. Halloween, Bronwyn informed me, was by far San Francisco's favorite holiday, but Carnaval was growing in popularity. Though San Francisco wasn't a traditionally Catholic city, like New Orleans, and relatively few actually practiced Lent, apparently the local residents grasped at any chance to dress up in costumes, overindulge in wine and song, and spill out into the streets. You had to like that in a people.

Speaking of loose morals, I noticed Oscar kept slipping under the curtains while women were trying on clothes. He claimed he was trying to curtail shoplifting, but such theft wasn't much of a problem for me. Before opening Aunt Cora's Closet to the public, I had filled a red bag with caraway seeds and three old keys, charged it with an incantation, then hung it over the door. That kept the problem at bay. Many was the time I had watched a customer on the way out stop in the doorway as though they'd forgotten something, turn around, and come back into the store, then surreptitiously take something out from underneath their shirt and put it back before leaving. That little red bag might not stop evildoers in their tracks, but it gave people something to think about. And upon reflection, a lot of would-be shoplifters opted, wisely, against developing bad karma.

When not helping customers to find just the right size or style, or chasing Oscar, I spent my time making minor repairs on newly laundered items—sewing up fallen hems or replacing missing buttons. I enjoyed these moments, watching people try on hats and scarves and dresses of all kinds, making small talk, soaking in the laughter and high spirits. And among other things, the rush didn't give me much time to dwell on recent events. Still, my eyes kept glazing over as I tried to sew up the hem on a newly acquired pink satin nightgown.

"Lily, why don't you go upstairs and take a break?" Bronwyn said. "You look like death warmed over."

"I haven't been sleeping well lately." The understatement of the year.

"Go on. I can take it from here," she said as she moved toward the main counter.

"I *am* a bit tuckered out," I said. "I guess I could use a quick nap."

I trudged up the back stairs, washed my face, then lay down on my still-made bed. I closed my eyes, hoping to drop off and get some rest, but I kept thinking about Max. Before the fear and anxiety of the night rushed back to me this morning, there had been one instant of sweetness, waking up next to a man. A really good-smelling man, despite the drama we had shared.

On the other hand, he had stormed out without a backward glance when I tried to tell him the truth about what happened. Funny to be disbelieved when I was finally being honest about myself.

I sighed and rolled over, willing myself to put the man out of my mind. But rather than falling asleep, I started thinking about last night's discovery.

Why in the world would Frances set up an altar in her home? It seemed so very out of character. Or could I be making unfair assumptions about the altar? Voodoo—or vodou, as it is sometimes called—is a religion just as legitimate as any other. I had no way of knowing whether the altar was simply for worship, or protection, or something actively evil. Obviously there were spirits who didn't want us there, but they could have been acting independently, or could have been the result of a powerful protection spell run amok.

On the other hand, someone had lit those candles recently. . . .

That reminded me—I still had Max's camera from the other night, the digital one with the photos of the altar. I remembered sticking it in my backpack in the flurry of activity when Max was injured. I got up and retrieved my woven backpack from the sofa, where I had dropped it last night. I opened it and remembered the strange handlike candleholder I had shoved in there as well.

Pushing it aside for now, I found the camera at the very bottom of the pack. Turning it over in my hands, I studied the various knobs and dials. It looked expensive. I tried to see the images on the screen, but the pictures were tiny and the images hard to make out.

Finally admitting there was no way I was going to sleep, I went into the kitchen and made myself a snack of toast with huckleberry jam and a mug of peppermint tea. I flipped through my Book of Shadows, reading some of the quotes and observations I had collected over the years, words of peace and reflection that always brought me comfort. Today I found solace from an unexpected source, Helen Keller. She said: "Avoiding danger is no safer in the long run than outright exposure. Life is either a daring adventure, or nothing."

This from a woman who was blind and deaf. Maybe I needed an attitude shift. So life was dangerous; it was also a daring adventure.

Ten minutes later, I went back downstairs to the still-bustling shop.

"Bronwyn, do you know how to work these things?" I asked after she finished ringing up twin sisters who were thrilled to have found matching 1960s sundresses.

"New camera?" Bronwyn asked as she studied it. "Looks like a nice one."

"It's not actually mine; I'm just borrowing it. I need to get access to the photos, but I don't have the cord thingy to attach it to the computer."

"Cord thingy?"

"I think you need the thingy to get the photos out."

"Oh, right," said Bronwyn, who was about as technologically savvy as I was. "That's too bad."

"Just take the memory card out," said a voice from behind us.

We turned to see that Maya had arrived. She smiled and dumped several copies of the *San Francisco Chronicle* on the counter, then took the camera from Bronwyn and extracted the tiny memory card, holding it up like exhibit A.

"By the way, great article in the paper this morning. I bought a few extra copies in case you wanted to send them around to anyone."

"Thank you, Maya, that was thoughtful."

"No problem. Um, Lily, do you have a minute? Could I talk to you in private?"

"Of course," I said as I led the way to the back room.

"I assume the police came to tell you about Frances," she said as we sat at the table. "Can you believe that happened? Right after we were there?"

"It's so sad."

"They were asking me a lot of weird questions about you."

"What kinds of questions?"

"Like what you knew about poisonous plants . . . and witchcraft."

Our eyes met.

"Lily, I have the sense something's going on here, something more than murder and a child's kidnapping, and it seems like they're related. Can you tell me what it is?"

I wasn't sure how Maya felt about the whole magical-herbs thing, much less the witch thing. I knew she had been raised in the Baptist church, and her mother was still active there. As far as I knew, there really wasn't too much about the Wiccan religion that was at odds with her church, except of course for the whole God/Goddess dispute. And concepts of heaven and hell, and the religious hierarchy and . . . Okay, I guess there were a few areas of disagreement. But both believed in helping one's community and being kind and good, and that seemed like a lot to build on.

But how would I explain my own version of witchcraft? I took Maya's hand in mine. She was calm and warm, and not the type to fly off the handle at the first sign of something unexpected. Maybe coming out to my friends—and an occasional police inspector—was just one more daunting step in settling down and becoming part of a community. I had to take the risk.

"I do have some abilities that are . . ."

"Magic?" she offered, looking doubtful.

"I was going to say freakish."

She frowned at me, dark eyes questioning.

"It's pretty hard to explain, but I can sometimes sense things. And if I concentrate, I can affect things."

"Uh-huh. Things like . . . ?"

"All sorts of things. I don't do it very often." Or at least, I tried not to.

"Why do the police think you're involved with Frances's death?"

"Because they don't understand what they found. Frances's body was found in—"

"A pentagram. The cops asked me about that. I've

noticed you guys have some of those around. I assumed they had to do with Bronwyn's Wicca group."

"They do; that is, they're a common sign of protection."

Maya nodded. "I even looked them up on the Internet, because at first I thought they were some sort of satanic something or other. But it said they were for protection, too. Sort of like the swastika being taken over by the Nazis, right? It used to be a Buddhist symbol of peace."

"Something like that, yes."

She nodded and squeezed my hand. "Well, I trust you, Lily. I don't really understand you, but I trust you."

"Thanks, Maya."

Her eyes shifted over my shoulder. "Bronwyn's got a line at the register; looks like you should get back out there. Hey, why don't I take the camera's memory card down the street to get the pictures developed?"

"That would be great, if you wouldn't mind."

"Nah, I'm at loose ends. I'm supposed to be looking for a job, but it hasn't been easy to find one that fits in with my school schedule."

We walked back toward the register.

"You know, I was actually thinking you should just come work for me officially," I offered on impulse.

"Work here?"

"We could use a third person to run errands, and to cover us when we're not here. Besides, we like having you around, right, Bronwyn?"

"Especially if it stays this busy." Bronwyn nodded with an enthusiastic smile. "We'll need you. But you have to promise—no more jokes about 'the other white meat.'"

She laughed. "I promise, no more jokes. I'd love to work here!"

She may have regretted her eager acceptance when she returned with the photos half an hour later. Maya's head was bent low over the pictures, and she was grimacing.

Chapter 12

"What *is* all this?"

The photos brought the horror of last night back to me in living color. At the time I had been involved and concentrating, operating on a different level. That was one reason I wasn't watching out for Max, intent only on what I was doing. But now, the animal sacrifice seemed even more gruesome when taken out of context. The blood, the candles, the blackened bones, the dirt and stones . . . it was all just plain old creepy.

"It's . . . pretty bad, right? I found that altar . . . It's kind of hard to explain."

She handed them over with two fingers, as though they were a noxious item, or a snake. "Better you than me; that's all I can say."

Suddenly an odd sensation came over me: I didn't want to be alone tonight. Having never had friends before, I didn't quite know how to ask Bronwyn and Maya to stay. So I just blurted it out.

"Bronwyn, Maya, would y'all hang out with me tonight?" I felt myself blush.

"Sure," said Maya. "What do you want to do?"

"I'm free," said Bronwyn. "My granddaughter can't make our movie night; she's at a sleepover with some friends."

And it was as simple as that. After closing the store at seven, we ordered Chinese food to be delivered and I grabbed a bottle from the collection of California wines I was slowly acquiring. This one was a zinfandel from Seghesio Winery. The man at the wine shop couldn't stop raving about it. One of these days, I promised myself, when I wasn't so swamped with all this demon business, I was going to take a day trip up to the Napa and Sonoma valleys to go wine tasting. I heard it was just like Tuscany.

Once the food arrived we brought everything up to my apartment, lit some candles, and sat in the living room around the coffee table. Oscar had trotted upstairs with us, and since he couldn't transform in front of Maya and Bronwyn, I made him a couple of grilled cheese sandwiches and put them on a plate for him on the kitchen floor.

I brewed a pot of loose-leaf green tea to go with the Kung Pao tofu and gluten-based mock Mongolian beef—which tasted much better than it sounded—and then Bronwyn volunteered to read our tea leaves. We giggled over her outrageously incorrect readings, and then I started making the leaves form funny shapes, which led to some rather obscene interpretations. We laughed some more.

"Why do women's private discussions always devolve into sex talk?" Bronwyn said, wiping her eyes.

"You think men's don't?" asked Maya, smiling. She was lying on her stomach on the rug, her feet waving in the air, her chin on an orange satin pillow. "I've got brothers; I *know* how bad they can get. Okay, so we know that Bronwyn has a million guys in love with her, most of them half her age."

"Not in love," Bronwyn clarified. "More like in lust."

"I tell you what, Bronwyn, you give fiftysomething a good name." I laughed.

She gave us a cat-and-the-canary smile. "You get to be my age, and like men as much as I do, you learn a few tricks. When I was younger I always worried about how I looked, or what the man was thinking. Now I just have fun."

"So, Lily, what's your story?" Maya said, turning to me. "Tell us about your love life."

"I . . . uh . . ."

Oscar trotted in and gazed at me. This was his kind of gabfest.

"There's not much to tell, I'm afraid. I've moved around a lot," I evaded. I heard an electronic sound. "Oh, Bronwyn, isn't that your cell phone ringing?"

Her phone made the sound of the music that accompanied the Wicked Witch from *The Wizard of Oz*. I hoped I would soon be able to lighten up enough to find it funny.

"Oh! I guess it is. . . ." She pawed through her satchel until she unearthed the phone, then chatted for a moment.

"That was my friend Casey. He tends bar down at the Lucky Star. He says there's a great estate auction going on right down the street from him."

"At ten o'clock at night?" I asked.

"He says it's been going since noon, and they're closing at midnight no matter what, even if they have to give the stuff away for free."

I looked at Maya; she looked at Bronwyn; Bronwyn looked at me.

"Free's my favorite price," Maya said.

"Mine, too."

"Mine three," Bronwyn added with a grin.

We drove to the big warehouse down off Harrison, between Second and Third streets. The industrial metal doors were propped open, and a few dozen people milled about under harsh fluorescent lights, perusing red-lacquered armoires and end tables, wooden carvings, stone sculptures, oil paintings, woven rugs, carved brass dishes and cups. . . . According to the flyer, the man who had passed away was an inveterate traveler who couldn't help but buy something in every country he visited. No doubt about it, these were the leftovers of a fascinating life. He had rented the warehouse just to house all his goodies.

I understood the impulse. I could easily have wound up that way myself—that was one reason I opened my shop, to be able to acquire great old clothes and pass them on, rather than hoard them.

Since the auction had been going on for most of the day, there were a whole lot of bright red Sold stickers attached to precious objects, but dozens of lots were still unspoken for. We wandered around looking at the many offerings. Bronwyn was taken with a Japanese iron tea ceremony kettle and brazier, decorated with a spray of intricate flowers that managed to make the heavy metal object seem at once strong yet delicate. Maya lusted after a hundred-year-old cloisonné elephant-shaped jewelry box that opened under the colorful, decorated trunk. In typically strange fashion, I fell in love with a huge bag of brass goat bells; don't ask me why.

I had to learn the rudiments of auctions when I opened my business and realized that, despite all the clothes I had gathered in my travels, I still needed more inventory before opening the doors of Aunt Cora's Closet to the public. I had seen auctions in the movies, but the reality was a lot less glamorous. Perhaps if we were bidding at Christie's in New York City it would be a different ball game, but the auctions I had attended consisted of ordinary jeans-clad people, like me, vying for mildewed cardboard boxes full of classic LPs or ceramic pitchers shaped like cows.

My particular interest, of course, was textiles, with special attention to women's garments. But bidders couldn't be choosers. You bid on a "lot," which might be a single piece of furniture, but more often is a grouping of items either of a particular theme or from a particular seller. The winner of the bid takes all—you might want only one item in a lot, but you have to take the whole shebang. This could lead to the discovery of some little unexpected treasure that had been tucked under another item, but most times the real junk makes its way straight to the Goodwill donation box or, if beyond redemption, to the landfill.

A registration table was set up by the main doors. In exchange for my name and contact information I was given a wooden paddle marked with the number 32, then bid on and won a lot that included a bunch of silk pajamas and kimonos. I also landed a big, funny carved wood chair that looked a bit like a child's conception of a throne. The back was entirely decoupaged with a 1920s theme. It would look great in my store, right next to the coatrack. I even gave in to temptation and bought the goat bells, although if I had waited until midnight they would probably have been given away for free. Not a soul competed against me.

Finally I bid on an evil-looking, powerful stone statue, in large part to keep him out of the wrong hands. Only about a foot tall, he was squat and crudely formed, his features blunt and expressionless. According to the three-by-five card that listed his origin, he was acquired at a roadside stand not far from Machu Picchu, in Peru, though as far as I knew the Inca rarely produced freestanding sculpture like this one. The vibrations were powerful—not necessarily malevolent, but he was the sort who would appreciate being buried and left alone, or given his own altar with the proper respect. He could be a powerful ally, if you could keep him under control.

Someone was bidding steadily against me. This is by far the most annoying thing about auctions—you can't help but feel animosity toward the one or two bozos insisting on driving up the price. I looked around to take a look at my competition: an older guy with a full Santa Claus–type white beard, and a woman ... The voice sounded a little too familiar. She was hidden behind the crowd, but I craned my neck and scootched over about six inches to see who it was.

A small woman with pretty eyes and a habit of rising up on her toes, up and down, up and down. *Sandra.*

What was she doing here?

The old man dropped out of the bidding when we passed the two-hundred-dollar mark. Sandra seemed so intent that I backed off as well, and she clapped when she was awarded the cold stone statue.

I made my way to the back of the bidding floor and edged up to her.

"Hi, Sandra. What are you doing here?"

"I've been here for hours. Got lots of great stuff."

"Oh, good for you. Are you buying to sell in the shop, or just for you?"

"Oh, resale, or at least that's what I say," she said with a wink. A resale license allows a person to buy things without paying sales tax, the assumption being that you would in turn give the state its slice of the pie by charging sales tax upon reselling the item. A lot of people with resale licenses play a bit loosey-goosey with the tax-free privilege. But questionable business ethics were not paramount in my mind at the moment.

"Sandra, do you know anything about that little guy you just won?"

She looked at me with trepidation. "You backed off the bid, Lily. It's mine."

"I know that." I wondered how much to say, and how to say it. Sandra clearly believed in something beyond the concrete world, but she had a curious take on things. I couldn't help but think about the odd gleam in her eye when she showed me the *Malleus Maleficarum,* and the way she mentioned, oh, so casually, about Bronwyn being a witch. "I just think you should be careful. I know a little bit about—"

"I know everything I need to know, Lily, or soon will," snapped Sandra.

Before I could ask her what she meant, Bronwyn and Maya joined us. Maya was flushed with victory after scoring her very first auction buy: the cloisonné elephant.

"Maybe I should bid for the teakettle," Bronwyn pondered out loud. "I can't decide."

Maya's gaze met mine, and we shared a smile.

"Bronwyn, you have at least three kettles at the shop already," Maya pointed out. "I'm afraid to ask, but how many do you have at home?"

Bronwyn smiled, chagrined. "Several, but I only ever use the old copper one my mother gave me, anyway."

"Why would anyone need more than one teakettle?" Sandra demanded, her eyes darting about, looking at each one of us in turn.

We all laughed and shrugged.

"Well, I've got to run. Great to see you." Sandra quite literally trotted off to claim her sinister prize.

We watched her jog across the crowded room.

"Is it just me . . . ?" I began.

Maya shook her head with a rueful smile. "Sandra has not mastered the concept of personal space."

"So she seems kind of . . . odd . . . to you, too?" As one who had been looked on as an outsider all my life, I didn't make the accusation casually.

"Oh, yes, she's got her own way of doing things," Bronwyn said. "In fact, she wanted to join the coven at one point, but she just didn't fit in. It was quite awkward, since we pride ourselves on staying open to all. But there was something about her approach to the whole thing. . . ."

"I knew her from before," Maya added. "She's involved in the neighborhood association over by Frances, not Hunters Point per se but near India Basin. But she was always after Frances to sell her place. As a matter of fact, that's why I first asked to interview Frances, because Sandra sounded so sure she would be leaving the neighborhood soon."

"That reminds me: Have you ever heard about Frances renting out her house for tours?"

She shook her head. "I wouldn't be too surprised, though. She was always looking to make some cash, which is why she wanted to sell the clothes. It made me wonder why she didn't just sell that big old house and have done with it."

"Do you have any recordings from your interviews with her?"

Maya shook her head. "She wouldn't let me record her. And even the written notes I took . . . to tell you the truth, I couldn't get her to tell me much beyond what I told you the other day: when she married, the dates of her children's births, that sort of thing. I was hoping with time . . . You know how it is with some people: They take a while to open up. Frances seemed sweet and friendly, but she was actually pretty closed off."

I finally got home about midnight. Oscar was beside himself, walking along the backs of the furniture and jabbering nonstop about the day in the life of a neighborhood celebrity. He had already made his way through most of the Chinese leftovers, so I offered him a cookie, took a long shower, and pulled on some old flannel pajamas and new fluffy wool socks.

By the time I came out of the bedroom, Oscar was snoring in his nest of blankets on top of the refrigerator. When he first chose this spot for his bed I worried that he would get a crick in his neck—he had to fold himself up to fit in the little cubby. But he seemed content and refused my offer of the couch. He had found an old green wool blanket and a threadbare wedding-ring quilt in the linen closet, made them into a little nest, and settled right in.

I tiptoed around the kitchen as I made a cup of tea, though I had already learned that nothing short of a bomb would awaken this particular goblin when he was in deep slumber.

I looked at him with some envy. Despite my lack of sleep lately, I wasn't ready for bed, my thoughts still on the bizarre events of the past couple of days. Feeling rather foolish, I decided to practice some basic magic to be sure I hadn't lost my powers altogether. Sitting cross-legged on the floor in front of my coffee table, I commanded the electric lights on and off. I lit the candles scattered throughout the apartment without touching them. I closed and opened the bedroom door with my mind's energy.

Finally, I looked through my Book of Shadows, flipping the pages with the wind from my thoughts. I looked up *La Llorona* to see what the book had to say, in case there was anything obvious I had forgotten. I read about her story, her ghostly calling, her dragging people down into the water with her. Of course, Aidan was right: She wouldn't kill in a house, in a circle. And the only hope for Jessica was to trade a soul, and not just any soul. It had to be one *La Llorona* truly wanted.

I checked it against the book Aidan had lent me. There I found a snippet of an old song:

Don't go down to the river, child,
Don't go there alone;
For the sobbing woman, wet and wild,
Might claim you for her own.
She keens when the sun is murky red;
She wails when the moon is old;
She cries for her babies, still and dead,
Who drowned in the water cold.

It sent a shiver up my spine, but it didn't tell me anything new. The murky red sun was sunset, and the old moon was full. *La Llorona* would be strongest during the full moon, which was coming up in two days.

While I was looking through Aidan's tome, the pages of my Book of Shadows started flipping on their own, stopping at a recipe for a sweetness charm. Strange, I didn't remember this page. Which was odd, since I had read through this Book of Shadows for so many years that the pages were soft as cloth from the frequency of their turning. On the other hand, it wasn't the first time something had been added to the book without my knowledge; all I could assume was that, like any living thing, it had its own life.

This page was written in Graciela's shaky pen. When she was a young woman her script was lovely and formal, but with age it had deteriorated until it looked like chicken scratches interrupted by an occasional loop-the-loop. I used to tease her about it. The thought made me miss her with a visceral, physical yearning deep in my gut. One reason Frances's death bothered me so much was that she reminded me of Graciela. But then again, maybe all sweet old ladies had a certain way about them. On the other hand, Graciela wasn't sweet as much as formidable and impressive.

I read the page that had opened for me. Sweetness charm bags usually took the form of sewn packets rather than bags that could be opened and their contents changed. This wasn't an easy spell to cast, much less to maintain. Changing one's physical or psychic appearance took great power and skill. In order to charge the bags, a spell was cast with a great sacrifice. A blood sacrifice.

The witch in "Hansel and Gretel" had used a sweetness charm to cover her evil intentions. *Nibble, nibble, little mouse.* Wasn't that how the refrain went in the story? I cast my mind back to the tale, remembering when my mother used to read to me, before she sent me away. We had a big, thick book of classic illustrated Grimm fairy tales that seemed as large and heavy as I was. I had a memory of snuggling in my mother's lap, holding the massive book on my knees while she read to me in her deep, lovely voice.

Closing my eyes I experienced the scent of my mother, the timbre of her voice, the part in the story where the starving children are eating from the magical house made of cookies and candy, and the old lady says, *Nibble, nibble, little mouse. Who's that nibbling at my house?*

I had a sudden image of Frances beckoning Maya and me down the hallway, just like a sweet witch luring us to our doom. Wasn't that what Tomás had said?

My cuckoo clock struck one, making me realize I had been staring at the books for nearly an hour.

Before retiring to bed I poured a small circle of salt on the coffee table and drew a pentagram within it, laid out two white candles, one blue candle, one red, one yellow, and one green, all of which had been dressed with olive oil. I combined two drops of rosemary oil, three of frankincense, and one-fourth teaspoon of dragon's blood resin in my oil censer, and set out stones of red jasper and Apache tears. Then I chanted a protection charm, asking for strength and clarity.

As I laid out a white cloth for the stones, I remembered: I still had Frances's wedding dresses! Why hadn't I thought of them before? Maybe they could tell me something. I ran down the stairs to the back room of the store, flicked on the overhead light, and opened the storage closet. I had stashed the gowns here shortly after the police confiscated the other clothes from Frances's house.

They weren't in the closet.

I checked all the changing rooms, out on the floor, behind the counter. Plenty of wedding dresses, but none were the ones I was looking for.

Frances's wedding gowns were gone.

Chapter 13

The next morning I dressed in another recently acquired vintage outfit, this one bought from a charming widow who lived in a palatial French-château style home in the hills of Piedmont, overlooking Oakland and the bay. On a clear day, the woman told me, one could see the Golden Gate Bridge and all the way through to the open ocean. When I had arrived for the clothes, she invited me to stay for lunch and proceeded to launch into a series of risqué stories about her many romantic escapades.

The garment was called a "wiggle dress" because it fit close to the body down to the knee-length ruffled hem, and, I could only presume, looked best when one wiggled as one walked. It was rather ridiculous, a black background with hot pink polka dots, but I felt the need for a little absurdity lately. More important, its vibrations were brash and gutsy. I wore a short pink jacket over the spaghetti straps for the sake of modesty and the cool, cloudy day.

About noon I looked up to see Frances's lawyer, Delores Keener, walking into the store. She paused and looked around briefly, then smiled warmly when she saw me.

"Lily, how *are* you? I would have come earlier, but I've been a bit under the weather," she said. She was beautifully dressed in a charcoal pantsuit, but her color was off, slightly grayish green, like those kids after the ill-fated camping trip so many years ago. "Can you *believe* what happened with poor Frances? I begged her to leave that neighborhood, but she said she'd never think of selling that house."

"I was just thinking about you yesterday," I said. Her unexpected presence in my store made me wonder if I had accidentally summoned her. "I saw the article in the paper about you running for the DA's office."

"Can you believe it? Me, district attorney?"

"I'm sure you'd be great."

"Speaking of such things, have the police spoken to you about the other day? They seem quite curious about you."

I looked around to see if anyone could overhear our conversation. The store was full of folks meandering through the aisles, laughing while they tried on hats and jackets. They seemed absorbed in their own business. Still, I decided to change the subject.

"I'm sorry to hear you've been sick," I said. "Are you feeling better?"

She waved it off. "Must have been something I ate. I could stand to lose a few pounds, anyway," she said with the conspiratorial smile known to women who understand the slimming potential of the stomach flu. "Speaking of newspaper articles, I saw the big spread about your store."

"I think everyone must have. The place has been jammed."

"Lily, this might not be the time and place for this, but we have some business we need to discuss," Delores said, her tone suddenly serious. "Would you prefer to come to my office, or do you have a minute now to talk privately?"

"Oh, of course," I said. I told Bronwyn I was stepping into the back room for a moment and led the way through the heavy velvet curtain to the old green table. "Can I get you anything? Tea? Juice?"

"No, thank you." She collapsed into a high-backed faded purple velvet chair. "Ahh, it feels good just to sit down. I love these shoes, but they sure don't love my feet."

Delores was wearing the kind of sophisticated high-heeled pumps I could never get used to, though I admired the look. One thing I liked about my vintage outfits was that so many of them looked good, in a funky way, with comfy shoes like Keds and sandals. Footwear that let me sell clothes on my feet all day, and outrun the occasional spirit at night. All in a day's work.

"I'll cut right to the chase," Delores said, leaning forward and fixing me with her soft brown eyes. "Frances Potts amended her will the night before she died. She left everything to you."

"I'm sorry?"

"She left you her entire estate."

"But . . . that doesn't make any sense. I don't want her estate."

"All I can do is make sure it goes to you. Afterward, it's yours to do whatever you like with." Delores shrugged and brought a slim file out of her maroon leather portfolio, handing it to me. "If you want to give it to that sad-looking man sitting on the curb outside your store, be my guest."

"How is this even possible? I only met Frances once, on the night she died."

"Technically it was the night before she died—the medical examiner placed the time of death at sometime around dawn the next day. Not that it matters. The night you and Maya visited, Frances and I had dinner. She asked me to change it at that time. It was a simple enough thing to do, a one-page document I printed off and had her sign right then and there."

I opened the file and read the paper, noting Frances's wobbly signature at the bottom of the page. Had I unconsciously influenced her somehow?

"I still don't understand. Why would she do such a thing?"

"She was quite impressed by you. She said something about your financing Maya's oral history project, doing something worthwhile with the money." She studied me for a moment, then gave me a quizzical smile. "Most people are happy to hear they've inherited. Does it matter why?"

"Yes, it matters. If Frances wanted Maya to have money for her project, why not give it to her directly? And what about her own daughter? She mentioned grandchildren, as well."

Delores shrugged. "Her daughter Katherine is . . . an interesting character. She's the one who found her mother, you know, poor thing. I feel terrible—I called Katherine after I left that night, suggesting that she drop by. First time she visits in years, and . . ." She shrugged. "Anyway, now she won't talk to me. Perhaps you'll have better luck. Here's her information." She handed me a piece of notepaper with Katherine Airey's phone number and address.

"You mean she lives right here in San Francisco?"

"Didn't you know?"

"I guess I assumed she lived farther away, and that's why she wasn't around more."

Delores just shook her head and sorted through a few other papers in her attaché case.

"Do you know anything about a redevelopment plan in the neighborhood?" I asked.

"All I know is, Frances didn't want to sell. One of your neighbors here in the Haight, Sandra Schmidt, met with her about it several times. She even came to me once."

"Why do you think she wanted it so badly?"

"She's involved in a neighborhood association nearby that's working with the city on a broad redevelopment plan for that whole area. As I'm sure you've noticed, it could use the help."

"And Sandra wanted the house?"

"I believe she wanted to tear it down, use the property for a park or some such. I didn't get into the details—Frances said no, so I relayed that to Schmidt."

"Could I ask . . . why are you representing Frances? What with running for office and all, it seems rather small potatoes for you."

"She and my mother were close," she said, gathering her papers and tucking them back in her briefcase. "I do a certain amount of pro bono work, and a lot of older folks have a hard time finding lawyers they feel comfortable with. Plus, I love a home-cooked meal from time to time. Slim-Fast shakes can only take a person so far."

"I'm sorry for your loss," I added. "I forgot she was an old family friend."

"Oh, by the way, Frances was very explicit about her burial in her will. She already had a plot picked out, so presuming the police release her body in time, the funeral will be tomorrow at eleven, in case you'd like to attend. Please invite your young friend Maya as well."

She took the notepaper back and wrote the name and address of the cemetery, the date, and the time. It was an Oakland address.

As we stood, I asked, "Have you heard anything more about Jessica?"

"Who?"

How could she have forgotten? "Little Jessica, Frances's neighbor?"

A pained expression passed across her face. She seemed so sad that I pushed aside my momentary misgivings. "*Jessica*. No, nothing. I grieve so for her family."

Delores told me she'd be sending me some more papers to sign within the week, and let herself out.

I stayed behind at the table for a moment, thinking. Why in the world would Frances change her will after meeting me? Had I somehow influenced her unconsciously? *Great.* Now I not only had opportunity for her murder, but I had clear motive. I wondered how long it would be before Inspector Romero came knocking on my door . . . this time with handcuffs.

This was ridiculous. I didn't need the Potts estate; I didn't *want* the Potts estate. I would give it back, as simple as that.

I picked up the phone extension and dialed the number Delores had given me.

A man answered the phone with a distinct Eastern European accent.

"This is Lily Ivory; I was hoping I could speak to Katherine Airey."

"Is this a telemarketer?"

"No, I—"

"What is the business you are calling about?" he asked.

"Her mother's lawyer gave me her number. It's about her mother's estate."

"One moment, please."

I heard a dog barking in the background, a large one by the deep, gruff sound of it. I immediately felt better about Katherine Airey. You had to like someone who liked dogs.

The man came back on the line.

"She has already receive the papers from the lawyer. This is no problem."

"It's not that there's a problem, exactly. . . . Could I speak directly with Ms. Airey? It's really a personal matter."

"What is your name?"

"Lily Ivory."

"One moment, please."

He set the handset down again. I heard a woman's voice in the distance, and though I could not make out the words, I thought I heard a cold tone in her voice. I could only imagine what she thought of me, a complete stranger who had just inherited her mother's estate. Not only was she grieving the violent death of her mother, but she probably thought I was a fortune-hunting scam artist who managed to worm her way into an old woman's heart.

Still, she relayed a message through the man on the phone: I was welcome to come by anytime this afternoon after two. He gave me an address on Vallejo Street. I jotted it down and slipped it into my jacket pocket.

After pondering for another moment, I got up and rechecked the storage closet for Frances's wedding gowns. The older I got, the more I had to look repeatedly in the same place to find things. I liked to blame the borrower imps, but it was probably nothing more supernatural than my own distracted mind.

Still no wedding dresses in the closet.

"Bronwyn, have you seen Frances Potts's wedding dresses anywhere?" I asked as I returned to the front of the store.

"I thought you put them in the storage closet."

"Yeah, I thought so, too. They're missing."

Just then Maya walked in, ready to begin her first day at work.

"Hi, Maya," I said. "You haven't happened to see Frances's wedding gowns anywhere, have you?"

She shook her head.

"Who would abscond with two old wedding dresses?" Bronwyn wondered.

"They're not old; they're vintage," intoned Maya, reciting the store's slogan.

I smiled. "She's got you there. But either way, they're still missing. Let me know if they turn up, will you?"

In between helping customers, I showed Maya how to operate the register, and started to train her on my rather intricate inventory-control system. I kept track of what eras and styles were most popular, and liked to keep a record of where we were getting the clothes from. She caught on quickly. I watched while she checked out several customers and was impressed with her ease and efficiency. I should have hired her weeks ago.

Two hours later the shop was empty of customers and we spent our time clearing the dressing rooms and straightening the hanging clothes and the always messy scarf shelves. I kept thinking ahead to my meeting with Frances's daughter Katherine. What should I say, exactly? I would tell her I was giving the estate back . . . but there was more: I was hoping she could tell me something about her mother, or the house, or the neighborhood that would help to explain some of what was going on.

Maybe setting up gruesome voodoo altars was an old family pastime, for example, and Katherine had stopped by to light the candles, and quite accidentally set off a chain of events that almost killed Max with a sacrificial knife. You never know.

Once again, I had the new-for-me sensation of not wanting to be alone. This friendship thing was addictive.

"This is sort of out of the blue," I said, my eyes sliding over to Maya, who was folding a pile of jewel-colored velvet scarves at my side, "but would you come with me to meet Frances's daughter?"

"Like a condolence call? That's thoughtful."

"In part. But there's more to it than that. Delores Keener came by earlier today. Remember her?"

"The lawyer?"

I nodded. "She told me that after we left that night,

Frances changed her will and left her entire estate to me."

Maya cocked her head, frowned slightly, and gazed at me. "I thought that was the first time you met Mrs. Potts."

"It was."

"Why would she do that?"

"That's what I said. If she was going to leave it to someone so suddenly, why not to you, for instance?"

"Well, that part's easy. Because my family's from the 'hood."

I stopped folding scarves and looked at her. "What does that have to do with anything?"

"Frances was pretty cool in lots of ways, but she was hung up on the color thing. I think the neighborhood changed around her so quickly that she had a hard time dealing with it. She got mugged once. And overall she's a little, you know, odd. I still liked her, though, for some reason. She reminded me of my Grammy."

"Funny, she reminded me of mine, as well. How long have you known Frances?"

"You know my sister lives over near there, and my aunt. My mom grew up just a few blocks away as well, so I guess they've known about the family in the big house for a while."

"The big house?"

"That's what they call it."

We both worked on the scarves in silence for a few moments more.

"Some people say . . . that she was even stranger," Maya continued. "Those guys who mugged her? They both wound up disappearing. She's not what you would call well liked. On the other hand, some kids played jokes, broke in there on Halloween—that place is so big someone could live in there and you'd never know it." She shivered, her shoulders pulled up. "I never did understand why she stayed so long."

I checked my watch. It was after two.

"I called her daughter and she invited me to come by," I said. "I want to talk to her about the inheritance—I'm not going to accept it."

"Sure, I'll go with you. I just have to see if I can get off work. It's my first day and all."

"I think your boss will understand," I said with a smile. "Though I hear tell she can be as mean as a skilletful of rattlesnakes."

San Francisco's Pacific Heights neighborhood owes its name to soaring hills that offer residents views of Angel and Alcatraz islands, the Marin County villages of Sausalito and Tiburon, the Golden Gate Bridge, and the mouth of the bay opening onto the Pacific Ocean. Historic mansions and carefully detailed townhomes sat crowded in on narrow lots; small but formal well-tended gardens offered burbling fountains and European-style topiaries.

As I parallel-parked, an open-topped minivan tourist bus passed us, a guide on a megaphone pointing at houses and spewing unintelligible proclamations.

At my quizzical look, Maya explained. "This is one of the fanciest neighborhoods in the city. Danielle Steele's house is somewhere around here, and the Gettys', and one of our senators and a congresswoman live here, too."

"Frances Potts's daughter must have done very well for herself."

Maya nodded as we crossed the street to the address I had written down. "I doubt there's a house in sight worth less than several million dollars."

The only other people on the street were construction workers and gardeners. Two small bulldozers were loudly excavating the hill behind a house that was sheathed in scaffolding. The alleys between the houses were a scant three feet across, so the equipment was accessing the backyard through the garage. Next door a woman in an apron came out with a bucket and mop in hand and started to scrub the driveway free of invisible dirt. A man in faded gray coveralls rolled garbage cans into the street, marring the neighborhood's otherwise pristine beauty.

Though Katherine Airey, née Katherine Potts, had grown up just on the other side of this compact city, she now lived worlds away from the creaky old home of her youth. Her house was either brand-new or had been renovated to within an inch of its life. As with most modernist buildings, it was constructed of steel, concrete, and glass. It put me in mind of a corporate headquarters.

The door sat right on the sidewalk beside the garage, with no stairs or stoop. Six abstract sculpted plates were the patterned door's only adornment. I stared at them for a moment, but noted nothing sinister. I rang the bell beside it.

The dog barked, his voice deep and full. Katherine and I had something in common already, I tried to tell myself. Still, a shared love for canines didn't quite make up for my inheriting her mother's estate. My stomach quailed at the idea of Katherine's reaction to such an unfair and, I was sure, unanticipated development. I was grateful to have Maya at my side, her calm demeanor steadying me. I was becoming a true convert to the buddy system.

After a few moments a man answered the door. He was tall and thickly muscled; his hair and eyes appeared jet-black. He was dressed in jeans and a plain white T-shirt, but he had an air of self-possession that made me imagine that this wasn't the gardener answering the door.

"I'm here to see Katherine Airey."

"You're Lily Ivory?" he asked in the heavily accented voice I remembered from the phone.

I nodded. "And this is my friend Maya Jackson."

His eyes flickered over Maya, then back to me. I supposed I should have checked to see whether it was appropriate to bring a friend. On the other hand, Maya was wearing a skirt and T-shirt, and I was still in my vintage polka-dot wiggle dress. We were both on the small-to-average side. We might not make the most businesslike impression, but neither could I imagine this muscled man would see us as any kind of threat.

"Come on in," he said with a nod.

He turned and led the way up a narrow stairway. The main living area was located on the second story. It had an open floor plan, what designers like to call a great room. Our feet sank into the thick, plush, cream-colored carpet. Silk throw pillows in muted tones of taupe, putty, and beige offered the only color in the room. The rest of the upholstery was white, as were the walls and ceiling.

Glass floor-to-ceiling shelves lined one wall, showcasing stark black abstract ceramics. Not a book in sight.

The home itself had very few historic vibrations; in fact, the streamlined architecture and furniture inspired very little reaction in me, either way. But the entire front wall of the house was made of plate-glass windows, offering an unparalleled, unobstructed view of the water and the Golden Gate Bridge, and flooding the room with light.

Not exactly comfy, but undeniably impressive.

Our escort disappeared, but Maya inched behind me as a dog took his place, trotting up to check us out. He was a great black Lab, huge, his head like an anvil. *Katherine must be a brave woman to have a black Lab in a city home decorated primarily in white*, I thought to myself. Either that or a devoted housekeeping staff of twenty-five.

I put my hand out to the dog and he sniffed it, looking up into my face. Unlike many Labs I've known in my day, he had an intelligent gleam in his eye. He let me pet him for a brief moment before trotting over to his mistress, who was reclining on an ivory leather sofa.

Dressed in an immaculate white satin caftanlike gown, Katherine had blond, carefully streaked and styled hair. She had to be in her fifties, so I was sure she had some help from the salon; she had a well-preserved look about her. But what struck me most was her almost total lack of affect. Overuse of Botox, perhaps?

Without saying a word, Katherine gestured for us to take our seats in the matching love seat across a low glass-and-chrome coffee table.

"Hello, Katherine. I'm Lily Ivory, and this is Maya

Jackson," I said. "Maya knew your mother as well, and wanted to pay her respects."

"I'm so sorry for your loss," Maya said.

Katherine's light brown eyes looked me up and down before shifting over to assess Maya. Then she rose from the sofa and glided over to a small wet bar. Her movements were smooth, practiced. I had the oddest sensation that we had just stepped into a performance art piece. The only problem was, I didn't know what role Maya and I were supposed to be playing.

"Vodka tonic?" Katherine asked us over one satin-clad shoulder.

"No, no, thank you. I'm fine," I said.

"Me neither, thank you," said Maya.

We perched on the love seat and watched as Katherine placed ice cubes in a highball glass, poured it about half-full with premium vodka, and then added a splash of diet tonic water and a squeeze of lime. She took a generous pull on her concoction before turning back to us and walking toward the couch.

"So . . . I've been dying of anticipation," Katherine said with an amused smile that did not reach her eyes. She arranged herself on the sofa, lying back and putting her feet up. The dog came to sit on the floor next to the couch, resting his great head on her ankles. "Do tell, Lily, darling. How did you manage to get Frances to leave everything to you?"

"I don't understand it, either. I barely knew your mother."

"You act as though I care," Katherine said with a dramatic flourish of her left hand, as though waving off my concern. "As you can see, I have no need of her money.

That place is yours—enjoy. It's a house of horrors as far as I'm concerned."

"A house of horrors?"

"The place is a rattrap. You saw it. It's in a crappy part of town, surrounded by crappy neighbors. You would do the world a service by burning the place down. I'm just glad I don't have to think about it."

"But I don't want it. I plan to renounce the inheritance. It's not in great shape but it's still worth something. You have children; surely they could—"

"Leave them out of this," she snapped.

"I just mean it rightfully belongs to y'all."

" 'Y'all'?" She smiled her tight smile again. "Where are you from?"

"Texas."

"My mother was from New Orleans." For the first time I noted a faraway look in her eyes, as though she were thinking of her loss.

"Yes, she told me."

There was a long silence, only the tinkling of the ice cubes in Katherine's glass breaking the quiet. I noticed the drink was nearly gone already.

"I understand you were the one who found your mother's body."

She nodded.

"Could you . . . I don't suppose you could tell me anything about the scene?"

"The scene? You mean the fact that she was lying in a pool of her own vomit, on the floor, in a pentagram drawn of blood?"

I opened my mouth, but found it hard to know what to say. I glanced over at Maya, who looked ashen.

"I'd rather not think about it," Katherine added, smiling again.

"Would you mind if I asked you a few questions about your sister's disappearance?"

"What does that have to do with anything? That was a lifetime ago."

"I know that. But there might be some connection between—"

"My sister," she hissed, her voice dripping with loathing. "Everything has been about her, and her disappearance, since I was a kid."

Katherine leaned over to put her empty glass on the coffee table. As she moved I noticed a medallion fall out of the neck of the caftan. She grabbed it, slipping it back under the cloth before I could see what it was, exactly—a protective amulet?

Our eyes held for a moment.

"My sister wasn't the only one, you know," Katherine said. "There was nothing special about Elisabeth's disappearance. It was a tragedy, just like the tragedies that befall people every day all over the world. There are some things we should just accept and move on."

"I understand it was a very long time ago. But something's happened that might, possibly, be connected to that."

The dog sat up and started a rumble deep and low in his broad chest. I imagined he was picking up on his human's stress. He gazed across the room at me. Again, I got the sense that he was smarter than most of his breed.

"I don't want to talk about Elisabeth's disappearance. If you don't want the house, give it away," said Katherine as she rose and looked out the huge pane of glass to the street below. "I don't care about any of it."

"What about the pictures, the personal items?" Maya asked. "I was collecting some stories—"

"Especially those. My mother and I did not have a particularly close relationship, as you apparently are unaware." She studied her French-manicured nails for a moment before continuing. "Do you know that she has never, not once, acknowledged her grandchildren? I have a boy and a girl, both teenagers, and neither has ever even met their grandmother. She has plenty of time for the neighborhood children, none for them. She never wanted any of us in her house. So don't expect me to mourn for her, or for some long-dead sister."

"I don't—"

"You know what my mother did after my sister disappeared? She couldn't move on, couldn't deal with it, so essentially she abandoned me. Went back to her precious New Orleans for months at a time. My father had a fit."

"It wasn't a happy marriage, then?"

She looked at me in disbelief and let out a scoffing breath. "No, not precisely."

"I . . . Could I ask how your father died?"

"He hanged himself. Couldn't deal. Apparently I wasn't enough without his precious Elisabeth."

"I'm so sorry." I knew how it felt to grow up without a father. His absence was a void, a dull ache throughout my life. Not intolerable, but undeniable. It left a scar. But at least I hadn't known him. . . . I couldn't imagine losing a loving father to suicide.

She shrugged and with a slight inclination of her head sent the dog out of the room.

"And your father's parents?"

"They died not long after my sister disappeared. Then Mother sent me off to boarding school so she wouldn't have to deal with me. All told, it was a fabulous adolescence."

"But you made it through," I pointed out. "You have a lovely home, children. . . ."

"I found my own way. Let's leave it at that."

Since we arrived I had been trying to sense Katherine's vibrations, but she had been difficult to read. She didn't shake hands, so I couldn't rely on the more evocative skin-to-skin contact. But now she was emitting plenty; unfortunately, scared and angry vibrations feel very nearly the same, as they are two sides of the same coin. Her facial expression was so flat that it was hard to figure out which of the two emotions she was experiencing. Or could it be both?

I looked up to see that the young man had arrived again. Was he the modern equivalent of a houseboy? A boyfriend? He hadn't introduced himself, and there was no obvious husband-wife interaction, so we were left to speculate.

My gaze shifted back to Katherine. Overall, hers seemed a sad, sterile, bitter life . . . but who was I to say? Perhaps she was a relaxed laugh riot when not speaking of death and childhood trauma. Maybe she kept the Pacific Heights ladies-who-lunch rolling in the aisles with her clever quips.

"Please see these two out," Katherine said to the

man. He nodded and gestured that we should start down the stairs.

"Thank you for speaking with us, Katherine," I said as Maya and I stood. "I really am sorry about your mother. I didn't know her well, but she was very kind to me. You . . . Your eyes are very much like hers."

"My condolences," said Maya quietly.

Katherine remained mute.

Maya and I crossed the room, headed down the narrow staircase, and let ourselves out the heavy wood-and-bronze door.

We both paused outside on the sidewalk, breathing deeply of the fresh air. Maya lifted her face to the last rays of the sun; after dawning overcast, the day had turned warm and sunny, but now there was a thick fog rolling in.

The construction workers across the street were still making a racket, their Bobcats disappearing into the garage. We both watched the lurching, noisy movement for a moment.

Finally, our eyes met.

"That was truly bizarre," said Maya.

"Good, it wasn't just me," I said, relieved to know my judgment was sound. "I think we need hot chocolate."

"With marshmallows."

"*Lots* of marshmallows."

"A shot of rum in it wouldn't be such a bad idea, for that matter." Maya smiled.

"You missed your chance with that vodka tonic upstairs."

"Emphasis on the vodka."

We laughed and started across the quiet residential street. I began to dig around in my backpack for the car keys.

To our right, I noticed a red sedan coming down the steep hill. It seemed to be picking up speed, so I hurried a bit to get across the street and urged Maya to do the same.

The car sped up.

We increased our pace and reached the curb on the other side.

Suddenly the vehicle swerved toward us.

Chapter 14

I grasped Maya by the arm to get her attention. We broke into a run and leaped over the sidewalk.

The car was still headed straight toward us.

Racing up the short driveway, we ducked into the small alley between the house and its neighbor. A barred metal security gate kept us from going back farther than a few feet. Maya and I plastered ourselves to the wall, huddling in the farthest corner.

The car careened into the metal garbage cans, sending the heavy missiles sailing toward us.

A fraction of a second later we heard the terrible screech of steel on concrete as the car itself crashed into the buildings. The force of the impact shook the ground. Part of the nose of the car jutted through the opening between the two houses, coming to a stop a mere two feet from us.

Everything seemed to freeze for a moment. Even the Bobcats had stopped their roar. All I could hear was my own ragged breathing, and that of Maya. We were clutching each other, squeezing our eyes shut.

Finally we looked up. The grille of the car was close to us, far too close, trapping us between the walls of the houses and the metal gate at our backs.

We stood, still shaky, to peer inside the car.

There was no driver. No one in the car at all.

I turned back to Maya. "Are you all right? Are you hurt?"

"Just bruised, I think. But you're bleeding."

I looked down to see a gash on my knee bleeding profusely. What a day to wear a wiggle dress.

A small crowd gathered, a few neighboring housekeepers and the men from the bulldozers. One of them handed me a clean handkerchief for my knee. Another helped Maya and me over the wrecked hood of the car to stand on the driveway.

"It must have been a runaway," said a rather ashen-faced man in an orange and black Giants baseball cap. "Sometimes people forget to curb their wheels."

"Yes, I'm sure you're right," I said with a nod. It was the logical explanation, except for the fact that the car steered straight toward us.

"Lily, look," said Maya, and I followed her gaze up to the sheer glass wall of Katherine's house across the street. She stood at the window, her big black dog at her side.

Katherine looked neither shocked nor pleased, simply . . . unmoved.

As I looked closer, her lips seemed to be moving, as though she were invoking a charm.

* * *

"My cousin doesn't live very far," said Maya after the bystanders helped to extricate us from the wreckage. "He works at home—I'll call him and see if we can clean up there, gather our wits."

She must have noticed my shaking hands. It took all my concentration to steer us the two miles to the marina. It took us only five minutes to drive there, but another ten to find a parking place—I didn't want to use my special parking charm in front of Maya. She'd had enough surprises for one day.

Maya's cousin Russell had decorated his 1920s town house in early English gentleman: There was plenty of cherry furniture, and Ralph Lauren prints everywhere. Russell was on the small side, and the family resemblance was plain. He and Maya shared similarly delicate features, and a serious, calm nature.

He had already put on a kettle for tea, and fussed over us. We used the medicine cabinet in his well-appointed bathroom, got cleaned up, and applied a bandage to my knee. I would put a healing poultice on it when I got home, but right now it stung and made me clumsy.

Maya brewed us a pot of soothing chamomile tea and Russell brought out a box of chocolates and a platter of homemade oatmeal-chocolate-chip cookies. Normally I was a great believer in the healing magic of chocolate, but at the moment I was feeling beyond redemption.

I couldn't *believe* that I had invited Maya along on this trip, putting her in the path of danger. She could easily have been seriously hurt or killed. I changed my mind about the buddy system; I should go back to my solo ways. It seemed anyone around me lately was bound to be hurt.

Sitting on his couch, Russell and Maya chatted about

family members while I tried to distract myself by picking up today's newspaper lying on the coffee table. I found the article about Jessica that I had read earlier this morning. It made my heart hurt. Her grinning face, the horror of the whole thing. How many parents would have to know the kind of tragedy that had befallen these families? Frances and her husband, Felipa Rodriguez . . . How many others in between? Katherine said her sister wasn't the only one; the article had noted that, too. Numerous children had been disappearing from the neighborhood over the years.

I wasn't the only one with missing children on her mind. I overheard Maya telling Russell about what happened with Jessica's disappearance and our visit to Mrs. Potts the night before she died. They started to talk about the neighborhood redevelopment plan, putting me in mind of Sandra Schmidt. I used to think I could recognize fellow witches, but could I have been fooled in Sandra's case? Could there be more than met the eye, with her interest in the *Malleus Maleficarum*, her purchase of the stone statue at the auction, and her fervent desire to see Frances's clothes? And what about Katherine Airey, chanting while watching us nearly get run over by a driverless car?

La Llorona wasn't responsible for trying to run us down, any more than she had killed Frances. It wasn't her style. She pulled people into the water with her, reeling them into her watery grave to join her. *Llorona*'s violence arose from gut-wrenching guilt and anguish, not from the desire to see a particular person dead . . . or silenced.

No, trying to run us down with a driverless car was the trick of a witch.

Now I just had to figure out which witch.

* * *

I used Russell's telephone to call Bronwyn and make sure she was okay alone at the store for the rest of the afternoon; then I called the offices of the *San Francisco Chronicle*. I didn't quite know what to say—I wasn't a detective or a private eye, not a member of any of the affected families. But when Nigel Thorne's gruff voice came on the phone he didn't ask why I was interested in the subject, but simply invited me to stop by his office.

Maya decided to stay and have dinner with Russell, so I made my way alone to busy Van Ness Avenue and drove past a number of car dealerships, the opera house, the San Francisco Symphony building, and the grand domed City Hall. I enjoyed the sightseeing, but as I sat at yet another interminable stoplight I realized that Van Ness was the sort of clogged, stoplight-infested city thoroughfare that no native would ever use. Clearly I needed to make some time to get to know how to drive in San Francisco—the urban center is geographically compact, but unlike many other major cities there are so few taxis that everyone seems committed to driving. Even the public transportation is limited—when I first arrived I made the outsider's mistake of thinking people actually used cable cars to get to and from work, but the quaint historic trams are almost exclusively for the tourist trade these days. The bus system is complicated, and the subway serves only one narrow corridor of the city, though it stretches from the Peninsula to the far reaches of the East Bay.

Twenty minutes later, after missing a few turns, I arrived at the intersection of Mission and Fifth, right downtown. The *Chronicle* building boasted so much intricate plasterwork that it looked akin to a tiered wedding cake. I left my car in the underground garage, but hesitated as I was climbing out. Didn't Inspector Romero mention that Max Carmichael worked for the *Chronicle*? I frustrated myself by stopping to make sure my hair was smooth, applied a little lipstick, and even refreshed my mascara.

Pathetic. A witch in search of love. Sounded like the sort of self-help book Sandra would carry in her store.

The elevator was slow. While I waited I perused the bronze plaque on the wall, learning that two teenage brothers, Charles and Michael de Young, borrowed twenty dollars from their landlord to begin their rag in 1865 as "a daily record of affairs—local, critical, and theatrical." San Francisco was a relatively new city at that point—in 1848, before the discovery of gold at Sutter's Mill, the population was listed at a mere eight hundred and fifty souls. One year later that number ballooned to twenty-five thousand, and it would continue to double for the next several decades. By 1868 the de Youngs' paper was renamed the *Morning Chronicle* and moved into its current building.

It was sort of sweet. I'd spent years in ancient parts of the world, in neighborhoods and buildings dating back to the Holy Roman Empire or the Qing dynasty. Now I lived in a city where urban history was counted in fewer than a couple of centuries.

The elevator finally arrived and I rode it to the third floor, where I found Nigel sitting in a nondescript cubicle, hunched over a computer terminal at a beige office desk. In his late fifties, he had male-pattern baldness and unruly eyebrows that gave him a hawklike visage. Three framed pictures sat on his desk: a younger version of himself with a plump brunette at a Christmas party, kissing; and two young girls, not pretty, exactly, but gleaming with the loveliness of youth, wrapped in the black off-the-shoulder wrap typical of high school graduation photos.

"You came right over," he commented as he wrapped up the remains of a sub sandwich and dabbed at a drop of mustard on the front of his shirt.

"I appreciate your seeing me on such short notice." I took a seat in the extra chair by his desk. "I noticed the article you wrote about the child abductions in Hunters Point."

He nodded.

"I wanted to ask you about the disappearance of Elisabeth Potts. Do you remember her?"

His ergonomically correct desk chair squeaked as he leaned back, lacing his fingers together behind his head.

"Sure I do. It was one of my first big stories, back when I first started here at the *Chron*. That's when I had lots of energy; I was determined to figure it all out." He shrugged, his shoulder straining against the plaid cotton of his short-sleeved button-up shirt. "The police investigated the hell out of the parents—that's standard. Grandparents, too. Didn't find a thing."

"Did you suspect any of the relatives were involved?"

"Usually they are. Stranger abductions are relatively rare, s'matter of fact. I'm pretty cynical after all these years, seen too much, but in this case I would have been surprised. They just didn't have the vibe, if you know what I mean. It was Frances herself who kept pushing the police to do more. Even a year later she was still calling me to see whether there was any new information on the crime. She went half out of her mind, poor gal. Besides . . . it's not as though they were the only ones."

"How do you mean?"

He shook his head and blew out a long breath. "There've been kids disappearing from that neighborhood, one at a time, for years. They're all treated separately, so no one wants to put them together. I talked with the cops, suggested it might be a serial. But frankly, there are so many marginal folks living over there, I don't think they gave it much credence."

"A serial? As in the same . . . perpetrator?"

"Possibly."

"It's been thirty-five years."

"True. Not too long before little Elisabeth Potts disappeared, in early March of that year, there was one of those really sad cases that come along every once in a while, where a woman was abandoned by her husband and wound up drowning their kids in the bay out near what became India Basin park. Ever since then, far as I can tell, every coupla years, 'round about early March, like clockwork, a kid disappears from that neighborhood."

"Elisabeth was snatched . . ."

"On March fifth."

"But we don't know whether she was the first?"

"As far as I know, she was. But like I say, it's hard to know for sure. The people over there are transitory; not a lot of folks stick around as long as the Potts family."

"This may seem like a strange question, but was there any sort of evidence of something . . . otherworldly?"

"Ah, you've been listening to rumors."

"Rumors?"

"About the lady ghost who comes and gathers up the kids."

A shiver ran up my spine. "Could you tell me more about that?"

He leaned forward, resting his elbows on his thighs, the chair squeaking loudly. "Not like I believe it. But it's one of those urban legends, always interesting. Some of the descriptions are pretty graphic. According to some of the folks, voodoo can help keep the ghost at bay, which is interesting, since the community that believes in the ghost lady is mostly Spanish."

"Latino," I corrected. "They speak Spanish, but they're mostly from Mexico and Central America."

"Right. Anyhoo, for some reason they felt like their own *botánica* magic wasn't effective, so they turned to voodoo for help. I even spoke to a voodoo priestess at one point. She passed away a few years ago, but her protégé has taken over. Still works with that group occasionally. Goes by the name of Hervé something or other."

Voodoo again. I couldn't avoid it any longer.

"Do you have contact information for him?"

"Sure. I wrote a whole article on it a while back."

"Could I read it?"

Nigel took off his wire glasses, leaned toward me, and fixed me with a hawk-eyed look.

"You don't actually believe this crap, do you? I mean, that whole satanic-ritual abuse scare has been largely discredited. Turns out child abuse is pretty standard."

"I like to keep an open mind. And I believe that others believe."

With a sigh, he put his glasses back on, turned to his computer screen, lifted his head as though looking out the bottom lens of the bifocals, scrolled through options, and finally clicked his mouse several times.

"I'll be right back." He got up and headed to the large office printer across the room.

I sat for a moment before giving in to curiosity and getting up to look at what was on the computer screen. With my typical grace, I managed to knock a stack of papers from the desktop to the floor. Stooping down, I started to gather them together.

"Fancy meeting you here."

I saw muscular thighs first, then looked up to see Max Carmichael crouching down on the other side of the pile. He helped pick up the papers.

"Um . . . hi," I said, smooth as always.

"I'm glad you're here. I need to talk to you."

"This isn't really the best time."

"You're not here to see me? I'm crushed."

Despite his light tone, he looked down at me with an accusatory gleam in his eyes, which were as gray and clouded as the foggy afternoon. Though I had to admit I had been looking forward to seeing him again, his skeptical attitude came back to me loud and clear.

"Gosnold refuses to take me out on the bay."

Grabbing the stack of papers, I finally stood up and set them on the desk. I turned to face Max as he straightened as well.

I nodded. "It's for the best."

"I had a whole film crew lined up."

I noticed the same woman who had lingered in the doorway of Aunt Cora's Closet the other day in one of the glassed-in offices. She was looking over at Max and me, a distinctly possessive look in her beautiful eyes.

"You're being watched," I said.

Max glanced over at the woman, then back at me. "Violet? She's harmless."

"She's . . . proprietary."

He looked down at me with a crooked grin. "Jealous?"

"Listen." I avoided his eyes, and his question. "I told you it was dangerous to go out on the bay with Gosnold. Why don't you let him show you the nice ghost over at the Queen Anne Hotel?"

"Because I was after Gosnold, not some mythical ghost. And in case you forgot, the other 'haunted mansion' he agreed to show me was something of a bust, as well."

"Back off, Carmichael; I saw her first," Nigel interrupted in a teasing voice as he returned to his desk.

"You old fraud," Max replied. "You'd never look at another woman."

Nigel just grunted and sat in his desk chair, handing me the printout. I tried to shield the headline—*Child Snatcher or Supernatural Specter?*—from Max as I slipped the article into my backpack.

"You two know each other?" Nigel asked.

"Not as well as we'd like," Max said.

Nigel raised his eyebrows and his gaze shifted from one of us to the other before he spoke to me directly. "Anyhoo, more likely it's their parents on crack, but whatever. By the way, here's the newest one. It's no surprise, second week of March."

He handed me a piece of paper with a bulletin with the huge headline: *Missing Girl.* The photo was a school portrait of Jessica Rodriguez, grinning. I couldn't stop recalling the image of her smiling over her shoulder at us as she hopped out of the house. My heart rose to my throat. I swallowed hard.

"Thank you for your help, Nigel," I managed.

He nodded and handed me two business cards, one of his own, and one for an Hervé LaMansec, along with his shop address on Valencia Avenue. He stood.

"Let me know if you unearth anything, and I'd be more than willing to look into it further. Sometimes a case like this just takes a new pair of eyes." We shook hands, and Nigel's kind gaze held mine. "Just . . . be careful."

"Thanks again." I nodded, gathered my things, and started across the room to the elevator. My knee had stiffened while I sat, so I walked with a decided limp.

"What happened to you?" Max asked as he trailed me.

"I tripped," I said over my shoulder. "Why are you following me? You're a mythbuster, right? You don't buy all this witchy stuff."

"Something like that." He reached toward me, and for a crazy moment I thought he was going to embrace me. For an even crazier moment, I thought I would let him. I caught a whiff of his scent—soap, laundry detergent, and an underlying musk that was purely him.

His arm snaked around me to push the elevator call button.

"Then why are you following me?" I asked, clearing my throat in an attempt to recover my wits.

"Morbid fascination."

"Just what I always wanted," I said as I watched the

elevator indicator numbers slowly light up. "To inspire men with 'morbid' fascination."

He chuckled. "Where are you off to next?"

"A coven meeting. We're planning on sacrificing a virgin."

"I'll bet you're going to go see that voodoo guy Nigel mentioned."

"Gee, Max, you're like a mind reader. Are you sure you don't have magical powers?"

"I'll go with you."

"No, thanks. How are you feeling, by the way?"

"I'm feeling fine. My sister's a doctor. She took a look." The elevator arrived and a young woman with an armful of files stepped off as I got on. Max held the door open, staring down at me. "She says there's no way the wound's only a day old. It healed too fast."

"You're welcome."

"You shouldn't go alone to see this guy."

"Any particular reason?"

"He calls himself a voodoo priest. Isn't that reason enough?"

"I can handle it. I'm a big girl."

"I noticed. That's quite a dress you have on," he murmured as his eyes drifted over me, down and back up. Then he stepped onto the elevator and allowed the doors to close behind him. "I'll drive."

"Look, Max, take it from one who knows: The last thing a voodoo priest is going to respond to is your blatant disdain and disbelief."

"I'll keep it under wraps."

"Even if you were a great actor—which, I hate to break it to you, you *aren't*—if this practitioner is worth his salt, he'll sense your cynicism immediately, like I did. This isn't Charles Gosnold we're dealing with here."

"I'll be good. I promise."

The elevator pinged its arrival at the garage level. I wasn't sure why I was considering letting Max come with me, except that I found his presence oddly comforting. Of course, the last time he was in my company he got hurt . . . as did Maya when she joined me at Katherine's home.

On the other hand . . . chances were good that Hervé something-or-other was a fake, like so many so-called "priests." And we were going to be in a public shop, after all. But just in case he wasn't, and something were to go terribly wrong, Max should have a talisman.

"Do you still have my medicine bag?"

He nodded. "I wanted to ask you about that. . . ."

"Just keep it for now. Let me see. . . ." I started fishing around in the bottom of my backpack as Max led me over to a dark blue pickup truck. "Aha! Here it is."

"This is the second time you've brought out necklaces when we're together."

I slipped it over his head and paused, my arms on his broad shoulders, and murmured a brief incantation.

"There," I said as I patted it. His chest was broad and strong. Our eyes held just a little too long.

"I'm not really a medallion-wearing kind of guy."

"I don't know much about voodoo, Max, but I reckon it's powerful. Did I steer you wrong last time?"

"Last time I wound up with a couple of inches gouged out of my torso."

"It would have been a dang sight worse without my protection; I guarantee you that."

"Hmm," Max said.

"What does 'hmm' mean?" I asked as I climbed into the cab of the truck. It was an older model, but not full of trash like my van. I keep my vintage Mustang immaculate, but the work van's another story.

"It's my attempt to be diplomatic. I'm not used to women giving me jewelry. Not to mention being chased by ghosts."

As we traveled across town to the Mission District, I was glad that Max was at the wheel. He drove like a local, weaving our way through quiet residential streets, down an alley, through a parking lot, then back out to a main thoroughfare. I was lost within the first five minutes.

"How long have you written for the *Chronicle*?" I asked.

"I'm freelance. I was a correspondent for Reuters for the last five years, mostly in Europe and Africa. But my dad lives up in Marin, and he's getting up there, so I decided to come home for a bit. And you? You mentioned you're from Texas?"

I nodded. "I only moved here about six weeks ago."

"How do you like it so far?"

"I love it. The people here are . . ."

"Whack-jobs?"

I laughed. "Wonderfully eccentric. I've never been anywhere like it."

"Mark Twain used to write for the *Chron*; did you know that? He once said San Francisco was the most cordial city in the nation, and that he was better treated here than he actually deserved."

"I think I feel a little like that."

"Better than you deserve?" His eyes shifted over to me. "I doubt that."

I turned to look out the window, feeling a rare blush stain my cheeks. Max reached forward and turned on the radio, trying a few stations before settling on an oldies channel playing a love song. The strains of "When a Man Loves a Woman" filled the cab, and Max hummed along under his breath. Cute. The man liked sappy oldies music.

When he pulled the truck onto Valencia we rolled along slowly until I spotted the address across the broad boulevard.

"There it is."

"Looks like a dive," grumbled Max as he parallel-parked in a space about a block down.

"It's just a regular old voodoo shop."

"Uh-huh. I don't use 'regular' and 'voodoo' in the same sentence."

"Stop being such a curmudgeon. You wanted to come, remember? Maybe you should go get yourself something to drink while I talk to LaMansec."

"Nah, I'll stick with you," Max responded, as though he were doing me a favor. He held my arm protectively as we crossed the wide, busy street. When we approached the cobalt blue door of the shop, he looked down at me and added: "But morbid fascination can only take a man so far. If there are any virgin sacrifices, I'm telling."

Chapter 15

Detalier's looked like a typical store from the front display window, which showed keepsakes similar to the things one finds in a lot of shops in the Haight: carved statuettes, embroidered runners, inlaid pipes. Inside, Max had to duck to avoid hitting his head on the carved gourds and brightly painted wooden animals that hung from the ceiling. Two teenage girls were giggling over a hand-sewn hex doll, and a Japanese couple lingered near the black candles. Shallow shelves presented various body parts made of wax, which seemed a little gruesome until I realized that they were no stranger than the small metal *milagros* sold in *botánicas*. Skulls, bones, and wax-sealed bottles filled with various concoctions crowded a turquoise bookshelf. In one corner was an incongruous display of Che Guevara paraphernalia, along with a selection of cigars. Most disturbing was a statue of a large, horned, goatlike creature with a human body, sporting a pentagram carved on his forehead.

The pretty young woman sitting behind the register

wore colorful swaths of batik and African mud-cloth prints, her long dreadlocks tied up in a brightly patterned scarf. She had traditional tattooing on her face: blue-black dots in a spiral on her cheeks and across her smooth forehead.

She smiled at us in welcome. Without being called, a man came out from the back of the store, ducking through a brightly beaded curtain that clacked loudly behind him. He was heavy but not fat, of average height but with a football player's physique. His eyes were wide-set and startling, his skin so dark it gleamed. From his air of authority I assumed he was the shop owner I was looking for: Hervé LaMansec.

"I'm Lily Ivory," I said. "I was hoping to ask you a few questions."

We locked eyes for a long moment. He gestured toward Max with his chin, and spoke in a sonorous, deeply inflected voice.

"Who he?"

"A friend."

"No friend to us, I think."

"He'll be fine. Just a bit skeptical."

He nodded and grunted. "What you want?"

By now we had attracted the attention of the other shoppers.

"Could we talk in private?" I asked.

He held my eyes a moment more before nodding. "You alone. He stays here."

Max opened his mouth to protest, but I had anticipated him.

"Max, please." I held his gaze briefly. Then he and LaMansec shared a manly moment of trying to stare each other down before Max finally shrugged and took a seat in a colorful painted wooden chair next to the reception counter.

LaMansec led the way through the beaded curtain, down a short, narrow, unadorned hall, and into his private office.

The interior decor surprised me: I might as well have been visiting my local DMV. A large, standard-issue gray metal desk was topped by a desktop computer; the walls were lined with shelves containing reference books, stacks of papers, and dozens of files. Atop a beige metal file cabinet sat a small television tuned in to *The Oprah Winfrey Show*. LaMansec picked up a remote and switched it off, then waved me toward a folding chair.

"Please, make yourself comfortable," he said in an uninflected voice.

"What happened to your accent?" I asked.

"It's strictly for the tourists." He shrugged one brawny shoulder. "They feel cheated if they know they're speaking to a guy born and raised in L.A. Tea?"

"Please." I nodded.

He poured hot water from an electric kettle into two blue-glazed mugs, added bags of mint leaves, and stirred in a dollop of amber honey. Handing one to me, he took a seat behind his desk and fixed me with his intense gaze.

"I heard a powerful witch had come to town. It's a pleasure."

"You heard about me? From whom?"

"Let's just say your reputation precedes you."

Reputation? I had a reputation?

"I was hoping you might be able to tell me something

about children disappearing from the Bayview–Hunters Point neighborhood."

The pleasant smile dropped from his face. "Another one?"

"Just the other day."

He shook his head and ran his hand across his forehead in a weary gesture.

"Is it *La Llorona*?" I asked.

"That's their name for her."

"And you're powerless against her?"

A flash of anger passed over his face. "Powerless? Not at all. I've given them salts and talismans, along with the basic advice to keep their children by their sides at all times, especially at night. But I'm not a miracle worker. For most of these people, vodou is not part of their belief system. And as you well know—"

"If you don't believe, it won't work."

"Precisely."

"Have you ever had direct contact with the demon?"

He shook his head. "No. She won't be summoned."

"How hard have you tried?"

He gazed at me for a long moment.

"Not hard. To tell you the truth, she is an evil I'd rather not deal with. I try to help when people come to me, but I can only do so much. This is my living. I have paying clients—true believers—to worry about."

"I understand," I said, and I did. This sort of thing could consume a person; those of us born with supernatural abilities came to appreciate that early. This was especially the case for those who used their powers to make a living instead of, say, selling vintage clothes. But all of us had to become adept at what Oprah would call "drawing boundaries."

"If they don't believe in vodou, why do they come to you? Why not turn to their own *curanderos*?"

"Early on they decided their own magic was limited. I'm not sure why. I inherited this practice from my mentor, and she had been working with them for years already."

"Could I show you some photos I took of a personal altar? I think it might be vodou."

"Of course."

I brought the envelope of photos out of my backpack. They weren't the best pictures in the world, in part because there were so many halo effects and orbs that it was hard to see everything on the altar. But they gave the general idea.

Hervé looked at the photos carefully, spreading them out on the desk before him. His dark eyes then shifted back up to meet mine. "Where did you say you took these photos?"

"I'd rather not say. Why?"

"That looks like a Hand of Glory." He pointed to the strange candleholder that I had taken with me. "Do you have any idea what that is?"

I shook my head.

"A genuine Hand of Glory is the dried and pickled hand—usually the left—of a hanged man. When a particular kind of magic candle is made and set within the Hand of Glory, like it is here in the picture"—he showed it to me—"it gives light only to the holder, and can unlock any door it comes across. Including spiritual doors."

Our eyes met for a long moment. "So this would be beyond the average personal altar."

"I should say so, yes. And the blackened bones . . . it is hard to tell, but they may well be black-cat bones."

"As in actual cat bones?" I felt a little green around the gills.

"I won't tell you how they obtain them."

"I do appreciate that. I'm afraid to ask, but they do what, exactly?"

"They can impart invisibility when held in the mouth of a practitioner."

"Invisibility?"

He nodded. "This altar must belong to a practitioner."

Sweet little Frances Potts, a voodoo practitioner? "Can you tell whether the practitioner would be acting for good or for ill?"

"Much of my practice can be used for both purposes, just as in the craft you practice." LaMansec hesitated for a beat. "But from the presence of the Hand of Glory and the black-cat bones, I would assume this person is working for evil."

"One more thing," I said as I put the photos back in my backpack. "I want to summon *La Llorona*."

"To what end?"

I unfolded the missing-child flyer and set it on the desk before him.

"I want this child's soul back."

"What about the others? Will you ask for them all back?"

This is the problem with such things. You open up a can of paranormal worms. But the sad truth is that, over time, the children cannot return. They are no longer the same after too much time in another dimension. It might already be too late even for Jessica.

"I should have been able to protect her. I should have sensed that she was in danger."

"Is this about the child, or about you?"

I ignored that. I wasn't sure. "Is there anyone who can help me?"

Sigh. "You need to speak to my teacher, Mother Decotier."

"Where can I find her?"

"She moved on to the next dimension almost ten years ago."

I shook my head. "I'm not a necromancer."

"You can't call spirits?"

"Not in so many words. I mean, I attract demons and spirits like flies to honey, but I'm not a medium: I know when souls of the departed are near, but I can't understand what they say."

He raised his eyebrows. "Really."

"I can't read cards or tea leaves or palms, either."

Hervé was grinning by now. "But you *are* a witch, are you not?"

"I feel vibrations in old things, and can sometimes feel, or even smell, the auras of people and objects. But the only truly 'witchy' thing I'm really good at is brewing."

"You don't see much of that these days."

He was right; brewing as an art has largely lost favor amongst modern witches. Though many were clever at mixing herbs, teas, or poultices, few actually used the old-fashioned cauldron, which relied upon the magic of the fire, the process of boiling, and the transformation from liquid to steam to condense and focus one's intentions.

"I blame Shakespeare," I said.

"How so?"

"Remember the witches in *Macbeth*? Not a very flattering portrayal." He smiled, but I was serious. Things just haven't been the same since those infamous witches mixed ghastly ingredients and chanted, "Double, double toil and trouble, fire burn, and cauldron bubble."

"In any case," Hervé said, "there's no need for necromancy. Presuming Mother is willing to speak with you, she will find a way. Do you know the small park dedicated to Mary Ellen Pleasant?"

"Who?"

"Pleasant has been called the mother of civil rights here in San Francisco. She was a remarkable woman, an entrepreneur born as a slave, who went on to use her personal fortune to help fund the abolitionist movement. Following the Civil War she fought several high-profile court battles in San Francisco over crimes such as riding the streetcar while black. She won."

"I'm embarrassed to say I've never heard of her."

"Few have. When they couldn't destroy her any other way, rumors started to fly that she was a voodoo queen, and a prostitute. The slander accomplished what nothing else had—she lost everything. Still, without her legacy San Francisco would be a very different city today. She was a very powerful soul." He wrote on a notepad. "At 1661 Octavia Street there is a plaque in her honor. She used to live in a grand mansion there, and planted the eucalyptus trees that remain. Now Mother Decotier haunts the place from time to time in a sort of personal tribute. She likes to scare the tourists and remind them of who Pleasant was. Presuming she agrees to talk with you, she'll require payment."

"I understand. But just so we're clear, I won't sacrifice life."

He threw back his head and laughed, a full-throated guffaw. For the first time in his presence, I felt a tingle of trepidation. His laugh was formidable, almost alarming.

"A witch with standards. I love it. Tell you what, Lily the witch. I will arrange a meeting, and inquire as to the payment—short of taking life." He laughed again. "I will do it as a . . . professional courtesy."

"Thank you."

"Do you have a cell phone?"

"No." I was a teensy bit phobic about portable electronic devices. They scrambled my sense of vibrations. "But here's my card with my home number."

"You have e-mail?" he asked.

"Yes, but I don't check it very often." I took back the card and wrote the address below my phone number.

"Check it. I'll e-mail you her reply and the meeting time."

What was it with all these tech-savvy spooks? Sometimes I felt I would have done better as a sixteenth-century witch . . . except for the massacres, of course.

As we rose to go, Hervé went over to a cupboard and extracted a small jar of what looked like dirt. He sprinkled a little of it into a tiny plastic Baggie.

"My gift to you. For your charm bag."

"What is it?"

"Dirt from a prison gateway in New Orleans. It will help to keep evildoers from you. Powerful protection."

"Thank you, Hervé. I really appreciate it, and your taking the trouble to talk with me."

"My pleasure."

By the time we returned to the front, Max appeared to have gotten over his snit. He stood with the dread-locked woman by a display of scented oils. He was holding her wrist up to his nose, apparently assessing one of the perfumes. She laughed at something he was saying. Twin boys, about eight, joked with him, and he looked down and teased them about their New Orleans Saints T-shirts.

The smile left his face when he looked over to see me standing with LaMansec. He glared. Hervé grinned.

"Tell you what, Lily, you bring this one along. Mother would love to meet him."

"I don't think that would be a good idea—" I began.

"I'll be there," Max said. He reached into his pocket and pulled out a business card. "Just let me know where and when."

I thanked Hervé again, and Max and I left the shop.

I paused for a moment out on the sidewalk. Closing my eyes, I breathed deeply and let the smells and sounds surround me. Spicy fried meats, refried beans, ranchero music and rap with booming bass moving by from a car. A million vibrations, mostly good. This was a pulsating, vibrant neighborhood, peopled by up-and-coming immigrants, students, and artists. It might be scruffy, but it was full of hope. These people were looking forward, toward the future.

"You okay?" Max asked.

I nodded, opened my eyes, and smiled up at him. "Mmm."

"What exactly did that voodoo priest do to make you smile like that?"

I laughed and shook my head. "It's this neighborhood. Isn't it great?"

Max glanced around us and then fixed me with a doubtful look. "Which part are you talking about? The overflowing Dumpster or the rampant graffiti?"

I cocked my head and studied the bright spray-painted tags on an otherwise uninspired cement wall. Not that I approved of such vandalism, but the vivid colors did enliven the place.

"You have to admit it's well-done. I mean, they obviously take pride in their work."

Max chuckled. "I'll say one thing for this neighborhood: They've got some of the best tacos in town. Come on, tiger; you owe me dinner."

"I don't owe you a darned thing."

Nonetheless, I let Max lead me a few noisy blocks down Valencia Street to an informal restaurant called Taqueria El Toro. He spoke in Spanish at the counter, ordering tacos of *pollo asado*, *mole*, *chile verde*, and *al pastor*, as well as cold beers for both of us. I almost asked for *carnitas*, but since spending time with Oscar, the thought of eating pork was hard to stomach. Despite his earlier words, Max insisted on paying.

We took our bottles of Dos Equis, each adorned with a wedge of lime, to a clean booth near the back. Max nabbed a basket of chips and a small bowl of salsa, then set them on the table and took a seat across from me.

"You want to tell me what's going on?" he said.

"Not particularly, no."

"Carlos Romero is a homicide inspector."

"Mm, this looks like good salsa." I dipped a chip, still warm from the fryer, into freshly made tomato salsa and popped it in my mouth. The chip was a crisp, salty explosion, and the salsa was flavorful and perfectly spiced. I hadn't realized how hungry I was.

"What's a homicide investigation got to do with a witch?" Max pushed.

"Keep your voice down." I glanced around us to see who might be overhearing our conversation. There were still a lot of people in the world who believed in the power of witches, for good or for ill.

"I thought wi—"

I gave him a look.

"Er, your type of people were proud of who you are. Your . . . heritage, or whatever you call it."

"I doubt you know the first thing about my people."

"Enlighten me."

I sat back and took a long pull on my ice-cold beer. "Any idea how many people—mostly women—were killed during the hysteria in Europe?"

"Hundreds, I would imagine," he said as he dug into the chips and salsa. "Maybe thousands."

"Conservative estimates put the number between fifty and eighty thousand."

He stopped chewing.

"More than the entire population of London at the time. Up there with the Black Death. And those are the ones we have court records for; a lot were taken care of in a rather less formal fashion. Countless others were tortured and driven from their homes. So when you speak so flippantly about a 'heritage' of witchcraft, you might want to consider what it would be like to walk around knowing you have that kind of history."

"Lily, I understand that it's a historical tragedy, and evidence of our misogynistic past as a society . . . but there's no proof the accused were actually witches. I've read *The Crucible*."

"It's true; a lot of the women killed were victims of personal vendettas. Some were so influential and respected that their very existence threatened the menfolk in charge. Some were simply guilty of being 'weird.' The last woman put to death for witchcraft in England was a senile old lady. But a lot were, in fact, natural witches and sorcerers."

"If they had supernatural powers, why didn't they just get themselves out of the situation?"

"Plenty did. They weren't able to catch us all, not by a long shot. I suppose if they had, I would never have been born."

Our eyes met for a long moment.

"And anyway, you don't understand how it works," I continued. "We can't just point a wand and make things happen the way you see in the movies. It's much more complex than that."

"Lily—"

Saved by the bell. A young man at the counter called his name, and Max got up to retrieve our food order. I gathered napkins and forks and knives from the stand, two more kinds of salsa from the salsa bar, and we sorted out our order at the table. *Al pastor* and *chile verde* for him, *pollo asado* and *mole* for me. Salsa and guacamole for us both. We dug in.

After a few minutes of eating in companionable silence, Max started to stare at me. Stretching one long leg out in front of him, he reached deep into the front pocket of his jeans and extracted my medicine bag, closed tight, and placed it upon the table. It was butter-soft red leather, decorated with colorful beads I had stitched on as a girl. Inside the leather was a second bag, made of black silk. Inside that . . . was magic.

I wrapped my hand around it. It was warm from Max's skin, and I could sense its welcoming hum. I let out a contented sigh and smiled. It was like being reunited with a long-lost friend.

"Tell me about the bag."

"It's called a medicine bag, or a charm bag. It's consecrated, and imbued with protective powers."

"A bunch of stones, a feather, powder . . ."

"You *opened* it?"

"Of course."

Of course. What had I expected?

"Did anything spill?"

He shook his head. "I was careful. Tell me about the contents. Dirt? Magic stones?" He couldn't quite cover up his disdain.

I had no pockets, and I wanted the bag next to my body rather than in my backpack, so I tucked the bundle into my bra and purposely ignored his question, if not his tone.

"Do you carry a picture of a loved one in your wallet?" I asked.

His eyebrows shot up in question. "Sure. I've got one of my mother."

"Could I see it?"

Looking at me curiously, he pulled out his wallet, flipped it open, and handed it to me. The photo showed a woman in her sixties with a broad, open smile. I slipped the snapshot out of its plastic jacket and laid it on the table facing Max. Then I held out a sharp knife.

"Gouge out her eyes."

"What?"

"Go ahead. What harm could it do?"

"Give me a break," he scoffed, and tried to sound condescending, but he wasn't as casual as he'd hoped. The horrified expression on his handsome face gave him away.

"Why not?" I challenged. "It's just a piece of paper stained with chemicals."

"Put down the goddamned knife already."

"Then curse her name. They're just words, right? According to you, they don't mean anything."

"I get your point." He snatched the photo back and slipped it into his wallet, refusing to meet my eyes.

"Don't you see, Max? We all ascribe meaning to inanimate objects; that's what we do as human beings. It's a bit of magic. Witches just tend to ascribe more meaning, and in a more conscious way. And we learn to direct that meaning. It's all about focusing intentions."

"What I believe is that you've cast a spell over *me*. Talking to you, a person could almost start to believe in this nonsense."

From him, that was high praise indeed. I smiled and returned my attention to polishing off the rest of my tacos. I sneaked a peek or two over at Max, watching the way his jaw worked while he ate, and the movements of his throat when he threw his head back and drank from his bottle of beer.

Why did he appeal to me? For one thing, he was smart, and I was a sucker for smart. And the chemistry was impossible to deny. And he was . . . normal. What would it be like to be able to be friends, or even something more, with someone perfectly normal like him?

Romance, not to mention sex, was problematic for me. The potent associations of sex and witchcraft was one favorite subject for the authors of the *Malleus Maleficarum.* They considered women to be temptresses, luring men to their doom, as in so much of the world and throughout so much history. But it is true that there is power in the intense feelings associated with sex. That kind of emotion can strengthen a witch's abilities, and for someone like me, who was not always in command of her own talents, the loss of control the emotions stirred up could be . . . significant.

My first boyfriend in high school, who I thought was decent and brave until I realized he was showing off to win a bet, wound up with a minor head injury. Graciela had gotten me out of that predicament, but not without a lot of effort and a stern warning. Later, in Geneva, I met a psychic with some knowledge of and sensitivity to my world. He and I had a brief relationship until I realized I was with him primarily because he wasn't afraid of me, and he was with me because he hoped to glean some of my powers. Luckily I was mature enough at that point to break it off without causing him bodily harm.

But how could I have feelings for someone like Max,

a man who not only didn't believe in my world, but despised it? I could *force* him to care for me; love spells are simple enough, and can be very potent. I knew I had that kind of power. But I didn't want to do that. That always smacks of something sordid to me, the idea of making love to someone who wouldn't be interested in their right mind. I might as well go out and hire myself a gigolo.

"So back to my question about the police . . ." Max said, breaking into my thoughts.

"It's really none of your business."

"I'm making it my business."

I took a deep breath, felt my medicine bag for moral support, and shrugged. "The house we were at . . . I told you a friend of mine was killed there."

"Was she a close friend?"

"Not really, no. As a matter of fact, I'd only met her once . . . twice, sort of. Once, really. But I still feel responsible."

"How could you be responsible for her death?"

"Not responsible, exactly, just . . . It's hard to explain. I feel like I should have protected her."

"I have to say, Lily, you strike me as someone who takes a lot on yourself."

"Oh, I don't know about that."

"Here's a for-instance: You meet a total stranger, and don't want him going out on a boat for some secret reason of your own. So besides giving him what seems to be your own personal good-luck charm, you also make sure the boat never picks him up."

I smiled at him, despite myself.

"Seems like a lot to take on yourself, seeing as how we had just met."

"Speaking of the cops, what's the story with you and Romero?"

He shrugged and took a drink. "He doesn't much care for me."

"Any particular reason?"

"I investigated a story about police corruption. . . ."

"He's a bad cop?"

"No, quite the opposite. But police don't like outsiders nosing around, making accusations. It's a hard thing: Their job is tough, and their closeness is necessary to deal with what they have to. But when there's a problem they close ranks."

"I guess that makes sense."

"Plus, my wife . . ." His gray eyes met mine, filled with a restless, deep sadness. "Let's just say that the circumstances of her death were . . . unusual."

"Unusual?"

"Romero doesn't trust me; let's leave it at that. He's actually more your kind of guy."

"How so?"

"I think his aunt or someone is a witch. I forget exactly. It came up when I was doing the story. He asked me to keep it out of the article, and I agreed."

I nodded. Our eyes met longer than was strictly polite.

"I'd better get going," I said. "I have to get back to the store."

He looked at me a moment more before inclining his head. We cleaned our table, walked to the truck, and headed back across town. Evening had fallen and traffic was thick, people rushing out to happy hour and home to their families.

"You know, now that we've had our first date, it's all downhill from here," Max said as we neared the *Chronicle* building.

"Excuse me?"

"First dates are where you get all the awkward things out of the way. . . ."

"Like being investigated for homicide?"

"Oh, sure, and being a witch, that sort of thing."

"Yes, that can be awkward."

He gave me a crooked grin as we pulled up to the entrance to the parking garage. "Luckily I'm not easily daunted."

The light from the streetlamps highlighted the masculine planes of Max's face, and made his light eyes sparkle. But wasn't this the man who so recently stalked out of my apartment, unable to deal with the idea of something otherworldly? Accusing me of lying to him, and to myself? Suspicion settled upon my shoulders like a heavy shroud. Could he be after something? Was he doing some sort of investigation, looking for an angle on a story? What was with his sudden change of attitude?

"Thanks for dinner," I said as I opened the door and slid out of the cab.

"So, may I see you again? This time I'll take you someplace with table service."

"I . . . I'm sort of involved." With spirits and witches.

"Involved."

I nodded, hesitating to meet his eyes. I wasn't great at lying.

"Too bad," he said, the doubt clear in his voice. "My loss, then."

He waited until I was safely in my car before taking off.

It was almost six thirty before I pulled up to a parking spot just down the block from Aunt Cora's Closet, which meant we were closing in less than half an hour. It was a good thing for me that Bronwyn was so flexible, I thought to myself. She had offered to watch the shop again tomorrow while I went to Oakland for Frances's funeral. I was going to have to start giving her a bigger commission.

As I neared the shop I walked right past Conrad, who sat with his back against a lamppost.

"Hi, Conrad."

"Oh, hey." He got up and followed me.

"Did you need something?" I stopped and turned toward him.

"Um . . . it's kinda awkward. . . ." He rocked back and forth slightly on unsteady feet.

"Well, that does seem to be the word of the day. What's up?"

"This morning right after you went to the café, your neighbor came by and said she left something in your store."

"What neighbor?"

"The nervous one. She doesn't like me."

"Sandra?"

"Yeah! That's the one. Sandra. I tried to talk her into waiting for you, but she was pretty insistent. I just thought you should know. Hope I didn't do anything wrong."

"No, of course not. Do you know if she took anything?"

"A bunch of white stuff. Looked like clouds."

"White stuff?" I asked. "Like fabric? Could they have been wedding gowns?"

He waved an index finger at me. "You know, I think you're right on the money. More likely wedding dresses than clouds."

"Thanks, Conrad."

"Dude. Anytime. Night."

"Good night."

He veered off to Golden Gate Park for the night. I headed straight to Sandra's shop.

I couldn't quite figure out Sandra's involvement in this whole mess, but there were too many bizarre incidents lately. Her bringing out the *Malleus Maleficarum*. The feverish need to get her hands on the stone statue at the auction. Her insistence on seeing Frances's clothes, and what I had found out about her interest in the Potts house. And now Sandra had taken Frances's wedding gowns. Unless she was planning an emergency double wedding, I bet she was trying to use the dresses to conjure. I just couldn't figure out why.

The Open sign was up in the door of Peaceful Things, but there wasn't a soul in the place.

"Sandra? Hello, anybody here?"

No response.

I started walking toward the back. About halfway across the store I felt it: a wave of nausea and dread. A pungent, metallic smell. I took my medicine bag out and held it in front of me as I made my way slowly and carefully past innocuous racks of T-shirts and love beads. By the time I reached the back of the store and could look through the archway to the back room, I spied a corner of cloudy white.

One of the stolen wedding dresses.

Sandra was dressed in Frances's bridal silk. The *Malleus Maleficarum* was open on the floor by her side.

She was sprawled on her back on the floor, writhing.

Silent but clutching at her neck, she looked up at me with terrified eyes.

Chapter 16

Sandra was choking. Her breath whistled as she labored to breathe.

I lurched toward her. The power of the circle hit me; she had cast a spell, but it was weak and was already dispersing. I was able to cross the lines of salt.

I didn't think her choking was caused by natural forces, but just in case, I opened her mouth to look for obstructions, then pulled her up to me and performed the Heimlich maneuver. To no avail.

As I held her, I felt strong vibrations from the dress. There was a layer of false feeling on top; it had fooled me before, when I didn't see any reason to be suspicious. But now I felt the undercurrents: Frances had not passed on to the other side. Was she haunting us? I hadn't felt her presence. Could she be possessing Sandra?

No. Intruding spirits don't like to kill their host. On the other hand . . . asphyxiation was a famous witches' hex. The *Malleus Maleficarum* included a whole section on suffocation from afar.

I laid Sandra back down. She looked up at me with horror. I could hear the wheezing, which was good—it meant that she was still able to get some air into her lungs. But she was panicking.

"Listen to me, Sandra. You have to stay as calm as you can," I told her, gazing into her pale green eyes. "I'll call an ambulance."

I ran and used her shop phone to call 911, then Bronwyn, who was still at Aunt Cora's Closet. She raced over.

"Oh, my Goddess!" Bronwyn exclaimed as she fell to her knees in front of Sandra. "Sandra, sweetie, what's wrong?"

Oscar had been following at her heels, but hit the brakes as soon as he felt the tremors of malevolent witchcraft. He looked up at me, then turned tail and ran back out of the store.

I started rifling through nearby drawers, then moved on to chests and boxes and trunks.

"What in the world are you doing, Lily?" Bronwyn asked.

"Looking for something causing this. It's witchcraft—there has to be a hex doll somewhere."

Sandra's movements became frantic as she gestured to me. I leaned down to her, and she clutched at the front of my dress to bring me to her. I put my ear right near her mouth, trying to hear over the dreadful wheezing.

"Fran . . . ces . . ." she managed.

"Frances is involved? But she's—"

"Her . . . house . . ." She started gagging, then released my dress and fell limp against the floor.

Of course. The hex doll wasn't here in the shop. I was looking in the wrong place.

Just then I heard sirens in the distance.

Grabbing a pair of scissors from the desk, I knelt beside Sandra and snipped a lock of her hair. At first I avoided her eyes, the look of panic there. But I stopped myself, took her by the shoulders, and looked into her wide, fearful gaze.

"Sandra, listen to me. Try to be as calm as you can. I'm going to find what's doing this to you, and I'll stop it. Do you believe me?"

She nodded.

"Just hang in there; breathe slowly." I looked up at Bronwyn. "Help her to breathe in and out, really slowly, like the opposite of the Lamaze method. I have to go."

"Go? Where?"

"Just tell the authorities you dropped by and found her. Leave my name out of it if you can."

"What are you going to do?"

"I think she's suffering under a curse, Bronwyn. I have to find the object used to cast the spell. Try to keep her calm. The more frightened she gets, the more she panics, the faster she'll . . . It will be better if she can remain calm."

Evil witches liked to use the person's complicity in their own demise.

With one more squeeze of Sandra's hand, and a silent promise as I looked into her eyes, I ran.

I pulled up to the back of Frances's house with a screech of my tires. As usual the house stood silent, dark and foreboding against the evening sky. I ran up the back walk, pulled the gruesome Hand of Glory out of my backpack, and the back door unlocked before me. Inside the kitchen the hand made it as bright as day; unlike a flashlight, it left no dark corners, illuminating everything. As long as I repressed the knowledge of what, exactly, I was holding in my hand, this was a neat little tool.

I ran up the stairs and to the bedroom door at the end of the hall. No spirits pestered me, unlike last time I was here. Could it be the effect of the hand, or had things changed?

Crossing through the room, I opened the closet and pushed aside the clothes hanging on the bar. As before, there was a soft light emerging from under the door. I flung it open.

No one was there. Only burning candles and the same items on the altar as last time. But added to these was a carved wooden box. I opened it to find a crudely formed hex doll with green eyes, a black string twined around its wax neck.

Setting the Hand of Glory on the altar, I grabbed the hex doll, picked up the sacrificial knife, and used it to snip the string.

I could practically feel the doll take a deep breath, and I did the same. I stashed the poppet in my backpack, along with the lock of hair I had taken from Sandra. As a part of her, the hair would help me rid the doll of its association with Sandra, just in case it fell back into malicious hands. Closing my eyes, I sagged in relief.

The light changed. I opened my eyes to see that the Hand of Glory had opened, allowing its candle to fall to the floor. The altar candles were knocking over, one after another. Within seconds a stream of fire raced along the black cloth, consuming the fringe along the altar.

I felt heat behind me. Turning, I watched as a wall of flames engulfed the clothes in the outer closet.

Sheer terror.

I fell to the floor, gasping for air, clutching my medicine bag. There was no way out but through the flames. I started coughing, quickly losing any sense or sight in the smoke and heat. I had to go, now, despite the flames . . . or die where I was.

Suddenly I heard something above the crackle of the blaze. A spurting, spitting sound . . . Foam was being sprayed in the closet! A fire extinguisher!

My eyes burned from the smoke, and I couldn't stop coughing. A strong hand reached into the altar room and wrapped around my arm, pulling me through the smoking closet and out into the bedroom, which was now going up in flames itself, fire licking at the old-fashioned curtains, swallowing the paneling like so much dried kindling.

As we raced through the bedroom I looked over to the man running beside me. Intricate tattoos ran up strong arms, all the way to his neck: Tomás. My savior.

The wall of flame was following us, reaching out toward us like a living entity. Tomás grabbed my upper arm to urge me faster as we ran down the upstairs hall. At the top of the stairs we paused. There was fire at the bottom, marching up in our direction. I pulled Tomás toward the other end of the hall until we reached the double-hung window I had climbed through the other night. Shoving the sash high, I breathed in the blessedly smoke-free air as I swung my leg over the ledge, and began to climb down the trellis. Tomás followed right behind me.

The lattice began cracking under our combined weight before we were halfway down. It started to pull away from the house, and we fell with it, jumping the last ten feet and rolling on the soft garden dirt below.

Looking back at the burning building, we scrambled another length from the structure and then lay on the dry, crackly lawn, coughing and hacking from the effects of the smoke.

"Thanks," I choked out when I could finally speak. I sat up and watched as flames began to lick outside the bedroom window.

Tomás pulled out his cell phone and dialed 911.

As we both sat there, stunned, my eyes fell to the neatly planted garden right beside our resting place on the lawn. A dark green, leafy bush sat in the corner nearest us. In the evening air I could smell the delicate apple-like scent of its fruit, in stark contrast to the acrid stench of the fire.

The mandrake bush.

I glanced back at the growing inferno in front of us. I was up against a powerful entity. I couldn't do this alone. I was going to need Aidan's help.

The kitchen door was open, the room still free of the flames. Given the age of the building and the dryness of its timbers, I imagined it wouldn't last long. Most homes burned beyond help within ten minutes, long before emergency vehicles were able to arrive. It was now or never.

I got up and rushed back in through the kitchen door.

Yanking open the refrigerator, I found an old-fashioned glass bottle of milk. On the breadboard was a loaf that looked homemade, and next to it a saltshaker. Perfect. On the shelf, in front of the heart-shaped sachets, was a jar full of pennies. Everything I needed.

"What are you, crazy, lady?" Tomás called out from the doorway. I looked over at him. He had so much black soot covering his face he looked as if he were wearing a mask. If it weren't for the dire circumstances, it would have been comical. "You're *looting* the place? I'm not going in after you again, *¿me entiendes?*"

"I'm coming!" I yelled, then turned back to the shelf and grabbed one of the stitched sachets.

My arms full of my plunder, I ran back through the door and out to the lawn, where I set everything down.

"Do you have a knife on you?" I asked Tomás.

"*Eres más loca que una cabra*," he grumbled, shaking his head. Graciela used to use that expression on me, as well; loosely translated, it meant that I was crazier than a she-goat. I supposed he had cause. Nonetheless, he dug into a pocket and handed over a penknife. His dark gaze kept shifting over to the street and then back down at me, as though he wanted to flee but felt duty-bound to stay. "Are you sure you're all right? What the hell are you doing?"

"I just need to take some of the root of this plant." I started chanting softly to the bush. Its scent wafted up to me, clearing my nostrils of the caustic scent of burning, replacing it with the freshness of green growth. I spoke to the plant, telling it of my need, and my situation. I asked if there was a root that would like to come and be part of the walking world.

The mandrake scream was famous for killing or driving into madness those who would pull it from the ground willy-nilly. But there was no need for such dramatics when obtaining the root. The bush simply needed to be approached with the respect and compassion due any living object.

My recipe for the mandragora called for milk to be brewed with three drowned bats, but not only did I not have any more bats on hand, I loathed making life sacrifices unless absolutely necessary. The bat, the chicken, the goat . . . their sacrifice was sometimes needed as a blood payment. But I hated it. Luckily I had some pretty potent stuff running through my own veins.

I made a small X on my palm and let three drops fall into the bottle of milk. Then I poured the milk, laid the bread, salt, and money on the ground, sat back, and waited. A high-pitched shriek emitted very briefly. Though it hurt my ears, it was over as quickly as it had begun.

I located where the brief cry had come from, and started to dig, using a flat stone from the garden border. All the while I spoke to the plant and chanted. Very carefully digging around the root, I loosened the earth, then pulled very, very gingerly, extricating a single bifurcated root that looked almost like a little person already: arms and stubby head, his legs crossed bashfully. Finally, I placed the offerings of bread, money, and salt into the hole and carefully covered everything with earth.

I bathed the root in the remainder of the milk, dried him with the corner of my skirt, and wrapped him in the only cloth I had with me, the black silk bag that had held the Hand of Glory. Normally the mandragora should be put to bed immediately in his own special box, but the best I could do was to make him a little nest in the bottom of my backpack.

"*De puta madre*," Tomás swore, breaking my concentration. "This place is crawling with you *brujas*."

Brujas means witches.

I looked up to see fear in Tomás's eyes. I couldn't blame him. I must look insane, kneeling, muddy, and covered in black soot, pulling roots and burying things while an inferno raged not twenty feet away.

A distant siren grew nearer.

"I needed to take some cuttings from the garden."

"This is evil stuff here. Let it all burn."

"Did you set fire to the house?"

"*What?* You really *are* crazy. I just saved your life." He coughed, then swore again in Spanish.

"I'm sorry," I said in a rush. And I was. "I just . . . Thank you, Tomás. Thank you so much. You're my savior."

He grunted and looked out toward the road.

"What were you doing here?" I asked.

"I . . . I was looking for something to do with Jessica. I keep thinking, keep wondering whether the old lady had something to do with her disappearance."

"How?"

He shook his head. "I don't know. I don't even know what I was looking for, a doll maybe, something of hers. Whenever kids hang around here . . . pretty soon they end up gone. I *told* Jessica to stay away from here, but she liked the old lady."

That reminded me: the heart-shaped sachet. I used Tomás's knife to cut into it. Out fell twigs and dirt, bits of bone, and hair, all matted with what looked like dried blood. Not your average sachet stitched by a sweet little old lady.

Tomás was looking down, a horrified expression on his face. "What *is* that?"

"A sweetness charm. It's how she convinced people that she meant no harm."

"I knew it. 'Hansel and Gretel' is my nephew's favorite story."

"You're smarter than I am." I pulled the poppet of Sandra from my pocket. It would have to be disposed of properly. "Could I use your phone?"

He handed over his cell phone, and I talked to Bronwyn at the hospital. She told me that after first being intubated, Sandra had suddenly started breathing on her own. I sagged in relief. At least I had gotten one thing right . . . though if it hadn't been for Tomás, I may well have forfeited my life for the sake of finding the hex doll. It was a little overwhelming.

We had come a mite too close to a witch burning tonight.

As I stood at the door of Aunt Cora's Closet, dreaming of a shower and fumbling with my keys, someone tapped me on the shoulder from behind. I jumped about three feet in the air and twisted around. Hervé LaMansec.

"My Lord in *heaven*, you scared me!"

"Sorry about that. You don't have a cell phone, and I doubted you'd checked your e-mail." His ebony eyes looked me over. "Are you all right? You look a bit . . . worse for wear."

"I'll be fine if you tell me you know what's going on.

Someone I know was almost killed by witchcraft tonight. And I barely escaped dying in a fire myself."

"That might explain why I was sent. Mother Decotier says she must speak to you tonight. Apparently time is of the essence."

"What's going on?"

"That I don't know. But she's expecting you."

I looked down at myself. The whole way home, the bitter smell of soot had overwhelmed my senses.

"Is there time for a shower?"

Hervé shook his head. "She's more of a come-as-you-are spirit. Don't worry about it."

I wasn't so much worried about insulting Mother Decotier as I was hoping to get this stench off of me, but I conceded to Hervé's sense of urgency.

Hervé led me to a green Prius hybrid with a bumper full of progressive political stickers. For the first time this evening, I smiled. Trust San Francisco to produce a hybrid-driving leftist voodoo priest from L.A. He drove swiftly through the darkened streets, parking illegally in a truck loading zone on Bush Street. Then we walked to the corner of Octavia, where Mary Ellen Pleasant's grand mansion once stood. A simple bronze plaque and a few eucalyptus trees commemorated the spot. This was a busy residential corner during the day ... I doubted many people took notice of its historical significance. But then again, isn't that true in most living cities? Every corner contains its own story, its own fascinating tale, but we are rarely made aware of it.

Hervé and I waited.

And waited.

I wasn't the most patient witch in the world under the

best of circumstances, and right now I was weary to the bone, smelled like a fireplace, and had lost faith in my magical abilities. All I wanted to do was take a shower for as long as the hot water lasted, then hide under my bed with Oscar at my side and a bottle of Cuban rum in my hand.

I was about to give up when a crow landed in the tree, then another and another. It was disturbing to see diurnal birds out at night. I looked over at my escort.

Hervé's hands were held out and up in supplication. His eyes rolled back in his head as he began chanting so quietly I couldn't make out the words. I felt the tingle of energy starting at the base of my spine and working its way up.

And there before us, standing between the trees, was an apparition.

I was speechless. I've never seen anything more than the occasional flashing light or glowing orb. Never an actual "ghost" that looks like Hollywood's version, like a person made of mist and light. Could it be some sort of trick? I looked around us. Were there projectors somewhere? I had no idea why Hervé would go to that kind of trouble, but lately I was feeling as suspicious as Max the mythbuster.

"Lily Ivory," the apparition intoned. The voice was melodious, strong and deep. It reminded me of velvet. It made you want to wrap yourself up in it. There was no faking that kind of voice, much less its effects.

"Yes," I replied. "Thank you for seeing me, Mother Decotier."

"You have a question for me?"

"Why didn't my spell work to save Frances Potts?"

"Look to the living threads. Next question."

I looked at Hervé. He looked a little nervous, which made me doubly so.

"What are living threads?"

She rolled her eyes. *A ghost just rolled her eyes at me.* Just when you think you've seen everything. . . .

"*Next question.*"

Apparently this was a twenty-questions sort of deal. I thought for a long moment. Graciela used to tell me that asking the right questions was the surest path to knowledge. Too bad I hadn't thought this out beforehand.

"Did Frances make some sort of deal to get her daughter Elisabeth back from *La Llorona*?"

"Yes."

There was a surge of light. Mother Decotier's figure disappeared in the brightness for a moment, then emerged again. She was manifesting for me, I realized. It wasn't that my power was any stronger, but that she was allowing me to see her in corporeal form. She probably assumed it was comforting. It wasn't.

"Where is Elisabeth?"

"Look to the name."

"The name Elisabeth?"

"No."

"Katherine?"

"No."

"Is Katherine actually Elisabeth?"

"No."

I sighed in frustration. "Is it too late to get Jessica back from *La Llorona*?"

Another surge of light. "*No*. Not too late. You must act immediately. Look to the moon."

She was fading. I watched the light dim until there was nothing but the slightest wisp of mist.

"Wait!" I called. "Who harmed Sandra?"

"*Hush*," said Hervé in an urgent whisper. "She has said all that she has to say. You can't call her back."

"But—"

"I require payment," came the voice. The corporeal vision was gone, but the voice wrapped around me, ephemeral but real, like a cloud. "Do you know what it is?"

And suddenly I did. An image came to me of a figure in the wax museum. Not of Mother Decotier, but of Mary Ellen Pleasant, San Francisco's mother of civil rights.

I nodded. "I'll take care of it."

"Look to the moon."

And the presence was gone.

As Hervé and I walked back to his car, he looked over at me.

"See that you do."

"Do what?"

"See that you fulfill your end of the bargain. I love her, but believe me—you don't want to make the woman mad."

I nodded and we climbed into his car.

We were silent as we started the drive across town. Finally, I turned to him.

"Hervé, do you know what the heck she was talking about?"

"Apparently you do."

"Excuse me?"

"I know she's cryptic, but she gives you the information you need. You must know enough to put the puzzle together. That's the way she operates."

"Wouldn't it be easier if she just said what she meant? What's with the guessing game?"

He shrugged. "I imagine it must be something about speaking from the next dimension—you know how Ouija boards are mostly about asking yes and no questions?"

"I think she just enjoys screwing with people's minds," I grumbled.

Hervé laughed. "Perhaps it's supposed to develop one's character. In any case, you must know what it all means. I'm impressed with your knowing what the payment is that she requires. I didn't pick up on that one at all."

"She wants a wax sculpture of Mary Ellen Pleasant. That part I've got covered. And going after Jessica—looking to the moon—that must be tomorrow night. It's the night of the full moon. *La Llorona* should be out in full force."

I looked over at Hervé's dramatic profile.

"I'm not strong enough to go up against *La Llorona* alone," I said.

He pulled to a stop at a traffic light on Market Street. His eyes slid over to me, resting on mine for a moment. He shook his head.

"I can't."

"Can't, or won't?"

"It's not my battle, Lily. I'm sorry."

I blew out a breath. Was I scared to go it alone? Of course. But even if I accepted the idea that I might die in the pursuit, the true tragedy would be not to save Jessica in the process.

Sacrifice another. That's the only way. La única manera.

If I were a mother, I could sacrifice myself without a second thought. I imagined that if I were a mother, I might sacrifice anyone, *anything*, for my child.

As Frances had done. I wanted to condemn the woman out of hand, but a tiny part of my heart went out to her. She must have gone a little crazy trying to get her daughter Elisabeth back. Finally, out of desperation, she returned to her native New Orleans to study the voodoo of her youth, and had come back and set up an altar. . . . But the candles were burning two days after her death, so there must be someone else involved. Perhaps that someone was the person responsible for killing her, and for laying her out in the pentagram. And what were the "living threads" Decotier mentioned?

Decotier had given me a firm "no" to my suspicion that Katherine and Elisabeth were somehow one and the same, or that Elisabeth had possessed Katherine. Still, Aidan's book on demonology had pointed out that a child brought back after so much time would have returned with powers similar to those of a natural witch. She might seem perfectly normal until challenged, but she would be altered, a sociopath in psychological terms. Would she be capable of murdering her own mother, or would she think of *La Llorona* as her only mother now?

Sandra must have somehow stumbled onto all of this while harassing Frances about selling her house to the neighborhood committee. Had she found out something about Elisabeth? Was that why she was being strangled, to silence her?

We pulled up to Aunt Cora's Closet. I was disappointed that Hervé wouldn't help me. But I also understood. He already had a lot to deal with in his regular practice, and better him than me. I'd had all the dealings with voodoo I wanted. From here on in, it was straight witchcraft as I knew it.

"Thanks for your help, Hervé," I said as I opened the car door.

Hervé reached out and put a hand on my shoulder. It was warm and comforting.

"May the strength of the gods be with you, and the mantle of goodness protect you."

"Thanks. I'll take all the help I can get."

I climbed out, unlocked the door, and let myself into the shop, turning to wave at Hervé as he drove away. Locking the front door behind me, I hoped to feel the warm embrace of my environment. But the subtle vibrations of the clothing didn't comfort me much tonight. I felt frustrated and insecure. What good were my talents if I wasn't strong enough to save a child, or to understand what was being asked of me?

Oscar sat on the next-to-last step of the stairs in the back room, head in hand, glowering like a worried mother waiting for her daughter to return from the prom.

"*Where* have you *been*?" he demanded.

"It's been a busy night," I said.

"So busy you couldn't call?"

"Oscar, please."

"I was worried."

"I'll bet you were more hungry than worried."

"That, too." As if on cue, his little belly rumbled so loudly I could hear it across the room.

On the green linoleum table was an empty carton of Annie's Cheddar Bunnies crackers that I kept on hand as emergency snacks for hungry children, and several wrappings from the hard candy I keep in a basket near the front register.

Guilt washed over me. There weren't any leftovers in the fridge, and I hadn't spared a thought for Oscar's welfare. I wasn't used to having a pet, or anyone at all, dependent upon me.

"I'm sorry, Oscar. I apologize. I'm going to have to teach you to cook, little guy. Let's go upstairs and I'll fix you something—how does pasta sound?"

As I moved toward the stairs, I noticed a couple of strands of pale hair on the back of the velvet chair glinting subtly in the overhead light.

Hair. Like silky threads. *Look to the living threads.* Look to them for what? I used Frances's hair in the protection spell. . . . Or did I? I had assumed it was hers. Was I inadvertently protecting someone else?

Upstairs I fixed Oscar some pasta with marinara sauce before taking a long shower, scrubbing myself until I was pink and glowing. I washed my hair twice but it still smelled vaguely of pungent, acrid smoke. I was glad the damned place had gone up in flames, I thought to myself. Bitterness started to edge out the sympathy I felt for Frances as a mother. The apparition had confirmed that Frances made a deal with *La Llorona* to get Elisabeth back. Had she cast the power of her life force in with the demon? Had her maternal anguish led her to do the unthinkable, keeping the cycle of violence alive? Could she have led neighborhood children to their doom, essentially feeding them to *La Llorona*?

By the time I emerged from the bedroom Oscar was snoring on top of the refrigerator. I pulled his covers up around him, smiling to myself. He'd been with me only a few days, but already he had his routine, had made himself a place in my home . . . and in my soul.

My heart fluttered in my chest. I was going to go up against *La Llorona* tomorrow. I had no way of knowing the outcome. Provisions had to be made for Oscar, just in case. Bronwyn would love to take him, but he wouldn't be able to revert to his natural form around her. I wondered how difficult that would be for him. Perhaps he'd best go back to Aidan.

Which reminded me . . . I was going to need Aidan's help even to summon *La Llorona*, much less to fight her. I also needed for him to arrange for the addition to the Wax Museum. My original plan to steer clear of Aidan and local witchy politics now appeared naive, laughable. By virtue of the powers I was born with, I was involved, whether I wanted to be or not. *You can't run from yourself*, m'hija, Graciela used to tell me. But that was exactly what I had been trying to do for years now.

I was going to be in Aidan's debt, no matter how I looked at it. Best make sure he had his mandragora, at the very least. I reached into my backpack and pulled out the little wrapped root at the bottom of the satchel. I was out of my league with humans lately, but herbs and roots I could handle.

I unwrapped him very gently. My whole life I've had an affinity for plants. As a small child I had coaxed juicy tomatoes, plump chiles, and fragrant herbs from the unforgiving, hard-packed west Texas soil. Plants give us clean air and beauty and sustenance, and, perhaps most important, they represent eternal life. Even when they die they rise again. Their vibrations are green and bright. All as it was meant to be.

I brought out my Book of Shadows and opened it to the page for creating a mandragora. I read:

> Would you like to make a mandragora as powerful as the homunculus so praised by Paracelsus? Then find a root of the plant called mandrake. Take it out of the ground on a Monday (the day of the moon), a little time after the vernal equinox. Cut off the ends of the root and bury it at night in some country churchyard in a dead man's grave. For thirty days water it with cow's milk in which three bats have been drowned. When the thirty-first day arrives, take out the root in the middle of the night and dry it in an oven heated with branches of verbena. Then wrap it up in a piece of a dead man's winding-sheet and carry it with you everywhere.

One thing about spells: Sometimes they have to be modified. Like any recipe, you make substitutions. You don't have access to a dead man's winding-sheet, you might use some gauze blessed with juniper and rose of Jericho instead. My blood would do instead of drowning the bats, and rather than actually burying the little guy in a dead man's grave, all we needed was some freshly overturned cemetery dirt.

Luckily the mandrake root is not poisonous to handle, unlike wolfsbane, which is so toxic that even touching the plant can cause irritation. Still, mandrake is a member of the nightshade family, so its berries, especially, can be deadly. I'd best not leave any lying around, lest Oscar decide he needed a snack. Funny that Frances had both wolfsbane and mandrake growing in her garden. Thinking back on it, I had even noticed lethal mistletoe clinging to a few of her trees.

I spoke to the mandrake root as I handled him, then hummed a snippet of a long-ago lullaby while I carefully carved just a little here and there to free his arms and give him facial features. His legs were already fully formed. He would be a cute little imp. Finally, I brewed an appropriate milk bath with herbs, seeds, and several more drops of my blood, and bathed him carefully. I wrapped him in clean black silk, thanked him, and put him to bed in a little wooden cigar box.

Once again I wondered why Aidan wanted a mandragora. Was it for a client? Or could he have been telling the truth—could he be lonely? It was hard to believe, but then, I hadn't realized I was so lonesome until Oscar barged into my life.

I went to bed, fell right asleep, and dreamed of fire and Frances's deadly garden.

Chapter 17

"Mistress, quick! You have to come!" Oscar yelled, jumping on my bed at a little before eight in the morning.

Bleary, I rushed after him into the other room. He had opened the mandragora's cigar box and stood gaping at it.

"Why did you wake him, Oscar?"

"What is he?"

"He'll be a mandragora, but he's not finished yet."

"Why are you making *that*?" Oscar whined. "I don't like him."

"You don't know him. He's not even born."

"Yeah, but I know I don't like him."

"You sound jealous."

He shrugged and looked away, pouting. I tried not to laugh.

"Oscar, I'm not making him for myself. You're more than enough for me, I promise you."

He looked up at me.

"Really?"

"Really. It's actually for Aidan."

"What for?"

"Good question. Maybe you could ask him next time you talk to him."

He stared at me for a moment.

"What's for breakfast?"

I whipped up some biscuits, which we ate with strawberry jam. Presuming I survived the day—or, more specifically, the night—I would have to start shopping more regularly, keep food on hand. Not only for Oscar, but for friends dropping by. I'd had only wine to offer Maya and Bronwyn the other day. People who had friends over offered things like cheese and crackers, right? It was the neighborly thing to do.

I felt a stab of fear, and dread, and yearning. I was finally starting to fit in here in this crazy San Francisco neighborhood, making friends, creating a sort of family. Suddenly I wanted to meet Bronwyn's coven, to celebrate the good, the strength and kindness of the Goddess and sisterhood. As a natural witch I couldn't really cry, but that didn't keep tears from stinging the back of my eyes. What would happen tonight, when the sun went down? How could I possibly be strong enough? Would Aidan Rhodes's help be sufficient to vanquish *La Llorona*, presuming he agreed to assist me? And if so, what would he demand in return? At the very least, I needed to tell him his mandragora was in the process of being born.

Speaking of which . . . I needed dirt from a fresh grave. It occurred to me that I hadn't noticed any graveyards since I had moved to the City by the Bay.

"Are there any cemeteries in San Francisco?" I asked Oscar.

Oscar shook his head. "All the active ones were moved out to Colma and Oakland to make room for living people. Now there's only the military cemetery out at the Presidio, and a little historic one at Mission Dolores."

"I guess it's lucky I'm headed to a funeral in Oakland this very afternoon," I thought out loud to myself.

"Why do the Catholics name their places after sorrow and pain?" Oscar asked as he followed me down the stairs to the shop.

"What?"

"Mission Dolores. It means 'Mission of Pain,' right? And there's a church called Our Lady of Perpetual Sorrow. It's kind of a downer."

I smiled. "I guess I never thought of it that way. But it's important to remember the supreme sacrifice. I think that's what it refers to."

"It's still kind of a downer. What time do we go to the funeral?"

"I'm sorry, Oscar, you can't come today."

"But I *love* cemeteries!"

"It's a solemn event."

"How come *he* gets to go?" Oscar gestured to the mandragora-to-be, which I carried in its box, under my arm.

"He has to stay with me until he's buried. Besides, he's not even alive yet. He sits quietly in his box."

"*I'll* sit quietly."

"Oscar, how am I supposed to explain bringing my potbellied pig to a funeral?"

He sat back on his haunches, his glass-green eyes huge, hurt, and filling with tears.

"Look, it's nothing personal, it's just . . ." His jowls began to tremble. I knew I was being manipulated, but my heart couldn't take it. I relented. "All right. But you'll have to stay in the car."

"Thank you, mistress! What time?"

"I'll open the shop and then Bronwyn's coming in early. We'll leave in about an hour." I consulted my cuckoo clock. "I have to talk to Aidan today after the funeral. Do you know if there's any way I can get in touch without going all the way downtown to his office?"

"I can get word to him."

"You can? How?"

"Er . . . I'll just, sort of, like, use telepathy."

"You have telepathic powers?"

"Hmm?" Oscar suddenly found his toenails very interesting.

"Why do I get the feeling you're not telling me something?"

"Are there any more biscuits, mistress?"

First things first. Before opening the store, I wanted to check in on Sandra Schmidt. I dressed in a simple early-1960s skirt and sweater and drove to San Francisco General.

When I arrived on the third floor I found Inspectors Romero and Nordstrom were in the room, talking with Sandra. My first impulse was to run away, but I squelched it. While I waited for the police to finish up their questioning, I asked a nurse for Sandra's prognosis. The nurse hesitated, but after I told her Sandra was my sister she informed me the doctors were running some tests to try to figure out what had happened, but the outcome looked good, no lasting effects. I sagged in relief.

The SFPD inspectors came out of Sandra's room. Romero's dark eyes looked me over and he nodded in greeting.

"Fancy meeting you here," he said.

"Hello, Inspector Romero, Inspector Nordstrom. How's Sandra doing?"

"Better now. She says you saved her life."

"I . . . uh . . ." Had Sandra told him about my going to Frances's house to find the poppet? Did they now suspect me of arson on top of everything else?

"She says you found her and called an ambulance."

"Oh! Right. I guess I was in the right place at the right time." Something occurred to me. "But why are you here? I thought you were homicide?"

"Sandra was able to tell us a few things pertinent to the Frances Potts case."

Best to deal with this up front.

"Look, Inspector, I know the whole inheritance thing looks bad, but I think you should know I'm renouncing it. I don't want it."

"Inheritance?" Romero glanced over at Nordstrom, who shrugged.

"From Frances Potts."

Still no recognition.

"Her lawyer came to see me and told me Mrs. Potts rewrote her will the night she died. I assumed you knew." By the look of surprise on both the inspectors' faces, I now guessed not.

"It just happened. You probably haven't heard yet." I felt kind of bad for them. It must be a professional slap in the face to have your murder suspect feeding you important pieces of evidence. "You would have turned it up soon enough, I'm sure. The pertinent point here is that I'm renouncing the inheritance, so it's not a real motive, per se."

Romero shook his head and blew out a breath. "Relax. The death has been ruled a suicide."

"Frances killed herself?"

He nodded. "She used some poisonous plants she was growing in the garden. Seemed to know what she was doing, according to the toxicologist. But it was clear from the evidence that she processed the stuff herself, and then prepared the meal. Her lawyer was sickened as well."

"But she seemed all right when I saw her that night . . ." I protested, thinking back on the last time I had seen Frances. She had been moaning slightly, and holding her arms over her stomach. But I had no idea she had been dying, slain by her own hand.

"Like I said, the toxicologist said she seemed to know what she was doing, and came up with a slow-acting cocktail of poisons, which she used to spike the meat."

"Oh."

"We're less clear on who laid her out in the pentagram, and why. I don't suppose anything's occurred to you . . . ?"

I shook my head.

"Miss?" I looked up to see the nurse I had spoken to earlier. "If you want some time with your sister, you should see her now, before the doctors come by on their rounds."

"Thank you," I said. She hurried off.

"Your sister?" Romero queried.

"I asked her about Sandra's prognosis. If you don't say you're a relative, they won't tell you anything."

"It makes me nervous that you lie so easily."

"I don't actually. I'm terrible at lying about anything important. It makes me sick to my stomach."

He chuckled. "Well then, best to tell the truth, I guess. Talk to you soon, Ms. Ivory."

"Inspector Romero . . ."

He turned back to me.

"Never mind. Bye." It had been on the tip of my tongue to ask him about the process tonight. Presuming we found Jessica, did we bring her to the police or straight to her family? For that matter, how would we explain her rescue? But like my mother used to say, *Don't borrow trouble*. We would figure that part out when, and if, I had the little girl safe in my arms.

"Lily? Is that you?"

I went into the room. Sandra was sitting up in bed, her gaze darting around as usual, like a nervous bird. It was good to see her back to her old self.

"I tried to stop Frances," she said in a fierce whisper. "I think she was an evil witch."

"She wasn't a witch, exactly . . ." I began, though Sandra wasn't listening.

"Those poor kids. Even after Frances died, they still weren't safe. None of us are safe. . . . I figured it out as I got to know her, spent time in that house. I found some of her witch's paraphernalia. Then I read the *Malleus Maleficarum*. I've been studying, you know. I thought I could stop her myself with the help of that sculpture from the auction, and then the dresses."

"That was brave of you, Sandra. She was very powerful."

"She asked me about you, you know. But her daughter Elisabeth—she's the one who did this—tried to shut me up." Her voice dropped and she leaned toward me. "I think she still lives."

A chill coursed through me, running up my extremities and settling in my core. My mind flitted back to the invisible presence that challenged me while I cast my useless spell of protection over Frances. I was almost sure now it had been Elisabeth herself.

"Sandra, who is she? Do you know who Elisabeth has become?"

She shook her head. "But I know what she isn't. She isn't human."

An hour later I had opened the shop, turned it over to Bronwyn's care, and headed to Frances's funeral. Maya was conducting an interview in Piedmont in the morning and said she'd meet us at the cemetery, so I drove over alone with Oscar. I made it across the Bay Bridge with no problem, but then I started to get nervous—each time I exit the freeway in Oakland, I get lost. Apparently they don't have much of a budget for street signs. Though Oakland is a smaller city than San Francisco, population-wise, it covers a vast amount of acreage. There are plenty of beautiful, historic, and quaint neighborhoods of Oakland, but I had wandered around the sordid underbelly enough to know that there are sections where it is best not to leave the freeway. Particularly in a bright red vintage Mustang convertible.

Today was no exception. I clamped down on my frustration and tried to reframe the whole thing as an educational experience: For instance, I learned that goblins can't read road maps. Oscar tried his best, I'll give him that, but he wound up wrapping himself up in the unfolded map and screeching. By the time we circled downtown for the third time the map was a torn, wadded-up ball on the floor of the Mustang.

We wandered past humble apartment buildings and elegant mansions, skirted the charming Lake Merritt, and finally pulled over in Chinatown at a little factory store that advertised custom-made fortune cookies. I had a pleasant chat with a kind man of very limited English skills who showed me the way to the cemetery on a map pinned to the wall, handed me a brochure, and gave me a small sample sack of adult-themed fortune cookies just for stopping by.

Back in the car Oscar nabbed the cookies and crunched loudly, reading me a few choice fortunes as I turned around and headed northeast on Broadway. I turned right at Pleasant Valley and then hung a left onto Piedmont Avenue. At long last I spotted the formal wrought-iron gates of Mountain View Cemetery straight ahead.

Some of the fortunes Oscar was reading were pretty funny, but it felt somehow unseemly to be hearing dirty jokes from a goblin as we drove through a cemetery. I told him to transform into his piggy mode—that way no one would see his natural appearance, and I was spared his running commentary. Pigs can't talk.

The main cemetery drive was newly paved, almost stark, and wound in a circle around a simple, gushing fountain. But in contrast to the newness of the pavement, the historic roots of the park were evident in the gothic revivalist architecture of the main buildings and the fascinating, lichen-encrusted hodgepodge of headstones, markers, and crypts. To the left I noticed a large plot of land with all the markers huddled to one side, and a new irrigation pipe running across the recently turned earth. I considered stopping to gather some dirt for my mandragora, but then realized this was a very old plot. It would be better to find fresher dirt. Each monument was tagged with blue tape indicating a number, and I found myself hoping they had a workable system. I couldn't even keep my invoices straight at the store. If it were up to me, I would mix things up and wind up returning half the headstones to the wrong graves.

Mountain View had clearly been the place to be buried back in the day. Elaborate crypts marched up the hill and looked out over a multimillion-dollar view of Oakland, the bay, and San Francisco beyond. Adorning these were ornate carved marble and granite sculptures, bronze plaques, stained-glass windows, and colorful mosaics. The grounds were landscaped in a crazy medley that reminded me of California itself: Towering palm trees stood shoulder-to-shoulder with grand redwoods, magnolias edged out pines and oak, and wisteria fought with English ivy.

I like cemeteries. The vibrations of grief can be overwhelming at the new burial sites, but otherwise there is a calm solemnity and acceptance tinged with sadness that can be strangely comforting. Yes, it is sad when people pass on. Their loved ones mourn them. But mourning indicates that there was once love, and that's a good thing.

The last time I was in a cemetery was in rural France. I remembered watching the black-clad old women tending their family graves and wondering, Would anyone mourn me when I was gone? My mother, perhaps, and certainly my grandmother, but few else. I realized in that moment that I wanted to find a community, make a home, create a web of friends . . . and perhaps even start a family. It was this revelation that led me to settle down in the Bay Area. That and a crazy parrot in Hong Kong, what felt like a lifetime ago.

I kept driving until I found Frances's final resting spot. My unscheduled tour of downtown Oakland had made me fifteen minutes late, but it looked as though the minister was just beginning. A dozen folding chairs had been set out, but the few mourners present stood beside a single stand of flowers. Maya and Delores were standing next to each other, holding hands. I recognized a couple of faces from Frances's neighborhood. But the biggest surprise was seeing Tomás on the other side of the grave. I crossed over to him.

"I'm surprised to see you here," I whispered.

"My family's at the cemetery to tend my cousin Juan's grave. That's what we do on the weekends. I saw the old lady was being buried, so I thought I'd come watch."

"I wanted to thank you again for saving me the other night."

He looked down at me, bitterness in his eyes. "No offense, lady, but I don't got no business with *brujas*, good or bad. I'm only here 'cause I wanted to see this one go in the ground."

What could I say to that?

As the preacher droned on, I looked out over the hillside. This was a new section of the graveyard; here the headstones were flat rectangles of granite on the ground, horizontal rather than vertical. I supposed the riding lawn mowers could go right over the top of them, so they made sense for maintenance, but like so many modern concessions to convenience they lacked the drama and dignity of the historic stones.

My gaze landed on a figure dressed in white standing a good forty feet away amidst a small copse of eucalyptus trees. Katherine. As I watched, it seemed as though she was rhythmically rocking.... Was she mumbling something? An incantation? She had her big black Lab with her—he was sitting obediently at her feet. Could that dog be her familiar?

The preacher wound up his talk, and Katherine turned to leave. I trotted up beside her before she could run away.

"Katherine," I called. "Wait, are you all right?"

"Of course," she said, hiding her hands behind her back.

I looked at her for a long moment. If I could trust my instincts—which were in question lately, what with sweetness charms and false assumptions—what I sensed from Frances's daughter was fear and sadness, not evil.

"What do you have in your hands, Katherine? What are you hiding?" I held my hand out, palm up, as though I were a schoolmarm demanding a student turn over her gum.

To my surprise, Katherine complied. She brought her hands out from behind her back and placed a chain made of black beads and a cross in my hand. It was a beautiful carved-wood rosary.

"You were praying?"

Katherine nodded. She hadn't been casting a spell; she was reciting the rosary.

"I have to tell you—" Katherine began.

"Katherine!" yelled the young man we had met at her house. He stood some twenty feet away, beside a sleek champagne-colored Jaguar. Katherine looked over at him briefly, then back down to me.

"I see you burned the house. Thank you for that."

"I didn't—"

"My sister . . ." She grabbed my hands. Her own were icy. "She's not dead."

I nodded. "I know. Do you know what happened to her?"

"She's not . . . human."

"I understand, but, Katherine, where is she?"

She began to say something, then swallowed the words. She was scared to death. She looked over to the car again, then back to the grave of her mother.

She shook her head. "I don't know. I have to go."

"Listen, Katherine. You should know . . . what your mother did, how she sent you away, how she never saw your children—she was trying to protect you."

She nodded, and the flatness of her countenance began to dissolve. A palpable wave of sadness enveloped her. She started to cry, and hugged me, taking me by surprise. Not knowing quite what to do in return, I hugged her back. I awkwardly patted her carefully coiffed blond hair, trying not to muss it.

The young man came up to us, nodded at me, wrapped his arm around her, and led her back to the luxury car. They drove slowly off down the twisting drive.

I condoled for a few minutes with Delores and Maya and thanked the minister for his service, and then trudged back over to my Mustang, emotionally spent. Oscar jumped back and forth over the seat, wanting to get out, having conveniently forgotten his solemn promise to be still and silent. I finally relented and drove to an older section of the cemetery, where I noticed a few people walking their dogs.

"What is *that*?" Oscar demanded, looking aghast at the collar and leash I brought out of my bag.

"Dogs have to be on leashes. I assume the same rules apply to potbellied pigs."

"You have *got* to be kidding me!" He cowered in the footwell of the passenger's seat.

"Come on, Oscar, I don't have a lot of patience right now. This is the deal; take it or leave it."

Fuming, he transformed into his pig guise and allowed me to put the collar on, but he wouldn't look me in the eye.

It was a great afternoon for a walk, and I savored the sunny, cool day as we strolled through old-fashioned plots proudly labeled with their family names: Pridham, Downey, Coop, Dixon. I liked to read the names off the stones and try to piece together the relations. Here lay the Marsh family, mother Abbie and father John, their daughter Alice and her husband, Cyrus, a baby named

Gracie who had passed away too young. Such a beautiful monument to a loving family.

On the other hand, I passed an obelisk that read merely: *My husband died. May 18, 1881.* Short and to the point. Still, she had a husband. I had no one. Except for an ugly goblin who, I was sure, had been sent as a spy for reasons I still did not understand.

Said goblin was chafing at his collar, pulling hard on the lead.

"Oscar, stop it!" I pulled back.

Oscar changed into his natural form, snapping the collar. He glared at me with his knobby arms crossed over his chest. Worried someone would see him, I looked around, but there wasn't a soul in sight. I had to hand it to Oscar: So far he had been pretty safe about changing whenever normal humans were around.

"*That* is the most humiliating thing anyone's ever done to me."

"Don't be such a drama queen."

He sniffed and held up his chin, refusing to meet my eyes. I took another look around and sighed.

"Okay, go off and play for a few minutes. But be careful."

He loped off through the monuments.

I had my own surreptitious activity I needed to pursue. I went back to the car and grabbed a small garden spade and a plastic container, then crossed over to a recent burial by the cyclone fence in an inconspicuous spot beneath a tree. I filled my container with fresh dirt from the grave. I would take it back with me and use it to bury the mandragora in my rooftop garden.

Looking through the cyclone fence, I spied several

members of Jessica's family gathered around what must have been Juan's grave. In true Mexican style, they had brought a picnic blanket and food; several children ran about, laughing. Felipa and a younger woman were digging bright orange and yellow marigolds into the border. Funny how differently we all mourn our loved ones.

If all went well tonight, I thought while I caressed my medicine bag, Jessica's family would be celebrating reunion in a few short hours. If all went well, they would no longer mourn her—they would have their precious little girl back in their arms. It would be worth the sacrifice.

A groundskeeper in green coveralls strolled by with a shovel and a hoe resting on his shoulder. He nodded and wished me a good afternoon. I tucked the container full of dirt behind my back along with the leash and returned his smile. Then I realized I couldn't see Oscar anywhere.

"Oscar?" I called in a loud whisper, not wanting the personnel to think there was a dog loose.

I looked behind headstones and in crypts, until finally spotting him perched on top of a moss-encrusted mausoleum, crouched and looking down with a sinister scowl upon passersby, just like a real stone gargoyle.

"Come on down from there, Oscar. That's not funny."

"Didja see that? That gardener didn't even *see* me!"

"Okay, you fit right in at the cemetery. You make a great gargoyle. Is that what you want me to say?" My eyes wandered to two elderly women standing at a serviceman's grave, placing a wreath of flowers and an American flag upon it. "Come on down now, Oscar; this isn't a place for joking around."

"Why not?" Oscar asked me as he obeyed, easily scaling the side of the crypt. "Why *do* cowans take it all so seriously? They're so solemn about it. Don't they know there's nothing to fear?"

Don't we, indeed?

Chapter 18

Half an hour later I was back at work, slowly making my way through yesterday's invoices, when I looked up to see Aidan swinging through the door of Aunt Cora's Closet with aplomb.

As before, the bell failed to tinkle. But this time Aidan stopped, looked up at it until it rang, then turned back to me and grinned with an aw-shucks duck of his blond head.

"Lily, I'm so glad you called. I've been thinking about you."

I didn't call. I didn't even know his phone number.

Oscar ran around his legs, overly eager to be appreciated.

Maya and Bronwyn were sorting through a recently acquired bag of clothes, doing a terrible job of pretending not to overhear.

"Hi, Aidan. These are my friends Bronwyn and Maya."

"So good to meet you both," he said, taking their

hand in his, each in turn, and presenting them with a smile. They appeared speechless.

"Bronwyn, would you mind taking the store for a few minutes?" I asked.

"You two go on and have fun. Don't worry about a thing; I'll take care of the shop."

"I'll only be a few minutes. . . ."

"Why don't you take your time?" Bronwyn urged, eager as a mother in pursuit of a bride-price.

"Perfect," said Aidan just as I opened my mouth to protest. "You can buy me that drink you owe me."

"It's only three o'clock."

"Is it?" He glanced down at a sleek silver watch. "I suppose you're right; it does seem a bit early to start in. A coffee, then."

We walked out into a clear, warm day. The streets, as usual, were filled to overflowing with tourists, street kids, aging hippies, and the newest wave of yuppies in search of tasty caffeine and microbrews. Seeing them today didn't bring me the usual delight; I was having a hard time thinking about anything besides tonight.

"I didn't call," I pointed out.

"But you wanted to see me, am I right?"

"Do you really want coffee, or could we take a little walk? I'm in need of some fresh air."

He inclined his head. "Lady's choice."

Haight Street is bordered by residential areas full of Victorian duplexes with tiny yards. I steered Aidan the few blocks toward Golden Gate Park. As we were walking by one home, we saw a middle-aged couple awkwardly lugging a bunch of protest signs down a broad wooden set of steps. They sported the pale, gaunt visages of strict vegans; their clothes were baggy and made of natural hemp. They both smiled hugely when they saw us.

Aidan sprang up the steps to help them with their signs, loading them into an old yellow and white VW bus. He held one up for me to read.

"'Make love. Not war,'" he read aloud before placing it on the pile. "Have truer words ever been written?"

The woman, emboldened by Aidan's enthusiasm, reached into the cab of the VW and brought out several pamphlets and photocopies on purple paper. I've noticed that a lot of activists have yet to internalize the "save a tree" mentality—they always seem to abound with flyers.

After politely refusing their offer of a soy chai latte, Aidan came back to my side and handed me one of the anti-nuke flyers.

"Are you trying to prove you're a nice guy?" I asked.

"I *am* a nice guy. I swear . . . the way you treat me simply because I'm a witch—"

"That's not the reason."

"Oh, yes, it is. You might want to examine this tendency . . . what with you being a witch yourself and all. Just a suggestion." Aidan continued to hand out the pamphlets to passersby.

"Have you been watching Dr. Phil, by any chance?"

"Don't be dissing Dr. Phil. The man's a genius. Speaking of geniuses, when's the last time you saw your father?"

"Let's leave him out of this."

My only childhood memory of my father was from when I was very young, so young that no one thought I remembered. But I did.

He was a handsome man, with dark hair and eyes like mine. He was leaving us, arguing with my mother about wanting to take me with him, to raise me—and train me—himself. At the last moment Graciela, who had raised my father when his own parents were killed, intervened. I remembered things flying about the living room, the whole place being torn apart. I had watched from my playpen, laughing. When it was over, Graciela picked me up and told me not to laugh, that it wasn't funny. My mother certainly took that advice to heart—I don't know that she ever laughed again.

As an adult, I had met my father only once face-to-face. It was not a happy reunion.

Aidan and I walked through a small tunnel beneath the Alvord Lake Bridge, and up the walking paths leading north just inside Golden Gate Park. Known as Hippie Hill, the grassy, southern-facing slope near the Haight entrance to the park always featured an interesting assortment of people. A drum circle played, a magician was holding several small children in his thrall, a number of young men played hacky sack, and here and there couples ate picnics and napped in the sunshine.

"I need to ask you for a favor," I said.

"*Another* favor?"

"This one's easy. I think. Do you know who Mary Ellen Pleasant is?"

"Sure. The mother of civil rights in San Francisco."

"If she's so important, why don't you have a sculpture of her at the Wax Museum?"

"I don't own the place, Lily. I just have my office there."

"Oh." I watched the magician make a boy's athletic

shoe disappear before I turned back to Aidan. "*Why* do you have your office there?"

"The guy owed me for a thing."

"Does he still owe you?"

"As in, enough to create a sculpture of Mary Ellen Pleasant?"

I nodded. He looked at me curiously for a long moment before inclining his head.

"I can get it done."

"Thank you. I want you to know I've started on your mandragora."

"Really? That's fabulous!"

"It will take thirty days before he's born."

He nodded. "Whatever's necessary. I've been making inquiries into Frances Potts's death. She was killed by slow-acting poison, and placed in the pentagram only after death, when someone tried to use her body as a sacrifice. But as you know, it was too late, since she was already dead."

"I know."

"How do you know?"

"Talked to the police inspector earlier today. It was ruled a suicide."

"Ah. Well, then, about *La Llorona* . . ."

"What is it?"

"She's here, out on the bay. . . ."

"I knew that much."

"You're very impatient, you know that? You should slow down, learn to enjoy yourself a little."

I bit the inside of my cheek, trying to control my frustration. It wouldn't do to lose my temper in front of this male witch.

"You have to stop this crazy quest against *La Llorona*, Lily," he said, suddenly serious. "I was able to make contact with her. She knew you were here, even from before."

I remembered the articles about me on the altar. Apparently Frances had known about my past as well. I guess I really did have a reputation.

"Interestingly, she's afraid of you. She wanted to appease you with the inheritance."

"That was supposed to appease me?"

He shrugged. "The point is, you're not strong enough to go up against her."

"I have to talk with her. I want to offer her a deal."

"*La Llorona* is not what you'd call a pillar of reason."

"I know that. That brings me to my next question: Are you willing to combine forces against her?"

He held my eyes for a very long time.

"I thought you didn't want to be beholden to me."

"I'm making you a mandragora."

He laughed. "A mandragora in exchange for all this? Hardly seems fair."

"What else do you want?"

He stopped walking and turned toward me. Holding my gaze for a long time, he took a deep breath and looked back out over the trees.

"You'll owe me. Big-time. Let's leave it at that for now. But you need to understand that *La Llorona* is more powerful than she used to be. It took some serious work just to summon her."

I nodded. "Frances Potts fooled me—and many others—with a sweetness charm. She was actually working with *La Llorona*."

"Why would she do that?"

"To get her own child back. Elisabeth was snatched thirty-five years ago."

"Ah. That makes sense, then. She threw her soul's power toward *La Llorona* when she died. That explains the demon's recent surge in power."

"Tonight's the full moon. I have to act now before it's too late. I want to get Jessica back, and I want to send that you-know-what back to where she came from."

"So she can terrorize others?"

"At least most folks along the Rio Grande know what they're up against. With San Franciscans . . . they're like lambs to the slaughter."

"I suppose you're right about that."

"And I need a couple of other things from you."

He looked down at me, amusement clear in his bright blue eyes. "Oh, sure, why stop now?"

I handed him a scrap of paper with a name on it. "Would you be sure this person comes tonight? Just before three a.m., at India Basin park."

He looked down at it, then back to me, and nodded.

"I'm not sure how things will play out tonight," I continued. "Your mandragora will be buried beneath the potted lemon tree on my terrace. Thirty days—this is very important. If you take him out too early, he'll fail to thrive. If you leave him there beyond that, he'll suffocate. And when you unearth him he needs to be warmed in an oven with lemon verbena. I'll write it all down."

"Why won't you be doing it?"

"I'm just saying . . ."

"Saying what?"

"Nothing. Just in case. Also, promise me you'll take Oscar back with you and take care of him, unless he wants to stay with my friend Bronwyn. I know I didn't want him at first, but he's been a really good guy."

"Lily, you're talking like you're about to move on to the next dimension."

"I want Jessica back, Aidan."

"What is she to you?"

"An innocent. And I want to banish *La Llorona* while I'm at it. I'm willing to do what it takes."

He sighed and looked at me for a long time. Gone was the slight mocking tone, the aw-shucks charm. Finally he took a deep breath and looked around at the trees and greenery of the park. Then he rubbed his hand over his cheek, as though assessing his whiskers.

"Well, Lily. You know as well as I do what you're inviting with that kind of attitude. I guess we'll just have to see that it doesn't come to that. I have to tell you, though, I feel like I'm being manipulated into helping you."

"It's not that at all, Aidan. I don't even know whether you *can* help me. Maybe this is my fate. Things do seem to be lining up that way."

"I don't believe that. I think for some reason you've talked yourself into this, as though you have to sacrifice yourself to prove something to somebody. Perhaps to yourself."

"Okay, I think we're going a little overboard on Dr. Phil at this point."

"I'm quite serious, Lily."

"I don't need your psychoanalysis, Aidan, just your powers. Will you be there tonight? Call her and hold her for me?"

He gave me a curt nod, then walked me back to the shop in silence.

Bronwyn and Maya held their tongues for all of thirty seconds after Aidan left.

"Who in the world was *that*?"

"Trouble," I said.

"Sexy trouble," said Maya, as she and Bronwyn shared a smile.

There were no customers in the store. I looked at my friends and knew I needed all the help I could get tonight. I flipped the sign on the door to CLOSED.

"Bronwyn, I have a proposition for you. I need your coven."

"You want to join the coven? That's wonderful news, Lily!"

"Actually, I'm asking more than that. Much more. I . . . I'm terrified I may be putting them in danger, but I need to piggyback on their power to go up against something very evil."

To my utter relief and undying gratitude, Bronwyn just nodded and waited for me to elucidate.

"Have you ever heard of a demon called *La Llorona*?"

"It's a Mexican folktale, right?"

"It's not just Mexican . . . more important, it's not just a folktale. *La Llorona* is here in San Francisco. She's been haunting the Hunters Point neighborhood."

"I even have a few stories from the seniors about her," Maya interjected. "I thought she was just an urban legend."

"I'm afraid not."

"That's pretty hard to believe," Bronwyn said. "I always imagined her out in the countryside somewhere. . . ."

"I guess she goes where she wants. There was a crime, many years ago, that might have attracted her. But I know she still haunts the Rio Grande, and others have reported her as far away as Peru and Montana," I said. "But I want to banish her from here, at least."

"That sounds . . . difficult. Dangerous," said Bronwyn.

That was an understatement.

"There's more," I said. "The most important part. She has the little girl, Jessica."

"Jessica?" Maya asked. I nodded.

"Together there's a chance we could get her back. It has to be tonight, with the full moon."

"There might be a problem if you need a full coven. . . ." Bronwyn trailed off. "I don't know if everyone will come. We might need extras."

We both looked at Maya.

"It could be dangerous," I said. "I think you'll all be safe—I'll do everything I can to make sure you are—but you have to know that it could be very dangerous. But the more women there are, the safer for everyone. Still, I wouldn't ask it of you, any of you, if I could think of any other way."

"I'll be there if it will help," Maya said. I could tell she didn't quite believe, but I had the sense that she would see enough tonight to make her a convert.

"I'll talk to the coven members," Bronwyn assured me. "They'll only come if they understand the danger."

"Also, could you ask Charles Gosnold to bring his boat to the India Basin dock, and keep it on standby?

We might need it. The plan is that we'll meet at India Basin Shoreline Park at two a.m."

"Not midnight?"

"*La Llorona* will be strongest, and therefore most present, at three a.m. It's the time between. We'll want to set up the altar and be in place ahead of time, and the circle must be cast by three o'clock. Any women attending should bring their talismans, any symbols of their strength as a group. Their solidarity, their faith in one another is their greatest power. Ask them all to wear black or white."

I rubbed my eyes. I was so very tired.

"What else?" I wondered aloud.

"Broomsticks?" Maya asked.

"Very funny."

"I wasn't exactly joking. I only know what I've seen on TV."

I smiled. "Sorry. No broomsticks. But chalices. I'll have to brew."

Bronwyn nodded.

Maya looked at me, her dark eyes sober, worried. "Are you sure about this, Lily? I've never seen you scared before."

"Yes, you have. I'm scared just about every day."

Bronwyn enveloped me in a bear hug, patting my back.

"And if . . . if anything happens," I said, pulling away, "I think Oscar will be going back to his owner, but if not, promise me you'll take care of him."

"Of course I will. But what could happen to you?"

"Nothing, I'm sure. Just in case."

* * *

After burying Aidan's mandragora-to-be under my lemon tree on the terrace and writing out the final instructions for his birth, I also wrote out a quick will. It felt rather maudlin, but I thought I should clarify things. The store and its contents would go to Bronwyn, and my savings and stock portfolio to Maya to continue her education and research. I also asked Maya to send my mother a regular allowance.

The rest of the evening hours I spent brewing. Oscar stuck by my side, aiding me with his very presence. I called on the spirits with an intensity that I'd never known. At the crucial moment my helping spirit appeared overhead, just as always, but this time I did not look away. Instead, I lifted my gaze to meet its eyes, and appealed to it with all my heart.

Afterward, I lifted Oscar onto the counter so we could speak face-to-face.

"I don't know exactly what's going to happen tonight, Oscar."

"Something big's going on, isn't it?"

"Bigger'n Dallas, as they say. And you're coming, because I'll need your help with the spell. But I want you to know that I've really loved having you around. You're a good guy. And if anything were to happen tonight—"

"Nothing will happen!"

"That's true. But if anything *were* to happen, you'll be taken care of."

His eyes got watery. I couldn't stand to look at him anymore.

"Okay, enough of that," I said, as businesslike as possible. "Help me carry this all out to the car, will you?"

We toted out several boxes filled with supplies. Leaving Oscar in the car, I returned to my apartment alone and took a few quiet moments to look around. My gaze took in hand-tatted lace curtains, the threadbare Turkish rug, the thrift-shop painting of red hills that reminded me of Texas. I cherished my apartment, my life here in San Francisco. I knew I could lose it all tonight. Still, I felt strangely calm, accepting of my fate, confident in my abilities.

As I was about to leave, I noticed my crystal ball still sitting out on the coffee table from my last unsuccessful effort.

What the heck.

I sat before it cross-legged, took a deep, calming breath, and gazed into its depths.

For the first time in my life, I saw something concrete: Graciela's lined face. Much older than I remembered her. Ancient. Gazing right back at me.

I felt tears prickle at the back of my eyes.

I picked up the phone and called the number I still remembered by heart.

Chapter 19

I arrived at the shore of the San Francisco Bay by one o'clock, and found that Bronwyn had come early with half a dozen women. They had set up a card table, covered it with a white cloth, and put out a thermos of hot apple cider and plates of homemade cookies. I had to smile. Just your average everyday midnight coven picnic . . .

Oscar was in his piggy form and wound around the women's feet, making friends and begging for cookies. The food, the pig, and the women's excited chatter lent a certain air of frivolity to the scene that I really appreciated. Sort of defused my tension.

I noticed when Aidan appeared on the dock, keeping his distance from the coven. He was ready to call in the fog, to compel *La Llorona* to show herself and then to keep her present. Meanwhile, I would confront Elisabeth, Frances's daughter—presuming Aidan's "invitation" was enough to compel her to show herself tonight, too. If all went well and I survived the night, I was going to be in serious debt to one powerful male witch.

Over the next hour the rest of the women arrived. There were some familiar faces: Maya came with her aunt Genevieve and her mother, Lucille, who insisted on bringing a warm casserole. Wendy from the café was there—apparently she was one of the regular coven priestesses—and I recognized a few other Haight Street neighbors. Many faces were new to me, but each woman met me warmly, holding my hands in hers, hugging me. The kindness and depth of their calm vibrations amazed me. They had shown up for no reason other than to help. How could I ever have been so dismissive of them?

When it was time I gathered them together and explained what we were doing and the role they would play. Once again I told them I would keep them from danger if I possibly could, but that I could not guarantee their safety. I invited anyone to leave right then, with no hard feelings.

"I know what I'm asking is impossible. But we're here for the sake of a child."

"We're ready," said Bronwyn. "You just take care of your part; we'll take care of ours. Trust us, Lily. That's what our group is all about."

The witching hour was upon us.

First came the closing of the circle.

"Hand to hand, and heart to heart." One after another the women clasped hands, touching the heart of the first woman, then the next. It continued, one by one, until the circle was closed.

Then a chant, led by Bronwyn, with a surprisingly steady, sweet voice.

She and the other priestesses stepped forward and began to draw down the moon.

I entered the circle and began to move with the chant, with the song. My spirit knife was in one hand, my medicine bag in the other. I moved without conscious thought, feeling the energy from these women surround me, enfold me. It was loving and safe, and so, so powerful. But it didn't feel out of control like my own powers often did; instead, it was smooth, mellow, secure and promising.

By the time the chant ended I realized I had gone into a semitrance, as easy as that.

Then came the offering of the brew.

The women held their chalices high, sending up the cone of power.

"*La Llorona*, we compel you!"

A wall of fog moved in. It was so thick it became hard to see more than fifteen feet away.

Then, loudly: a ghostly sobbing, wailing, keening noises.

"Where are my children? *¿Dónde están mis hijos?*"

Several of the coven members began to weep at the aching sadness of *La Llorona*'s voice. All the more reason to banish the demon—the coven members who heard her cry were now at risk themselves.

Wind whipping, I heard the mournful call of a foghorn and thought of normal life carrying on, cars racing across the bridge in the distance. Time hadn't stopped, because it didn't. That's not the way this sort of thing works.

"My children . . . where are my children?" Now the voice sounded far away, distant. That meant she was upon us. She felt strong, much stronger than she used to be. Frances had lent her power to the specter.

"Give us the child!" I commanded.

"A soul for a soul . . ."

"Lily!"

I looked up to see the woman I had asked Aidan to compel to come here tonight. The adult Elisabeth. The child who had returned to life, though not quite right, never truly human again after her time in the depths with *La Llorona*. The beloved daughter for whom Frances had sacrificed so much.

Delores Keener stood before us, atop an abandoned car. She seemed to shimmer with malevolence.

"Stop this, Lily. We can make you more powerful than you can imagine. Join us!"

As she spoke she seemed somehow larger, the planes of her face shifting like one of those children's puzzles where you moved the parts around to make up the picture. Was it just my imagination, the magic of the spell?

"Give us the child," I shouted. "Give us Jessica."

"Impossible. *La Llorona* is stronger now than ever."

"So am I."

Delores looked at me, her eyes piercing. "Yes. I can see that. But you couldn't take me on, much less her. But if you join us, a union born of sisterhood . . ."

I felt it then: temptation. A surge of pure power curling about me like a serpent, enticing me with the promise of never again doubting myself, of reigning supreme. The path to spiritual oblivion. My father had chosen that path. For the first time I understood how, and why. I thought of Graciela, the tiny woman who had stood against my father to save me as a baby. I concentrated on the coven of women, most of them previously unknown to me, who had come to support me in this treacherous, crazy quest.

"Your own mother tried to kill you," I shouted.

This time it wasn't my imagination—Delores swelled with rage. Vaguely, as though they were far away, I could hear the women of the coven whispering, their worried murmurs gathering strength to support me. Wendy had started them all in a chant of protection. They were brave; they had not broken the circle.

"She could not kill me," said Delores.

"But she tried. She poisoned your last meal, didn't she?"

"I always did love pot roast."

"She wanted to kill herself and you," I said. "But because I used the wrong hair in my spell, your hair, you were protected."

"I still got sick as a dog. I'm part human, after all."

"Were you there when I cast my spell?"

"It was my home. Where else would I be?"

"You lived up in the attic?"

"When I was a girl. As an adult I went wherever I wanted—I only had to make sure no one saw me. Sometimes the neighborhood brats would break into the house, but I took care of them. I found the trick of invisibility, read about black-cat bones in one of my mother's books."

"But why did you set her out in the pentagram . . . ?"

"I was watching you that night. Your magic was strong—I have to hand it to you. You might have saved her if I hadn't been working against your craft."

"You didn't want her to live?"

Suddenly Delores looked sad, younger. Unsure. She just shook her head.

"You were hoping to appease *La Llorona*."

"She gets so angry," she said in a voice that seemed more and more high-pitched, like a little girl's. "I want to stay in the human world. But now that Mother is gone, there won't be any more children surrendered to her . . . Mother traded the children for my soul, and pledged her own upon her death. It was a great sacrifice."

"You have to go back," I said.

"*No.* Sandra already tried. I fixed her."

"But I saved her."

She shrugged.

"I want Jessica back, Delores. She still has a chance for a normal life. Do the right thing."

"No!"

"I'm not leaving here without her."

"And what will you trade for her?" Delores asked, the little girl dropping away as her sneering, adult veneer returned. "Your own soul?"

"No."

"A soul for a soul. That's the only way."

"I know that. I have a soul in mind. One of her favorites. You."

My eyes flashed over to Aidan, who stood by the water's edge, holding his call for *La Llorona.*

The wind blew the fog around us in wraithlike streams, the salt air of the bay wrapping around us both.

Delores leaped down from the top of the car and ran toward me in a rage. When she hit the line of the circle she bounced off, as though she had hit a brick wall. I broke out of the protection of the circle and grabbed her, dragging her toward the water's edge.

She was being pulled in, feetfirst. She reached out to me. The planes in her face shifted, and all at once she looked like the little towheaded girl who had been lost so long ago, young Elisabeth.

"Help me!" she yelled.

My resolve faltered.

In that instant skeletal hands wrapped around my ankles with an inhuman force. They pulled my feet out from under me and just that quickly I was in the water. This was not the bathwater-warm sea of the Caribbean. The numbing cold made it hard to move; the horror made it hard to think. *La Llorona* was dragging me down with her, into the depths of the bay.

Fighting panic, I willed myself to concentrate on my goal.

Jessica.

The wind whipped, the water crashed, whitecaps appeared all around us.

I took a huge lungful of air before the water closed over my head. I had never been underwater before in my life—it was an odd, all-encompassing sensation. I was drowning. Once again I fought panic. Squeezing my eyes shut, I envisioned the coven of women on the shore helping me, all of whom were there for me, and for Jessica. I saw Graciela, and my helping spirit. Aidan. Max. Little Oscar.

Kicking at the skeletal fingers that clasped my ankles only caused them to tighten on me, pulling me down farther.

My eyes opened. I could see nothing in the murky darkness of the water. But I could hear the desperate cries of drowned souls, and the anguished, never-ending sobbing of the demon.

I forced the panic down deep in my belly and called

on my spirit guide to sustain me, to keep me from being driven mad by the pain and fear. I concentrated on accepting my fate, and on my goal: the salvation of a little girl.

Jessica.

I heard *La Llorona*'s screaming again, but it was different this time. It sounded closer and closer to me, indicating she was farther and farther away. The horrific keening wrapped around me until it was inside my head, becoming the whole of sensation for a brief, excruciating moment.

There was no more air. My lungs spasmed. Black spots danced in front of my eyes. I looked overhead to the subtle glow of the full moon through the fog, dancing on the surface of the water so far over my head. Since I was a baby, like every other natural witch, I had drawn strength from the moon, had responded to its phases and cycles. I yearned to be bathed in its light just one more time.

Suddenly I felt something drift into my arms. With my last ounce of strength I grabbed at it. Flesh, hair . . . a child.

The grip on my ankles slackened, then released.

I wasn't strong enough to swim to the surface, but luckily I didn't have to. As soon as I was free the waters thrust me up and out. Within seconds I bobbed up to the surface, corklike, with Jessica in my arms. We both took great gulps of air, coughing and sputtering. Jessica began to cry, but I couldn't keep from laughing with joy.

Witches don't sink.

Gosnold's boat came toward us. As it neared, I saw Max looking over the side, his face a study in worry and fear. He threw a life preserver to us and fished us out of the cold brine, pulling us up and over the side.

Gosnold turned the boat around and headed to the dock.

Max swore in a constant, profane stream as he wrapped Jessica and me in emergency blankets, then enfolded both of us in his arms to help warm us.

Jessica stopped crying and just looked at us with those huge dark eyes, vague and unfocused, as though she were sleepwalking.

"You okay, sugar?" I asked.

"What . . . what happened?"

"It's a little hard to explain. You're safe. We'll get you back to your family. Go back to sleep."

She gave a huge yawn, closed her eyes, and slept against Max's chest. She was breathing well; her pulse was strong. I wrapped an arm around her and concentrated, sagging with relief to feel her pure, clean, human vibrations.

The fog lifted suddenly and bright moonlight streamed down upon us. I looked overhead to the full moon and thanked the universe. Jessica was going to be all right. She wouldn't remember the trauma of the past few days as anything more than a vague, unpleasant dream.

"What in the *hell* happened out there?" Max demanded.

I was still grinning down at Jessica. The salt drops on my face felt like tears of joy.

"Lily? What happened?"

I looked up at Max. His face was close to mine as I huddled at his side, drawn to his warmth.

"In the old days, one of the tests they gave witches was to throw them in the sea or a lake. Do you remember what happened?"

His light gray eyes held mine. "If they sank and drowned they were innocent. . . ."

"But if they floated, they were true witches," I finished. Countless women—and not a few men—had died from the "ordeal of swimming," the *indicium aquae*. If they were innocent of being witches, they drowned. If they failed to drown, they were hanged or burned. Talk about your no-win situation.

"I can't sink," I said. I couldn't contain my grin. "Never even could swim worth a dang. I float like a proverbial witch."

Gosnold pulled up to the dock and Max climbed out, taking Jessica from my arms and setting her on the pier, and then turning back to help me out.

Oscar was squealing and trotting back and forth, his piggy hooves clopping loudly on the wooden-planked pier. I crouched down to give him a reassuring squeeze. His mere presence had helped tonight. He was a great familiar.

Looking farther down the dock, I saw Aidan. Our eyes met. *Thank you*, I mouthed. Aidan Rhodes, male witch, nodded and kept walking, just an ordinary guy out for a stroll at three in the morning.

"You know that guy?" Max asked.

"I wouldn't go that far," I said. "But I certainly owe him."

Maya ran toward us and enfolded Jessica in her arms. She and Bronwyn promised to take her straight home. I told them to stay back and let her go to the door herself, so they wouldn't have to answer a lot of uncomfortable questions. I imagined the police would have a hard time with this particular truth.

The coven women gathered around me, everyone hugging and crying and cheering. I had never been a big hugger, but I did my best to join in their euphoria, knowing that in a few minutes Jessica's family would have all their prayers answered. They had been touched by grace, and by the bravery of a bunch of courageous, caring strangers—and they would never know it.

After some time, I noticed Max standing to the side, arms crossed over his chest, frowning.

I extricated myself from the throng and went to him.

"You okay, Max?"

"I don't know. . . ." He shook his head and looked out over the water. "I can't quite wrap my mind around what happened here tonight."

"It's probably best not to think too much about it. The point is, it all worked out okay."

His face was sketched with worry, tugging at my heart. Time to change the subject.

"Too bad you didn't have your film crew, now that Gosnold finally took you out on his boat, right? Tell me, did he charge you for the privilege?"

Max smiled down at me, the light dancing in his eyes. "As a matter of fact, he did. He told me I might see something I would never forget."

"He's such a sleaze." I shook my head.

"He's a businessman." He shrugged.

Our gazes held for a long moment.

"You scared the hell out of me," Max said, his voice low and harsh.

"Do I still scare you?" I tried to keep my tone flippant, but I really wanted to know. Now that he had seen this part of me in action, would he turn away from me, like so many other cowans?

"You're a scary woman; no doubt about that . . ."

My heart sank.

". . . but you certainly haven't scared me off."

Max drew me into his arms, tilted my head back, and kissed me.

Slowly. Deeply. Thoroughly.

It was enough to make a witch swoon.

Chapter 20

That night, Maya and Bronwyn came back to my place after seeing Jessica home, and decided to sleep over at my apartment. Too giddy and stunned from our triumph to go to bed right away, we popped popcorn and brewed nothing more magical than hot chocolate. Oscar snoozed on the couch while we laughed and chatted. It was bliss.

My first ever slumber party, at the ripe old age of thirty-one.

"Don't you want to close the store for a few days, take a well-deserved break?" asked Bronwyn as we washed our dishes. I reveled in the ordinariness of the chore after our extraordinary night.

I shook my head. "All I want is to get things back to normal."

"So how did you know what spell to use, and that you needed the coven?" Maya asked.

"I finally broke down and called my grandmother Graciela. She taught me everything I know about the craft. Though I have to say, there's no way to really know about these things. There's a bit of improvisation that goes into it. But she was working a spell on her end . . . and I had some other help as well. And all you women, too. I could never have done it alone."

"I still can't believe that Delores Keener was . . . less than human," said Maya.

"Poor thing," I said. "I still feel bad for the child she once was, for Elisabeth."

"Why didn't Frances just say her child had been returned to her? Why the big secret, keeping her in the attic, of all things? Maybe that's what made her so nuts."

"It took Frances a couple of years to get strong enough to negotiate with *La Llorona*, during which time Elisabeth wouldn't have aged. Hard to explain. Plus, by the time her mother got her back she was changed . . . altered."

"Even her new name, Delores, meant pain," Maya mused. "And her last name, Keener, as in one who cries or wails, like *La Llorona*?"

"That's what I finally guessed, after a few hints."

"Now that I've seen you in action," Bronwyn said, hanging three Italian ceramic mugs on their cup hooks, "I have a hard time believing your protection spell didn't work for Frances."

"At first I thought it was because I had focused the brew on demons, rather than humans. But as it turns out, my spell was useless against suicide. Self-destruction is a powerful drive. And ironically enough, I made a mistake with an important ingredient—hair—that helped Delores survive the poison."

"And then she went on to try to run us down, and kill Sandra?" Maya asked. "How *is* Sandra, by the way?"

"Back to her old self since I called and told her I was giving Frances's property to the neighborhood association. She's nothing if not goal-oriented. She says they'll make it into a park."

"A haunted park?"

"That part's anybody's guess."

"Lily, sweetie, what's this?" Bronwyn picked up a piece of paper I had left out on the counter. My last will and testament.

"Um . . ."

"You really didn't think you were going to survive tonight, did you?"

"Well . . ."

"But you went anyway?" Maya asked.

My new friends looked at me, eyes huge.

"It was important," I mumbled.

"*You're* important," said Bronwyn.

"Important and a little bit crazy," added Maya, her voice edged with anger.

The cuckoo clock chimed five o'clock.

"So, does it still count as a slumber party if there's no sleeping involved?" I asked, hoping to change the subject.

"That's almost the very definition of a slumber party," said Maya with a reluctant smile and a little yawn. "But with that said, I call the couch. I'm even willing to share with the pig."

Despite my entreaties for them to get some more sleep, Maya and Bronwyn stuck to me like white on grits as I opened Aunt Cora's Closet that morning. Soon after I performed my cleansing ritual, the bell rang and we all looked up to see a man walk in, his faced obscured by two cellophane-wrapped supermarket floral bouquets and a shiny helium balloon that read, *Thank You.*

I knew who it was by the tattooed biceps.

"Tomás. How nice to see you."

"Hey." His dark eyes shifted to Bronwyn and Maya.

"Guys, could you give us a minute?" I asked.

"Sure. We'll go down to the café for coffee. Either of you want anything?"

I asked for a mocha latte. Tomás shook his head.

After they left, he and I looked at each other in silence for a long moment. Then he held out the flowers and balloon.

"These are for you. On behalf of my family. They don't . . . they don't know what you did for them, for all of us."

"It wasn't just me. A lot of people worked together. Does Jessica seem all right?" I asked as I accepted the flowers and cradled them to my chest, breathing in the scent of mums and carnations. "Her old self?"

"Just like the day she left. The police already came by, and we told them what we knew: that she just showed up at the door in the middle of the night, and can't remember a thing. That's all."

I nodded.

"She can't tell us anything about what happened. It's like she was asleep the whole time."

"That's for the best."

His dark eyes fixed on mine, intense and wary.

"But you and I both know she had some help. I saw those women who just left for the cafe, your friends, hiding out in their car last night, watching until Jessica came into the house."

"Some things are better left unsaid."

"And . . . *La Llorona*?"

"She's left town." The combination of the strength of the coven, my spell casting, and Aidan's power—mostly the latter—had convinced her to return home to the Rio Grande, where she belonged.

"I'm sorry about what I said, about you being a witch."

"You saved my life, remember? So we're even on that score. And the truth is, I *am* a witch."

He smiled slightly. "Well, then, I guess there are witches and then there are witches."

"I guess so," I said, returning his smile.

"If there's ever anything you need . . . all you gotta do is ask. I got your back."

"Thanks, Tomás. That means a lot."

"I'll see you around, then."

I nodded. "See you around. Thank you for the flowers."

He turned and walked out, just as another person walked in. The two men nodded at each other as they passed in the doorway.

Max. With a spray of wildflowers.

His eyes held mine for a beat; then he looked down at the flowers in my arms.

"Looks like I've got some competition."

"Yep. They're practically knocking down the door."

He smiled. "Well, as I believe I've mentioned before, I'm not easily daunted. Are you free for dinner on Saturday? There are things we should talk about."

"Oh, I can't on Saturday."

"Hot date with Mr. Biceps?"

"Not exactly. The provost at the San Francisco College of the Arts saw the article on Aunt Cora's Closet, and she promised me a bunch of Victorian clothes and old flapper costumes she found in a sealed storage closet under the eaves."

"Sounds intriguing. But why are you looking at this stuff at night?"

"Maya's a student at the school, and she mentioned that I might be able to help out with an unusual problem. Supposedly the students have been hearing odd noises in the middle of the night; the provost wants me to check it out in exchange for the clothes."

"Let me get this straight: You nearly drowned last night, and now you're chasing ghosts again?"

"I'm not chasing ghosts, Max. I don't know the first thing about ghosts. *La Llorona* was a demon. There's a big difference."

Max looked at me for a long time, an angry glint entering his light gray eyes. "You don't even realize quite how crazy you sound, do you?"

"The students are just spooked because they discovered the school was built over an old cemetery, but of course that doesn't guarantee spirits of any kind, much less malevolent ones. I'm just going to assure them there's nothing to worry about. I'm certain I won't see a thing more exotic than corsets and white cotton bloomers."

Max blew out an exasperated breath. "I don't know how I'm going to handle this sort of thing."

"We haven't even gone out on our first date yet and you're already giving up? What happened to Mr. Undaunted?"

"I never said I was giving up. And we had our first official date already, over tacos. I was thinking of something slightly more elegant for our second outing."

"Well, I do need an escort for this vintage wedding I was invited to." I handed him the gilt invitation I had received yesterday via Susan Rogers, fashion editor at the *Chronicle* and aunt to Natalie. "But you'll have to wear a tux. It's at the Palace Hotel, pretty fancy."

"I look great in a tux." He looked down at the invitation. "But this is months from now."

"You don't think you'll be around months from now?"

His eyes looked up into mine. At long last he gave me a slow, sexy smile. "Consider yourself escorted."

Bronwyn and Maya returned with hot beverages and bagels in hand. I introduced them to Max. After exchanging pleasantries he ducked out of the store, promising to call me later.

"Yet another good-looking man in here," said Maya as she handed me my mocha. "Things are looking up."

"Maya and I have a little present for you," said Bronwyn with a smile. "We saw it in Sandra's window—her niece is watching over the store—and we couldn't resist."

"A present? For me?" I felt like Oscar when I gave him his pendant. When was the last time someone had given me a gift? Then I remembered Oscar, currently snoring contentedly on his purple silk pillow. I guess it's true that the best things in life are accidents: My familiar turned out to be my favorite present ever.

Carefully I untied the yellow ribbon and the pretty pink wrapping on the flat package. It was a bumper sticker.

I couldn't stop laughing. We carried it outside, where

I proudly affixed it to the steel bumper of my vintage Mustang.

It read: *Rhymes with Bitch.*

"Oh, now, *that's* funny," a voice came from behind us.

I turned to see Aidan walking toward us. Maya and Bronwyn said a quick hello, then scooted back to the store to give us privacy.

"I'm glad to see you're finally embracing your witchy self," he said with a wicked smile. "Now, about that debt you've incurred . . ."

Author's Note

Most of the spells used throughout this book are based on information gathered from practicing witches in personal interviews, but none should be repeated.

The directions for creating a mandragora are found in a fascinating, massive collection of spells and incantations originally published by Paul Christian in 1870, and recently reissued: *The History and Practice of Magic* by Lida A. Churchill and Paul Christian, published by Kessinger Publishing, 1994. The directions are found on pages 401–402.

"I need something to guard against ghosts . . ." whispered the young woman slouching at the counter. She cast a nervous glance around the shop floor, which was empty except for racks of great vintage clothes, cases of costume jewelry, and shelves jammed with hats. "A protective . . . thingamajig."

"A talisman?" I asked.

"That's it."

"Talismans don't really guard against ghosts, per se—"

"Whatever." She shrugged. "It's better than nothing."

Her feathery bright pink hair brought to mind a silly children's toy, the kind one might win after stuffing ten dollars' worth of quarters into the mechanical contraption at the Escape from New York Pizza parlor a few blocks down Haight Street. But from the jaded look in her heavy-lidded amber eyes and the multiple piercings along her left eyebrow, I suspected the overall effect she was after was more “aggressively alienated youth” than “cuddly stuffed animal.”

“You’re a student at the San Francisco College of Fine Arts?” I said as I opened the back of the glass display case and pulled out the black velvet–covered tray that held my rapidly diminishing collection of hand-carved wooden medallions. There had been a run on them lately.

“How did you know that?” Her eyes flew up to meet mine. “Can you read minds?”

“No.” I shook my head and stifled a smile. “My assistant, Maya, goes to the College of Fine Arts. We’ve had a lot of students stop by in the last week, asking for protection.”

“Did I hear my name?” Maya emerged from the back room. She was petite, had delicate features, and wore her hair twisted into thick black locks that ended in a series of beads that clacked pleasantly against the silver rings and cuffs adorning each ear. “Oh, hey, Andromeda.”

“Um, hey,” the customer said to Maya with a nearly imperceptible lift of her chin. Pink hair swayed as she tilted her head in question. “Where do I know you from again?”

“Sculpture class,” Maya answered. “We’ve met a few times.”

“Oh, yeah—my bad. So, you’ve told her about the ghosts at the school?” Andromeda asked Maya. “The footsteps out in the hallways, the heavy breathing, doors opening and closing . . .”

“As a matter of fact, I have.”

“It turns out that the main building”—Andromeda leaned across the counter toward Maya and me, her voice dropping to a fierce whisper—"*was built on top of an old cemetery.*"

"That's mostly an issue in the movies," I pointed out. "It doesn't actually mean there are ghosts lingering."

"I've heard something, too, though, Lily, along with half the school," Maya said.

The trepidation in my assistant's serious dark eyes gave me pause. Maya rarely asked for—or needed—anyone's help, and she retained a healthy dose of cynicism about the world of the paranormal. So I had been more than a little surprised a few days ago when she had asked me for a protective talisman, and even more so when she brokered an unusual deal with the school's provost, Dr. Marlene Mueller: If I could calm the students' fears of ghosts running amok in the campus hallways, I could help myself to the contents of a recently discovered storage closet chock-full of Victorian-era gowns and frilly unmentionables.

As a purveyor of vintage clothing, I leapt at the chance.

But there was a fly in this supernatural ointment: I don't know much about ghosts.

I'm a witch, not a necromancer. Few outside the world of magick appreciate the difference, but trust me, the two vocations don't involve the same skill sets. For some reason, my energy attracts spirits like flies to honey, but I can't understand a cotton-pickin' word they say. "Interdimensional frustration" is what I call it.

One thing I *do* know is that all of us walk over interred corpses all the time. People are born; they live; they die. It's been the same story throughout the millennia, and the physical remnants of our earthly sojourns—

our bodies—have to go somewhere. If simply walking across a grave were enough to incur a curse from beyond, none of us would live long enough to attend kindergarten, much less college.

"We're supposed to meet Dr. Mueller's daughter, Ginny, at school tonight to take a look around," Maya told Andromeda.

"You're trying to see the ghost *on purpose*?" Andromeda gaped at both of us for a moment, then shivered as though a goose had just walked over her grave.

Looking down at the selection of talismans on the counter, she picked up a medallion, weighing the cool wooden disk in her hand. Each full moon, I make the talismans from the branch of a fruit tree, carving ancient symbols of protection on them and consecrating them in a ceremony of rebirth. However, just as in the natural world, there are few absolutes in the realm of the supernatural. The medallions are powerful sources of support, but on their own aren't enough to stop a determined force of evil. It's kind of like having a big dog in the house: He might not chase off every ne'er-do-well, but the average mischief makers go elsewhere.

"Does it matter which one I get?" Andromeda asked. "Or are they all the same, protectionwise?"

"They're—" I began.

Andromeda dropped the medallion and screamed, flattening herself against a stand of frothy wedding gowns. The clothes rack teetered under the pressure.

"What the eff is that?"

Oscar, my pot-bellied pig and wannabe witch's familiar, snorted at her feet.

"That's Oscar, the store mascot." Maya smiled. "He sort of grows on you."

"He won't hurt you, Andromeda," I said to the pink-haired young woman still cowering against the white wall of silks and satins. Clearly she wasn't a pet person. Or maybe she just wasn't a pet pig person. "Oscar, go back to your bed."

Oscar snorted again, looked up at me, rolled his pink piggy eyes, and trotted back to his purple silk pillow.

Andromeda wiped a thin hand across her brow. "I'm a nervous wreck. Ghosts, now pigs . . . I just wish everything would get back to normal."

"This one should help," I said as I held up a medallion carved with the ancient symbol of a deer and an Aramaic inscription. I had braided and knotted the cord from silk threads in five powerful colors: red, orange, turquoise, magenta, and black. It suited her.

Andromeda bowed her head to allow me to slip the talisman on, and I couldn't help but notice the pale, vulnerable curve of her slender neck. Her vibrations were clear as a bell—bright and frightened, almost tangible, and though I was only ten years her senior, I felt a surge of maternal protection. Like her mythical namesake, who had been offered as a naked sacrifice to a sea monster, this Andromeda had a lot on her mind.

As we used to say back in Texas, she was scareder than a sinner in a cyclone.

But not of a ghost, or even a pig.

Andromeda was scared of something altogether human.

* * *

"Don't you need any, you know, ghost-hunting stuff?" Maya asked later that night after I managed to squeeze my vintage Mustang convertible into an impossibly small spot in front of Bimbo's on Columbus Avenue. Proud of my parking finesse, I led the way up Chestnut toward the San Francisco College of Fine Arts. The cool night air was fragrant with a whiff of salt off the bay, the aroma of garlic from the North Beach restaurants, and a heady floral perfume—early blooming brugmansia and jasmine were my guess. San Franciscans did like their flowers.

Slung over the shoulder of my vintage dress was my trusty Filipino woven backpack, and on my feet were easy-to-flee-in Keds.

But no legitimate ghost-hunting stuff.

"Oops," I said. "Guess I left my catch-a-spirit kit in Hong Kong."

"Very funny. Seriously—you don't have any special equipment or anything?"

"Like what? Stakes and crosses?"

"Those are for vampires," Maya pointed out.

"Right, I get that mixed up. Stakes would be immaterial. Get it? Immaterial? Like ghosts?"

Maya gave me a pity smile. "The guys on that TV show haul a lot of equipment around with them. Mostly electronic stuff."

"They no doubt bought most of it at Radio Shack's annual clearance sale. Just how do they expect to capture energy on film?"

"I'm just saying." Maya shrugged. "You should get cable. It's very educational."

"But if I watched TV, when would I find the time to traipse around town looking for phantoms?"

Besides, I thought to myself, *I already know darned well that ghosts are real.*

We arrived at the campus. Our footsteps echoed off the ochre stucco walls of the covered walkway as we trod upon red saltillo tiles worn down by the feet of thousands of nuns, and now art students, for more than a century. The San Francisco College of Fine Arts was housed in a gorgeous example of Spanish revival architecture, complete with red-tiled roofs, intricate plasterwork, graceful arches, and a bell tower. So far the vibrations of this convent-turned–art school felt largely positive, with just enough negative thrown in to prove its claim of being a historic building.

After all, bad stuff is a part of life. Shadows are necessary, if only to emphasize the light.

"Just remember, ghosts aren't usually malevolent," I said after Maya and I met up with Ginny Mueller, the provost's daughter. "They're just remnants of a past life, or trapped energy from someone who used to be just as human as the next person. There's really nothing to fear."

Ginny snorted. "Have *you* tried to find the essence in a hunk of stone at three in the morning with a *ghost* breathing down your neck?"

"Can't say that I have," I conceded.

The place was as quiet as the proverbial tomb as the three of us climbed the broad, tiled staircase that swept up to the second floor. On the landing waited a tall young man wearing a security guard's uniform and a badge that read KEVIN MARINO.

He stood ramrod straight, shoulders back and chin

lifted, the very model of a rough, tough security guard prepared to protect the womenfolk. I wasn't sure how he intended to do that since as far as I could tell the most threatening item in his possession was his rusty tin badge. Still, I gave him points for effort.

"Hey." Kevin greeted us with a lift of his chin. He focused on me. "You the ghost buster?"

"Sort of. I'm Lily Ivory." We shook hands.

"Kevin." He paused. "Where's your, uh, ghost-huntin' stuff?"

"She left it in Hong Kong," Maya said.

"Oh. Well, all's quiet so far. There was a heckuva lot goin' on last night, though. Moaning, doors slamming . . . Thought it might be one o' them poultry heists."

"Someone's stealing chickens?" I asked, confused.

Maya nudged me. "He means *poltergeists*."

"Ah." No wonder I couldn't talk to the dead, I reflected. At times I could scarcely understand the living. "My mistake."

"Where'd you want to start?" asked Kevin.

"Let's start with the area of greatest activity," I suggested.

Kevin stared at me.

"The noisiest area," I clarified.

"Hmm. Lots o' those. Lots o' those, indeed."

"Which one's the worst?"

"Well, now, that's hard to say. Darned hard to say."

"Surely the noises emanate from *somewhere*?"

"Like I said, there's lots o' places like that."

Either Kevin was a dim bulb or he was stalling. Was he lonely and wanted to hang out with us? Was he afraid?

I forced myself to smile. "Pick one."

"The bell tower?"

"You tell me."

"Do you think . . ." Maya said hesitantly, her face looking pinched in the dim light of the hallway, "maybe we could start with the studios?"

I reminded myself that humans—normal humans, that is—aren't as sanguine as I am about the supernatural. All structures hold some ghosts, the whispery vestiges of the souls who have passed through. Most consist of little more than residual feelings and fleeting emotions, not the apparitions of lore. And most aren't a problem. They tend to keep a low profile, noticed only by those who, like me, are . . . different. A ghost's main impact on the human world is to lend its vibrations to a place, making it warm and welcoming, or cold and off-putting.

As someone who has lived a mostly solitary life, I revel in these vibrations, which make me feel connected to the past, to those who have gone before. The same feeling drew me to old clothes, which also carry a fragment of the energy of those who had worn them. Most people go through life unaware of the overlay of the past, which is just as well. On the rare occasions when they make a connection to the beyond it scares the you-know-what out of them.

"Has there been activity in the studios?" I asked Maya.

"Not really."

"Then let's not bother. Straight to the bell tower, I say. I want to get to the bottom of this. But listen—no need to come if you don't feel comfortable. I'll do my best to slay the critter and meet you in the café for a nightcap. No sweat."

"I'm coming." Maya wasn't the type to back down.

"Me, too," said Ginny.

"Yeah, we got your back," said Kevin.

I smiled, but I had to admit that our foursome was one sorry excuse for a ghost-hunting team: two jittery students, one security guard whose chief virtue was that he was not carrying a gun, and one bona fide witch who could not communicate with the dead if her life depended on it. And nary a ghost-catching electronic device to be found.

"Okay. Let's go see if we stir up anything at the bell tower," I said, heading down the corridor, which ended in a T a few yards in front of us.

Suddenly I heard something: the muffled sound of a girl weeping.

I looked back at my companions. "Do y'all hear that?"

"Yeah," Ginny said, "but that's not what we usually—"

I gestured for my companions to flatten themselves along the wall and wait, then carefully stuck my head around the corner. A young woman leaned up against the wall, weeping. Pink strands swayed with the shaking of her shoulders.

"Andromeda?" I said, approaching her. "What's wrong?"

She sniffed, wiped her arm over her wet face, threw her shoulders back, and looked up at me, as though she weren't sobbing a moment ago.

"Nothing's wrong. Hey," she said to the others with a slight lift of her chin.

"Hey," said Kevin, mimicking her chin raise.

"Hey," repeated Ginny.

"Hey," echoed Maya.

I gritted my teeth. I've been in California for only a couple of months, so perhaps with time I'll take to the local manner of exchanging *hey*s instead of actual greetings. But would a simple "How are you?" or "Pleased to meet you" kill these people?

"I gotta go," said Andromeda as she hurried past our group. "See you guys later."

We all watched as she beat a hasty retreat down the corridor and disappeared around the corner. After exchanging curious glances, we continued on our way.

"This way to the tower?" I asked.

Kevin nodded. "Straight ahead and to the right. Almost there."

I was beginning to wonder whether we'd find anything at all. From the students' stories, I expected to sense something supernatural from the moment I set foot on campus, but so far this evening the actions of the humans were the only odd behavior of note. Maybe it was the spooks' night off, or maybe the students had managed to freak themselves out with the combination of too little sleep, too much caffeine, and forlorn tales of lost loves. A potent brew, I knew from personal experience.

We turned the corner.

Ginny screamed.

About the Author

Juliet Blackwell is the pseudonym for a mystery author who, together with her sister, wrote the Art Lover's Mystery series. The first in that series, *Feint of Art*, was nominated for an Agatha Award for Best First Novel. Juliet's lifelong interest in the paranormal world was triggered when her favorite aunt visited and read her fortune—with startling results. As an anthropologist, the author studied systems of spirituality, magic, and health across cultures and throughout history. She currently resides in a happily haunted house in Oakland, California, where she paints and writes and fends off the overly zealous attentions of her neighbor's black cat, who seems to imagine himself Juliet's new familiar. Learn more about the author at www.julietblackwell.net.